LEGIONS
OF ORION

MICHAEL G. THOMAS

First published in the United Kingdom in 2012 by Swordworks Books.

ISBN 978-1-909149-03-8

Typeset by Swordworks Books
Printed and bound in the UK & US
A catalogue record of this book is available
from the British Library

Cover design by Swordworks Books
www.swordworks.co.uk

LEGIONS
OF ORION

MICHAEL G. THOMAS

CHAPTER ONE

The creation and expansion of the Centauri Alliance took place after a period of wars and uprisings that had gone on for over five decades. The scores of planets around six star systems were now home to billions, with each colony connected via the newly established Interstellar Network, a variant of the spacebridge technology discovered during the last war. These rifts in space were held open by spherical shells of exotic matter controlled by orbital monitoring platforms. The near instantaneous travel offered by the Network, and the opportunities the transportation web offered, turned a backward and disjointed collection of colonies into a thriving and bustling hive of enterprise within a decade of their discovery. It was this new age of optimism and hubris that pushed humanity on to its great adventure in the Orion Nebula and its destiny among the stars.

A Concise Guide to Interstellar Travel

It was ten years since the founding of the new Alliance. Ten years since the end of the bloody struggle that brought the first period of peace in a generation. With the fighting over, it was finally time for the scientific expertise of the Alliance to tackle some of its greatest mysteries. One of the most important of these lay within the jungle world of Hyperion. It was a strange, barely habitable planet due to its difficult atmosphere and frequent violent storms. Its breathable atmosphere contained a higher level of nitrogen dioxide than was normally safe for humans, though a small number were able to adjust in weeks or months. For the majority however the use of a respirator was vital until a person's body was given enough time to adjust, assuming it ever did.

The discovery of Hyperion had been early in the colonization of the Alpha Centauri sector, but had been quickly eclipsed by the rich jewel of Terra Nova, the most valuable planet ever discovered. Hyperion became little more than a backwater, as the other twenty-three planets spread out between Alpha Centauri and Proxima Centauri were thoroughly explored and exploited. Other than science teams, few had visited the planet until the discovery of the ruins in the last days of the Great Uprising. It was now a thriving colony of the Alliance and populated by the semi-synthetic humans known as the Jötnar.

A small flotilla of ships waited in orbit over the planet. Most were civilian transports and heavy haulers but mixed in with them were a handful of small military ships. At the core of the group was a single capital ship, one of the last remaining cruisers from the war and a prior visitor to the world, the Alliance Navy Ship Minotaur. She'd been involved in many battles, but her frequently repaired and upgraded superstructure gave little of her history away. From within her hull the dark shape of an Alliance shuttle appeared. It was a standard design used for everything from delivering cargo to landing Special Forces on remote moons. It moved away, making no sound in the cold vacuum of space with only the faint wisps of escaping dust and gas betraying the maneuvering thrusters as it pushed away. A pair of Lightning MK II fighters took up their positions alongside the shuttle and escorted the craft down to the atmosphere of the planet. Only when they reached the outer reaches of the atmosphere, did they pull up to avoid being pulled to the surface.

From the ruins of the archaeological site, a team of Alliance marines monitored the landing pattern of the shuttle. The site was apparently safe, but they were taking no chances. A single ground based fighter circled around the landing site and stayed on position as the craft finished its journey from space and down to the modern landing pad. The structure had been built in less than three months, as part of a permanent science station on the planet. Most of those in the shuttle moved off to the compound, each wearing the usual respirator as required for new arrivals on the planet. Two members of the party moved to a waiting groundcar that was being guarded by another two marines.

The journey from the science station to the dig site took almost forty minutes and took them through a rough track that had been cut through the thick jungle. A light mist hung over the land and reduced visibility to barely more than a hundred meters. The occasional insect or small animal could be seen, but the little life present on the planet soon kept away from the noisy machine. Most of the trees had been seeded along with the arrival of the colonists back when Terra Nova had been settled; little now remained of the indigenous vegetation other than on some of the more distant parts of the planet.

Eventually the vehicle reached a clearing before a series of large hills. Rocks and debris littered the site, but it was clear there had been something man-made here at some point recently. The groundcar pulled to a stop, and the doors hissed open to reveal the pair of civilians and their escort. Dr Katha Morgonz, a longhaired technological archaeologist, stepped out and shielded her eyes for a moment from the bright light. She was one of the most experienced and knowledgeable people in the entire Alliance when it came to unusual and ancient technology.

"Dr Morgonz, you're ahead of schedule," said a waiting marine as he moved up to the door.

She said nothing, other than making an impossible to

understand grunt. He showed her the way to the entrance of the site. It was little more than a crater in the rubble, and as he continued talking she dropped down from the thick stone slab to the group of marines waiting below. Two of them grabbed her and placed her behind their position at the entrance to the partially collapsed chamber. She shook some of the dirt from her face and then double-checked her file on the location. She wore a close fitting helmet that came down low over her ears and a lightweight respirator to help with the difficult atmosphere. It was breathable but with it taking over a week to acclimatize she didn't have the time. Not that she would have objected to spending more time on Hyperion, but this mission was both time critical and also extremely secretive.

"Are you sure this is the entrance? Teams Three and Four have found similar sites and are requesting more resources to continue their digs," asked Dr Neson, the special unit's technical officer.

Dr Morgonz nodded but said no more as she checked her data. A final look satisfied her that they were in the right place. She took a few steps forward to where the diggers had cleared an access point into the structure.

"No, this is the place. If you examine the satellite scans, this is definitely the location of the main data arrays. The reports from General Rivers during the fighting ten years ago confirm my findings. If there are any intact control computers, data or working systems, they will be here.

The other sites sustained substantially more damage in the explosion when the power cores vaporized almost everything underground."

"Look!" called out one of the small group of Alliance marines. He was pointing to a beautifully detailed carving that had been made directly into the wall. Doctor Morgonz moved to examine it, but spent no more than a cursory moment examining it before moving away.

"It's just another of the images showing the construction and use of the gateways. There are lots of them over this entire site. We are not here to sightsee, marine. This operation has one objective, and it lies inside there."

She looked about as if waiting for somebody.

"Where is our guide? I thought the Jötnar were providing us with one of their best?"

The marine that had spoken before pointed inside the crevice.

"Doctor, he's already inside with Captain Garcia. They're checking the route first. I think his name was Khan, and he is one of the Jötnar's most experienced commanders. He fought alongside Spartan and the other marines on Terra Nova. Amongst his people he's seen as something of a hero."

She moved to the gap and stepped inside while at the same time tapping the button on her arm. The high powered lamp on her helmet lit up and flooded the inner chamber to reveal little more that dirt and broken rock.

She glanced at the marine as she passed him.

"I need a scout, not a soldier."

She pushed on, and her assistant Jose followed a short distance behind her. The Alliance marines waited outside, each of them on the lookout for any of the creatures that were known to lurk on Hyperion. No one seemed particularly bothered that they were being left behind, and the attitude of Dr Morgonz did little to encourage them to show much interest. There was little action to be had these days, and the escort task on Hyperion was hardly a choice operation. The planet had been the home of a secret base used by the enemy at the end of the war and had housed untold numbers of Biomech creatures; many of which still roamed the jungle world. It had since been settled by the synthetic Jötnar, the close cousins of the Biomechs but now members of the Alliance.

"Watch where you're stepping, Jose. There might be some of those animals down here."

"Animals?" he asked in surprise.

"Yes, Jose, you know, of the four-legged kind."

Jose did his best not to stumble as he moved over the broken rock and dirt and followed the Doctor. He knew only a few scant details about the Biomechs, but the four-legged variety was now considered almost mythological in their status. They had been monsters created by fusing the dead and dying with synthetic technology to make violent and terrifying beasts. The Jötnar had hunted down most of the untamed survivors on the planet but a few remained, and he'd heard terrifying stories of the bear-sized creatures attacking visitors to the jungle world and being torn apart, limb from limb. It was rumored the Jötnar let some of them live so they could hunt and kill them as part of the juvenile's upbringing.

"This way!" called out a familiar voice. It was that of Captain Garcia, who had established a small supply dump about fifty meters inside the structure. They moved closer until moving through a low opening into a damaged room. A dump containing fuel, power cells and tracking equipment lay to one side, along with three marines.

"Yes, are you ready?" she answered it in a short and irritated tone.

A dark shape turned to face her. It was a Jötnar, and one of the nearly three-meter tall creatures that inhabited Hyperion. He was build like an ogre of legend and thickly muscled. He wore an odd uniform that bore some similarity to that of the old Confederate Marine Corps, but with newly fashioned armor plates around the chest and shoulders.

"We're ready. Are you sure you want to reach the lower levels?" he asked.

Dr Morgonz looked up to him and shook her head.

"I am no fool, Mr. Khan, and I am equally capable of taking care of myself. Now, we are running on a tight schedule, and my superiors require this information quickly. Let's go."

She moved to the dark opening at the end of the room and disappeared through it. Only the light on her head provided any illumination as she moved along the perimeter of a deep chasm. Jose followed close behind her, and the three marines that had been waiting joined in as well.

Khan shook his head as she left them.

"It isn't Mr, it's Captain," he said with amusement to himself.

Captain Garcia leaned in closely towards him.

"Is it just me, or are you tempted to stay here and leave her to get lost down there?"

Khan started to shake and laughed with a low rumble. They both paused for a moment, but in the end they had a job to do, and much as they might want to stay, they couldn't. Khan moved first, and the young Captain followed close behind. Another group of three researchers and two archaeologists arrived and moved behind them. Once through the gap, they could all see the great pit that according to their scans descended nearly three hundred meters straight down. Dr Morgonz pointed at one of the thick sets of power cabling, each one as thick as a man's arm, that ran like a snake around the structure.

"You see the pattern. It's the same as in the other mountain. The others were destroyed in the blast, but this one is still giving off trace interference."

She pointed over the edge and into the blackness.

"Something down there is still running. If it is anything to do with the control system for this site, then this could be the most significant breakthrough in science for the last decade."

The rest of the group mumbled in partial agreement, but it was clear most had no interest in being in such a place. The reputation of the last stronghold of the Zealots and their hordes of machines and creatures left a taste that could be eliminated only by leaving the underground site.

"Come on, we are running on a tight schedule here. If we don't strike gold by the end of today, we will have to give up on this part of the site and try the next hole."

They pushed on, and Khan watched her move ahead with amusement. He looked to Captain Garcia.

"What is she looking for exactly? I thought the research was going well."

The Alliance Captain shrugged.

"Not what I heard. The rumor I heard was that the last orb entry point just disintegrated whatever went inside. Without a system at the other end, there is no way to get through. Why do you think it's been taking so long to expand the network? She must be after technical information from the control system."

Khan nodded at that part.

"Makes sense. This was one of the main command sections of the base."

They moved on for almost an hour, each inching their way down the slippery surface until finally reaching a series of arches of which only three were still in one piece. The Doctor moved into the first and lit up the darkened space to reveal more of the cables that ran inside. The light revealed that the space was in fact a large open cavern full of damaged machines and cables.

"Look!" she said almost excitedly.

She stepped forward, but Khan called out.

"Stop!"

He pushed ahead to a position about ten meters in front and further inside the room. He stopped and sniffed the air.

"What is it?" asked Captain Garcia, who moved passed the civilians to join him.

Khan sniffed the air again but said nothing at first. He glanced about suspiciously, scratching his chin as he considered their situation.

"Well?" asked Captain Garcia, but this time with an impatient tone.

"I thought I heard something in there."

Dr Morgonz walked up to him and looked inside the chamber herself.

"What's the problem? Come on, we have work to do," she snapped, moving past him to enter the chamber. Khan shook his head angrily, but the woman ignored him and entered the open space. The rest of her team followed, only the marines waited. Khan looked at them and grinned before looking back to Captain Garcia.

"I see your men have the intelligence to be suspicious. Look at them," he said, pointing at the civilians that were already inside, completely unaware if there might be something dangerous lurking inside.

The Alliance Captain looked up to where they had entered, but it was too far away to be seen now and was no more than a glimmer of light hundreds of meters away from them. He tapped the radio unit built into his armored suit of marine armor, known as a PDS suit.

"Garcia here, we've reached the main control level and are moving inside. Contact the Commander, and give him our updates."

He then turned to Khan. "What do you think?"

Khan shrugged.

"We're underground with five guns between us. Could be interesting."

Captain Garcia shuddered slightly at his cavalier mention of the danger and the odds. He'd only been on a few missions with his kind in the past and had never quite understood their attitude. Their attitudes were an odd dichotomy of loving battle and action, yet were openly more cautious and sensible in battle than his battle-trained marines.

"Let's go," he said finally.

The four marines and the Jötnar pushed away from

their position and entered the large chamber. The civilians were already busy exploring the plethora of interesting items both on the floor and walls of the cavernous place. Khan moved along the right-hand wall and rubbed his large hand over the carved stonework.

"Interesting, they are like the ones we saw on the surface."

The one he seemed most interested in was of a glowing orb surrounded by walking machines. The design was basic, but it suggested they were bowing down to the orb, itself containing the shape of something.

Captain Garcia examined the same piece of art, although with less interest than that shown by Khan. He looked over to the Doctor who was walking towards a dark shape in the centre of the room.

"Hey, Doctor. Who did all this?"

She ignored him, but one of the archaeologists, a scruffy man with long hair, looked back to him.

"It's not that old here. I'd say maybe a hundred...two hundred years top. The tech is not that dissimilar to ours. We're thinking it is most likely one of the early colony ships. Over a dozen went missing during the first generation of exploration in this system."

Captain Garcia looked unimpressed.

"Colonists, how could they create the technology for something like this place?"

The archaeologist grinned at him, his face contorting

slightly beneath his respirator.

"How would I know? I'm not with the technical team. You need to speak to Doctor Morgonz about that."

Two of the technicians ran over to where the Doctor was busy wiping dust away from a number of large computer units. She actually seemed almost excited at what she had found hidden beneath layers of debris.

"What is it?" asked Captain Garcia from his position off to the side of the cavernous room.

With a flicker of energy, a dust covered display unit flashed and sprung to life. The whiteness of its display almost blinded them in the pitch-blackness so far underground. She turned and grinned at them, but no one could actually see her face for a few seconds as their eyes adjusted once more.

"This, gentlemen, is an antique. We have examples of this kind of equipment in the Alliance Archives back on Terra Nova."

"So it's one of ours, then?" continued the Captain.

Doctor Morgonz looked back at him incredulously.

"Well who were you expecting? Little green men?"

Two of the marines chuckled at her comment, but a stern look from the Captain put them back to their usual silent status. Doctor Morgonz finished working on the equipment and pulled a lever. More systems activated until at least a quarter of the equipment in the room was running. She examined the main screen for a little while longer and then reached out to touch the display. Jose stepped closer and lifted his hand.

"Hey, don't you want to check for any more gear before we start using this stuff?" he asked nervously.

The Doctor ignored him and brought up a schematic of the site. It was heavily detailed with multiple power sources around a central shaft near where the dome structure had been present. She spotted something off to the side and enlarged it to fill the screen.

"Wow!" she exclaimed.

Khan and Captain Garcia moved from where they had been checking the perimeter and approached her display. The image had shifted from the technical side and instead showed a network of nodes, each joined by a series of lines. Captain Garcia pointed to the shapes on the left-hand side.

"Isn't this Terra Nova and Earth?"

The Doctor looked back at him; an expression of pleasant surprise on her face.

"Well done, Captain. Yes, it is a map of sorts. This section contains three nodes, two of which are worlds in the Alliance. This third one I do not recognize."

Khan looked for just a second before speaking.

"Uh, that's this place, isn't it?"

The Doctor nodded but said nothing, evidently too embarrassed to have anything to say. The others gathered round the screen as she tapped a number of the nodes to reveal further details. The one at Terra Nova showed an icon that was different to any of the others. She tapped it, and it brought up technical data and schematics.

"Fascinating," she said to herself as she examined carefully examined the information.

"What is it?" asked Khan in a barely interested tone.

Jose looked over his shoulder at the towering creature and shuddered slightly at the thought of being so close to one of them. They might be their allies, but there were still rumors of their violence after the War.

"The data here confirms the location of the AI hub that was installed to control the enemy ships and Biomechs throughout the old Confederacy. It looks like the other nodes are for planetary based spacebridges."

Doctor Morgonz traced the lines with her hand and came to Earth. It showed just a few lines of data and several unidentifiable icons. When the Doctor tapped what appeared to be Hyperion, however, the story changed completely. The icon representing the jungle world moved off to the side, and instead a complex web of nodes took its place.

"What the hell?" spluttered out Jose in a surprised tone. "Is that what I think it is?"

Doctor Morgonz nodded and pressed an icon that shrunk the nodes as if it was zooming out. It continued for almost thirty seconds until stopping and showing a much smaller subset of nodes spread out over a vast area.

She sighed with pleasure and turned to look at the small group.

"What you're seeing here is a network between worlds. This area here is the Orion Nebula, and you'll note that there are nearly fifty marked nodes in this area alone. There were only three of them in our explored space. Interestingly though, there are no other nodes with AI Hub icons. We must have been the exception."

"Or the source?" suggested Captain Garcia, a comment that surprised the rest of the scientific team.

"Orion? Isn't that over a thousand light years away?" asked a skeptical Jose.

"Yes, a vast distance," she replied and then moved back to the display. As she examined the data further, she simultaneously pulled out a portable data drive and synced to the device.

"What are you doing?" asked Khan.

Doctor Morgonz continued working while answering his question.

"I am copying the telemetry and technical data from these systems. It will take weeks, maybe months, to lift all this equipment from out of here. I can have everything on this unit in less than a minute and transfer it back to Terra Nova."

She stopped for a second and turned back to the group.

"Do you realize the significance of this find? Not only can it show us how to access this technology, it also shows us that it has been used to travel to another part of the Orion-Cygnus Arm of the Milky Way. We have the exact coordinates of multiple nodes in this part of space. If they match the details for our own system, then there is a good chance we can use this technology to pinpoint and travel to other worlds in this network. This might be the missing link to creating stable long-distance bridges."

Khan shook his head in confusion.

"The Orion what?"

Doctor Morgonz returned to the display and continued examining the detailed information while Jose explained to Khan.

"The Orion–Cygnus Arm is a name we use for a minor spiral arm of the Milky Way galaxy. That's our galaxy by the way. It is big, we estimate about 3,500 light years across and anything up to 10,000 light years in length. Our own worlds and the Orion Nebula are all based in this part of space."

"Oh," replied Khan with a tone that suggested he was even less interested after receiving the explanation.

Jose continued talking, but it was clear to the rest of them that Khan had little interest in what he was talking about. He said a few more words but stopped when he noticed Khan sniffing the air and looking about the dark and damp open space. Captain Garcia spotted his movement.

"What is it?"

The Jötnar officer ignored the marine for a moment as he looked into the dark space for signs of trouble. The Doctor and her people continued to remove data from the antique computer systems, with not one of them spending even a second checking on what the marines were looking at.

"Khan!" hissed the Captain over the intercom. The Jötnar finally turned and looked back, but his face had changed from the calm creature from a minute earlier to one of tense suspicion.

"What is it?" he asked, now starting to become annoyed.

Khan sniffed once more and then pulled the L52 Mark II Assault Carbine from its sheath on his thigh. The weapon had been modified like all the stocks of weapons sent to the Jötnar. It featured an enlarged frame, bigger trigger assembly and larger magazine capacity. It was a big weapon for most people, but in his hands it looked barely larger than a submachine gun. He flicked off the safety before tilting his head to Captain Garcia.

"Animals...they're here!" he snapped.

The Captain lifted his own carbine and flipped off the safety.

"Marines, watch your corners," he called out as he ran back to the Doctor.

"Dr Morgonz, we've got a problem!"

Khan was already at the opening to the room and waving for the marines to join him.

"There isn't time. I can hear them. They are coming!" he growled.

Dr Morgonz glanced back to him and returned to her unit.

"We will leave when I am satisfied I have all the data. If there is any trouble, I will expect you to deal with, Captain Garcia. Now leave me alone!"

Jose and one of the other technicians had already abandoned their work and were making their way to the opening when the Doctor spotted them both.

"What do you think you're doing? Get back to the computers, and get me the power schematics!"

Jose hesitated, but a high-pitched howl reverberated up through the chamber and sent chills through his spine. More followed until the howl became a muddled mixture of screams and snarling. The entire group of civilians broke and ran for the opening that was being carefully guarded by Khan and the three marines. Captain Garcia approached her and pulled the small data storage device from the computer unit. The system started beeping as if panicking at the loss of the connection.

"Captain, what are you doing?" she screamed at him.

He grabbed her by the shoulder and dragged the startled woman behind him.

"I'm doing my job, Doctor! We need to get out of here, and fast!"

As if to emphasise the point, a section of the floor

about ten meters away in the middle of the room shook and broke open, sending shards of stone down into what sounded like an almost bottomless pit. From the newly created crevice emerged a dark, fast moving form.

"Biomechs!" hissed Khan under his breath.

They weren't the later synthetic creatures like him, but the early monstrosities that had been used as cannon fodder in the scores of battlefields. They came in a variety of shapes and sizes and were constructed from the body parts and organs of cannibalized human prisoners. Though simple in mind, they were strong, violent, and deadly at close-quarters.

"I thought you Jötnar hunted them to extinction here?" she said bitterly.

Khan lifted his carbine and selected the high-power mode. It activated all three coil-chambers of the weapon and boosted the power setting to the maximum. He pulled the trigger, and a pulse of light was all that could be seen as the magnetized projectiles flew out from the barrels at hypersonic speeds. The impact was devastating and shattered the creature's body in a spray of ink black blood and body parts. He twisted his head around to the Doctor.

"Not all of them."

More movement appeared in the breach, and one of the interior walls started to shake. It was clear that a sizable number of the creatures were trying to find their way through and into the room.

"Right, let's go!" Captain Garcia ordered.

The marines moved out first with the civilians following close behind. Jose and the Doctor followed towards the rear; Captain Garcia and Khan then brought up the rearguard. No sooner had they left the large room, and returned to the dangerous circular track, were they attacked. This time the creatures were actually climbing up the walls like animals climbing out of a well. One of the marines was grabbed and pulled over the edge, and fell screaming for many seconds.

"Move it!" shouted Captain Garcia.

With that final order the group moved as quickly as they could, each of them motivated by the fear of death and the increasingly loud sound of their pursuers closing the distance. Unsurprisingly, they covered the return journey in half the time of the route down and reached within fifty meters of the exit when the creatures finally caught up with them. The fight started with Khan blasting three of them as they lurched out from the dark pit. As he grappled with another two with his bare hands, a group of another dozen pushed past and into the surviving civilians and marines. Khan cast one back to the pit and snapped the neck of the second before rolling backwards to avoid the wild gunfire of Captain Garcia and his two marines. They managed to cut down a good number, but it wasn't enough. One grabbed the Captain and pinned him down, and another brought down a primitive edged weapon onto his head. The impact was heavy and cracked through his helmet to embed in his skull.

"Hold them back!" shouted Khan, and he did his best to stand firm alongside them, firing one blast after another at the growing swarm. They managed a continuous stream of projectiles and held them back for almost thirty seconds before they vanished as quickly as they had arrived.

"Good, now we need to keep moving," said Khan.

He turned around to find Dr Morgonz had rushed away with her team and was heading for the surface. Khan could see more movement near her position, but he already knew her fate was sealed.

"Idiot!" he muttered, chasing up the path.

If any creature stepped in his path, he smashed it aside with his fists or with a single shot from his carbine. He reached within three meters of the Doctor when the mortal blow was struck. One creature hacked brutally at her, managing to strike off her left arm with a single blow. Two more leapt on her, each hacking or biting into her as she screamed in terror. The other civilians split up like prey being hunted down by wild beasts. He jumped in and hacked wildly, but she was already dead by the time he reached her. Khan spotted the storage device drop from her hands before one of them leapt at him, knocking him down beside it. His carbine was torn from his arms, and a blade slew down, narrowly missing his face. From the corner of his eye, he spotted the marines being dragged down, and his blood felt as though it would boil. In a wild rage, he grabbed his nearest attacker around the throat and choked it with all his strength.

"Animals!" he roared.

* * *

The newly arrived unit of marines positioned themselves around the entrance of the dig site. The sound of battle had already eased off, and none appeared very keen on stepping into the darkness and the danger that lurked within. Technical Director Dr Neson knelt down and peered inside, to the worry of the others around him.

"Can you hear that?" he said nervously.

Before any of them could even move, the bloodied arm of one of the creatures reached out and grabbed at his head. In one quick movement, he was dragged inside screaming. The sounds of a struggle quickly ended with a sickening snapping sound. The marines stood in shock, each stunned by the suddenness of what had just occurred. One took a step closer, but another shape appeared in the shadows of the entrance. Each of them lifted their weapons and trained them on the blood soaked shape as Khan dragged himself out of the hole. He dropped to the ground, and from his hand the data storage unit rolled out and onto the floor. In his left hand, he carried the severed head of one of the creatures, presumably the one that had just brutally killed the Director.

"Captain Khan, are you hurt?" asked one of the corporals who ran over to him before any of the others made a fatal mistake and shot the wounded warrior. Khan shook his head and looked up at the bright light and small group of marines. He grinned at them, baring his chipped teeth.

"Close up the hole, and get in touch with Gun," he said, before looking back to the dark and dangerous place he had just left. He picked up the data unit he had dropped and placed it in the hands of the marine.

"I've got the Doctor's data from the site. Now get me Gun. It's time to do some hunting, and I think he's going to like it down there!"

The marine took the device and looked back to the others who stood by and watched with a mixture of dumbfounded surprise and horror. Not one of them could understand why Khan or anybody else would want to return to the scene of such violence. Khan was no ordinary man though, and neither were his kin.

CHAPTER TWO

The Crusader class of ships was the culmination of nearly a year's study into the creation of a universal ship design for the Alliance Navy. Gone was the fleet of cruisers, marine transports and battleships. To replace them, a brand new ship was designed to perform the tasks of all three, but in a package of about the size and cost of a cruiser. With improvements in technology and miniaturization, the new class could carry up to five hundred marines or an equivalent sized flight group plus eight craft, including shuttles or fighters. It was a bold experiment that would meets its first challenge in the Orion Incident.

Ships of the Alliance

Seven years later

Jenson moved along the poorly lit corridor and kept his head down low. He'd been waiting two decks lower now for almost two days, and fatigue was settling in. After what seemed like weeks, the engineering team finally packed up their equipment, and he was able to move. As he approached the main gantry, he could make out a two-man marine patrol that was busy inspecting a security-monitoring unit. Jenson took a step back and waited in the shadows. He reached down and pulled his sidearm from his belt. It was a modern low-velocity slug-thrower, and the kind of equipment that could be found at any main weapons dealer in the Alliance. What it lacked in complexity, it made up for with its ability to avoid detection in almost any scanner unit when broken up into its seven major components. It carried just five shots, but each was handmade and designed to kill at subsonic speeds, and the perfect weapon for use on a starship.

"What's that?" asked one of the marines.

The second of the two moved from the unit and peered into the shadows that lurked all around their position. The ship, for lack of a better word, had been constructed in a rush, and much of it was no more than glorified gantries and access corridors taken from other vessels and stations.

Jenson froze, every single muscle in his body turning to iron as he did his utmost to blend in with his surroundings. It hadn't been him, but anything that caught their attention could put them onto him. They looked about, but the more senior of the two quickly discarded the potential problem and returned to the monitoring unit. Jenson relaxed and continued forward until he was only fifteen meters away from the two men. On the wall to his right was the stencil identifier announcing this was Section 6B, the part of the ship where the rotational equipment and motors were based. Though not critical to the operation of the station, it did allow the use of artificially created gravity for those working on the ship. A door on the right-hand side, and near the sign, led into a brightly lit room.

That's the place, he thought, glancing back to the two marines.

They were still busy looking at the station. He took a deep breath, lurched across the space, and pushed open the door. Without thinking, he stepped inside and pulled the door shut behind him. Inside were two women playing cards. They wore engineer's overalls, and a series of displays ran along one side of the small room. He pointed the gun at them both, lifting his hand to his mouth for silence. The first, a middle-aged woman with short dark hair, fell from her chair in surprise. But the second, a much younger woman, just stared right back.

"You ready?" he asked.

The young woman nodded and then pulled a short, slightly curved blade from her waistband. She stood up and walked to her fallen friend, extending her free hand out to help her. As the fallen women reached up to hold her hand, the blade flashed across, slashing open her throat. Blood gushed from the deep wound, and she slipped to the floor, leaving an ever-growing pool of blood behind her. Jenson could almost make out the tattoo on her right arm, just above the wrist, of the Confederate Navy, the precursor to the Alliance. He smiled at the thought of what they were doing.

"I have full access to the habitation and rotation controls. That's all we can do from here. Will that be enough?"

Jenson nodded in satisfaction.

"That is enough. With this access, I will be able to carry out my tasks. Finally, we can ensure our brothers will not have died on Hyperion in vain."

He started to shudder; the memories and terror of what he had seen on that planet so many years ago was still fresh in his mind. The machines, the monsters; it was too much for him. The image of the dark, monstrous machine as it emerged from a glowing orb returned to his mind. It was an image that returned to him every time he closed his eyes. The metal followers ran about like beetles, each of them hacking and stabbing at friend and foe alike. It came to him so often now, he could no longer tell what was a real memory and what he had imagined. The entire scene was like an image from hell where the tortured bodies of the defenseless were shredded before his eyes. He shook his head, but the image refused to leave him.

"I...uh, I must..." he started and then almost fell back. The young woman stepped closer and placed a hand on his forearm. She felt warm and soft to the touch, snapping him out of his trance and back to the present.

"Jenson, it's alright. We'll never come into contact with them again, I promise you! Pontus and his brothers can stay buried, and we'll make sure it stays that way."

* * *

Governor Anderson, the grey-haired veteran of countless wars and campaigns, watched from the busy control room as the power systems were fired up for the test. They'd been used a dozen times already, but this was the first time they would power the experimental Rift-generator, the first one to ever be created for one-way travel. Ever since he'd taken command of the Alliance research base on Prometheus, he'd been involved with the unusual and the bizarre, from synthetic production of the war winning Biomechs to the dozens of new ships now plying the trade routes of the expanded Alliance. This was his second decade in charge of the facility, yet he still managed to maintain his slender frame. His still lightly freckled face and graying, unkempt hair, smartly trimmed sideburns and small moustache, betrayed his years of experience as a military governor and the second-in-command of a capital ship, now a senior Admiral in the Alliance military.

Captain Dirk Konicek, commander of his Marine Guards, approached and saluted smartly. He was a barrel-chested officer with coal black hair and a scarred complexion from a number of years working on some of the toughest environments in the Alliance.

"Admiral, the civilians are aboard and have asked permission to enter the control room."

"Sir, the plants are reporting maximum efficiency, computer systems are active, and the Rift-generator is ready for your signal," said the Chief Engineer on the program.

Anderson nodded and then looked about the room, and at the dozens of faces looking back to him. At least half had only joined the project in the last three years, but they had made massive progress. He thought back to the construction of the first Rift-generators that had been built with pride by his team. In just seventeen years, the Alliance had made massive strides in science, technology and exploration. The ever-present Alliance Marines were stationed discreetly at the entrances, though few expected trouble. The Prometheus research facility was now one of the most heavily guarded and improved sites in the entire Alliance.

So, it is time.

"Very well, bring them in," he said sternly.

One of the marines nodded and opened one of the small doors. In walked a small group of the press, including representatives from both Prime and Terra Nova, the two largest and most important planets in the Alliance. Their camera crews moved into position, each closely monitored by the marines. Admiral Anderson was no great fan of the press, but even he knew the importance of such an event in the history of the facility, the Alliance and humanity itself. He looked at the first anchorwoman, a young woman probably in her early thirties. She wore a stylish grey suit, and he was certain she was the head anchorwoman for one of the Terra Nova networks. She nodded fervently and pointed at the camera to her right, indicating they were also ready. The Admiral took a deep breath and smiled.

"Citizens of the Alliance, today is an auspicious day for all of us. In the seventeen years since the end of our terrible hardship in the War, we have come a long way. The network now exists between the major colonies, and trade and prosperity has returned to the long-suffering parts of our fledgling Alliance. This construction is the culmination of seven long years of work and the first stage in our exploration of the stars. Hundreds of years ago our ancestors launched colony ships on a generation's long journey to Alpha Centauri, now our home. With this first exploratory Rift, we reach out and continue our journey."

He turned from the camera and nodded to his Chief Engineer. The man moved several icons on his three-dimensional display and activated a start-up sequence.

"Generators at full power, Admiral."

A short distance away, another dozen engineers manned their own stations. Each called out and confirmed the status of their own equipment, including the cooling and backup systems.

"Cooling...check."

"Computer tracking...check."

"Security lockdown protocols now active."

The Chief engineer looked back to the Admiral.

"All systems are go, Sir."

Admiral Anderson paused just for a second before he gave the order. The tests in the past had all been successful, but never before had a Rift been targeted at an unknown location. The problems and potential dangers of creating a spacebridge with no end location for connection had been considered a deadly risk. It was only with the data recovered from the ruins on Hyperion seven years earlier had it been considered even a possibility.

"Activate the Rift," he said as calmly as possible.

The Chief Engineer returned to his system and entered his personal security clearance and override to start the system. As with most pieces of advanced technology, the actual final trigger was understated. No more than a simple activate button on his display. He reached out to touch it and could almost feel the eyes of billions burning into the back of his head as he pressed the button. His fingertip touched the unit, and around the room the screens changed color, as the diagnostic tools monitored the power and signal levels through the unit.

"Open them!" called out Admiral Anderson.

On cue, the entire right-hand side of the large control room lit up as thick metal shutters lowered down. Behind them was photoelectric glass, a substance able to instantly respond to adverse lighting condition in case of solar flares or other such problems. It only now became apparent that they were all situated aboard the old Prometheus Seven Trading Post. At almost two thousand meters in diameter, the station now housed almost a thousand of the best technicians, engineers and scientists. Well over a decade ago, it had been the home of trade and commerce in the sector. Little of that now remained with its new role of custodian of the Prometheus Rift. The view from the windows consisted first of the burning hot world of Prometheus, of which they orbited. Even more technicians and scientists were based there, but it was the orbiting station that was responsible for managing and maintaining the vast construction that floated in space next to it. Admiral Anderson pointed to the components.

"As you can see, the Prometheus Rift is complete and ready for its final test. We built this Rift to allow exploration of new star systems that are vast distances away. In the past, we have used the peak of our technology to travel distances of up to four light years. In the case of here, it took over a generation for the fastest and best-equipped colony ships to get here from Earth. This time we plan on sending a ship over a thousand light years to the Orion Nebula."

Unlike the orbs constructed on the colonies, the Rift equipment consisted of a dozen small orbital platforms, each of which was self-contained and connected via an array of thin cables to the station itself.

"As you may know, the power requirements to operate such a piece of technology are at the limit of our understanding. Over eighty percent of this entire station's power capacity will be used to run each of the platforms until the cycle is complete."

Even as they watched the group of platforms, each looking much like an improvised space station, they flickered and flashed as energy rippled across their structures. The clouds of dust and gas around Prometheus gave the streaks of energy odd hues and shades of color as they glinted off the dust and particles in space. At first, it was just the occasional flash, until a web of flashes and lines jumped back and forth. Admiral Anderson looked over his Chief Engineer's shoulder to check his screen. The man looked back at him.

"All systems nominal, Sir. The grid is holding. Capacitors are charging, thirty seconds..."

Anderson nodded, and although he gave the look of calm professionalism, he could feel the beads of sweat on his forehead. It wasn't just the money and resources that had been spent. It was the hopes and dreams of so many that had got them so far. The possibility of long-distance travel and exploration was one of the great dreams of so many in the Alliance. The opportunities and possibilities this technology had created had thousands of companies, and hundreds of thousands of people, waiting for the chance to make their names in the great unknown. He knew a lot was riding on this mission. He wondered how excited they would be if they realized where the exact coordinates in Orion had come from. He tried to shake that out of his head.

Hyperion is something for another day; right now we create the doorway.

The Chief Engineer nodded towards him.

"Sir, capacitors are fully charged."

Here we go.

"Activate the bridge!" he said smartly.

The last stage of the process was the actual creation of the Rift itself. Anderson had witnessed the activation of many rifts before, but without a Rift to connect to, there was a degree of uncertainty. Either way, it didn't matter now as the process was already firing up. The grid flashed with power, and the space between the platforms flickered one last time and then changed to a purple-blue glowing disc. He watched and waited as the disc settled down until it faded out to an almost transparent shape. He took in a deep breath, half expecting the fields to collapse. Instead, each of the technicians and engineers gave him an affirmative.

"Yes!" came a voice from one of the systems, and he

was quickly joined by dozens of other technicians and engineers. Back in the middle of the room, a large three-dimensional projected model showed the shape of the Rift entrance being created. Energy circles surrounded the platforms and ran in a stream back to the station in a continuous loop. One by one, each of the platforms changed color and flashed green on the model. The indication was clear and obvious to each of those watching that the system was working and settling down.

"Get me Commodore Lewis."

The image of the Commodore appeared in seconds and filled the large screen on the wall. The man was a seasoned officer and had been present at the last major action at Hyperion seventeen years earlier. He was now in charge of the defensive portion of the operation and commanded an impressive force of seven major warships, including the recently commissioned ANS Dragon. She was one of the newest of the Crusader class warships and the peak of Alliance technology. Her powerplants were heavily shielded and provided power to a battery of super-heavy railguns that were fitted in targetable mounts on the bow and stern. Dozens of smaller weapon mounts were fitted out with multi-barreled coilguns, all of them run by the advanced power system. She had the rough shape of a shark with a fattened forward section and an enlarged tail section. Many struts and antennae extended out, but it was the total lack of a rotating crew section that was the most revolutionary part of the vessel. No other military ship, until now, had been able to create such a force without the use of primitive rotating sections.

"Admiral Anderson, my forces are ready and awaiting your go order."

Anderson nodded and looked over to his team for confirmation on the stability of the Spacebridge. All lights appeared to be green, but there was a nagging doubt in his mind about the viability of the one-way Rift. He looked back to the display and the patient face of the Commodore. He watched for a moment, and his attention was drawn to the odd movement of the officers in the CIC (Combat Information Centre) of the ship. They moved with slow bounces that reminded him of the ancient but famous footage of mankind's first steps onto the lunar surface of the moon back in the twentieth century. The Crusader class of ship were all making use of the experimental gravito-magnetic drive developed on Terra Nova. It could only provide about one-fifth of normal Earth gravity, but it did allow the crew to go about their duties, without drifting around the spacecraft. The final indicator on the main display flashed several times and then settled down to a steady green.

This is it, he thought.

"Commodore, the Spacebridge is ready and stable. You are cleared to commence the operation."

There was a short pause, and for the briefest of

moments, he wondered if his message had failed to reach the Commodore. He was about to speak again when he received a response.

"Excellent. Congratulations to your team, Admiral. This is an auspicious day for the Alliance and for humanity itself."

From their position in orbit around Prometheus and directly alongside the Rift platforms, they had a perfect view of the assembled ships. ANS Dragon was the closest vessel to the Rift and the largest warship present. As the eleventh ship in her class, she represented the new Navy, one that was smaller but substantially more flexible. The ship was one of the new multipurpose warships being built for the fleet to replace the few functioning cruisers, battleships, transports and war barges still in service. She was more powerful than the old cruisers used. She was faster and had the capacity to carry up to five hundred marines or a similar sized flight group; almost half of the capacity of a dedicated transport, like the venerable ANS Santa Maria and ANS Santa Cruz. The remaining six ships included a motley collection of destroyers, each due for imminent replacement by the growing fleet of Crusader class warships.

"Look, there it is!" called out one of the media people. It was a young man, barely out of his twenties but dripping with enthusiasm and excitement. Anderson was hardly surprised, this was one of the biggest ever stories for the media.

Anderson knew immediately that they had spotted ANS Beagle. She had been hidden from view as she was positioned out of sight behind the structure of the station and guarded by three of the destroyers. She was substantially larger than any other ship present and of a bizarre design that included dozens of gantries and modules that seemed hastily attached to her fragile boom shaped hull.

"ANS Beagle," announced Admiral Anderson.

"As you all know, there is no point in us launching a mission over a thousand light years away if we have no ability to return and send data back. ANS Beagle is the first completely self-contained, mobile Rift generator, and as such, she is the most advanced vessel ever constructed."

He paused for a moment, letting that sink in.

"In fact, there are many that suggest the Beagle is the greatest engineering feat in our entire history. At more than a kilometer long, she can build, manage and power the reverse end of the Spacebridge for up to three months. Assuming the bridge is viable, we will be able to send engineers through to create a more permanent station that can manage a long distance bridge indefinitely."

Everybody in the room watched the massive ship as she used her maneuvering thrusters to position herself to face the entrance of the bridge. The entrance itself was substantial, but at the approach of the ship, seemed barely adequate. The outer sections of the entrance fired their own thrusters and moved apart at an incredibly slow speed. It took almost a minute before the hole had enlarged enough for ANS Beagle to safely fit.

"Sir, systems stable, bridge is secure and power systems are holding. We can keep it open for seven minutes, maybe eight with our reserves," confirmed the Chief Engineer.

"Good, send the signal."

It was the biggest problem with not having a Rift generator at the other end to lock down the Spacebridge. Whereas the bridge could operate for minutes, it would need an entire station to power it. Once hardware was installed at both ends, it could be operated for months and with far less power, while a permanent monitoring station was built at the other end. The longer the tunnel, the greater were the energy requirements, and the distance factor to the Orion Nebula was vast compared to the paltry distances so far used in the Alliance.

The mighty ship activated its main drive engines and pushed to the Rift at a crawl. In fact, it was almost impossible to identify the movement of the ship as she started her maiden voyage.

"Admiral Anderson, ANS Beagle is starting her run," said Commodore Lewis before cutting his video link. Anderson watched the small flotilla of warships change their position so that each ship was stationed with its thickest armor and maximum amount of weapons facing the Rift. None of the civilians noticed; as they were all too busy watching the bulk of ANS Beagle move ever closer to the Rift. It moved passed the station at a crawl, but with the slow speed came the added drama and excitement of such a behemoth moving to the gate. He noted ANS Dragon swivel on the spot and point her bow railguns directly at the Rift itself. As the previous XO of a Navy battlecruiser, Admiral Anderson was very familiar with the weaponry, and even he knew that these new weapons were substantially larger and more powerful than the weapons he had access to during the War.

If anything comes through the bridge, they'll handle it.

The front of the great vessel slipped inside the Rift and flickered and pulsed before vanishing from view. It took just seconds for the rest of the vessel to enter in its entirety and then it was gone. Admiral Anderson looked about the room and watched the look of confusion on the faces of the small group of press. This was in stark contrast to the large number of technicians and engineers who were busy maintaining the energy levels of the bridge.

* * *

ANS Beagle moved out from the violent exit of the Rift to the sound of emergency alarms blaring away. The structure shook and vibrated from the uncontrolled exit, and several parts of the vessel had ruptured and broken away. From his position in the CIC, Lieutenant Davies of the Alliance Marine Corps watched in confusion at their arrival. He had been placed in charge of the small contingent of a single platoon of marines to provide security for the vessel. It was a tiny number of people for such a great structure, but the risks of losing the ship had made it difficult to find more that would chance their lives on what could be a one-way mission.

"Captain, do we have a problem?" he asked Captain Raikes, the commander of the vessel and one of the Alliance's most experienced engineers.

More flashes rippled through the room, and a display sent shards of glass flying across the open space. Like most of the older ships, she made extensive use of a rotating section to produce artificial gravity, but it was flawed in execution. The pieces seemed to follow bizarre arcs and managed to strike two crewmembers in the face. Captain Raikes shielded his face and shouted out to the officers and crew in the CIC.

"I need a full report, now!"

He then turned to look back at him.

"This is just the consequence of an unsecured spacebridge, nothing for you to worry about."

With that short burst, he turned back to his crew and continued trying to get the situation under control. More flashes signaled the death of another display, the shuddering stopped, and the vessel appeared at peace, adrift in space.

"Sir, we're out of the Spacebridge. Reports are coming in now."

The Captain wasn't looking as he was much more interested in the video feed on the main screen. It looked as though he was looking out of a large window, like the bridge of an ancient water-based vessel, but in reality the image was a projection from external camera feeds. This meant the CIC could be placed deep within the ship for security and engineering reasons.

"Just look at that!" he said with a tone of awe and reverence in his voice. Lieutenant Davies looked to the display and gasped at the view. Not only was the left-hand side taken up with the massive shape of a burning hot star, but also directly in front of them was a planet surrounded by thick rings. The Captain glanced over his shoulder to the technicians.

"Look at that! You are the first people to ever look upon the planets of the Orion Nebula. This is truly a great day."

Silence greeted his words as they watched the shining orbs of light out in space. Many of them had visited other planets but few had travelled outside of Alpha Centauri, apart from those with long tours on military ships. This was a journey unlike any taken before by man, and every single one of them knew it.

"Sir, the gate is closing!" called out the Chief Engineer.

Captain Raikes looked at the display and watched as the

Rift in space flickered and then vanished as quickly as it had been made.

This is it then, he thought.

"You know what you need to do, people. This station needs to be operational, and I want it done carefully and by the numbers."

The crew went about their duties, and he relaxed for just a moment. It had been expected that they would take some damage while heading through the Rift, and that was one of the main reasons for bringing so much spare equipment. Until equipment was installed at both ends, it would be impossible to keep the bridge open for more than a few minutes. Even worse though, until his ship was made operational they had no way of getting home. In theory it should work, but there was a possible and very real chance they could hit problems. Nothing more was said for several minutes until one of the engineers called out after spotting something on his display.

"Uh...Captain...this isn't right!"

Captain Raikes barely even noticed his words until he noticed two more of the technicians moving over to the man's desk to look at his screen. He turned around and looked directly at him.

"What is it?"

"The nearest moon...I'm...well, Sir, I'm picking up a coded radio signal from its surface."

Captain Raikes was dumbfounded at the news. The

only way any coded radio signal could be sent was if something or somebody was there and had sent it. There was no possibility it could have come from them, they were the first visitors to this system.

"Sir, we're being scanned by something!" called out the same man.

Captain Raikes snapped to attention, his initial surprise now starting to worry him.

"What the hell is it?" he asked to the surprise of the rest of the crew. "Get me a long range view of the moon on the main screen."

It took just a few button presses to bring up a direct feed from one of the many stabilized camera mounts on the ship. The moon filled the display and looked like most moons, small, barren and desolate. He looked at it in detail but nothing of note appeared. He looked back to his crew that seemed equally perplexed.

"Get to work; I need a working Rift and fast!"

Command is going to want to hear about this, he thought.

But even more important to him was that he wanted to know they had a way back home. The thought of being stranded out in a star system this far out was the greatest fear any of them had on the ship. The only backup plan was that the Rift could be recreated back in Proxima Centauri, but that would not occur for another twenty-four hours. In the meantime, he had a damaged ship to repair, a Rift to create, and a strange foreign signal to investigate. He looked back at the image of the moon and tried to imagine what could be transmitting. None of the options were particularly appealing to him.

"Lieutenant!" he called out to the nearest science officer.

"Sir?"

"Prepare a reconnaissance drone. I want orbital scans by the end of today."

CHAPTER THREE

Admiral Jarvis first came to public significance during the attack on the Titian Naval Station. Her command of the Confederate counterattack has become legendary in the annals of the Navy. Her flagship, the battlecruiser CCS Crusader fought a long and bloody battle like none that had been seen for generations. She was present at the start of the War and her selfless actions at Terra Nova helped end it.

Heroes of the Great Uprising

"Thirty seconds until activation," said a pre-recorded voice over the ship's internal speaker system. It was nothing more than a simple reminder that they were about to move through. Spartan suspected the warning was more for insurance purposes, as at least half the trips through a Rift ended in minor injuries or at the very least some violent shakes.

He watched the glowing shape of the Spacebridge from the observation area of the liner. The entrance itself reminded him of a whirlpool, and no matter how many times he'd travelled through; it gave him a sickening feeling in his stomach. This wasn't the bridge that had been found in the middle of the War though. This was one of the first artificially made in the years since the War and had been lauded as the ultimate example of Alliance engineering. He knew where the technology had been found, and it had been won through blood and combat, not science and discovery.

Not that Spartan really cared too much about where it had come from. He'd made hundreds of such trips in his long career, but times had changed. In the past, he travelled to warzones or to fix problems, but now he was travelling to another private security post and yet another contract. He looked over his shoulder, half expecting to see one of his comrades from the Marine Corps or the Alliance Navy, but instead all he found were groups of civilians. It seemed a long time since he'd completed his ten years in the Marines, and there were still days when he missed the action. He looked at the people around him; most were specialists but a few were heading out to visit their families. He straightened his back, boredom now seeming to settle into his very bones.

How much longer till this damned journey is over? He wondered. Although unlike the rest of those on board, he knew almost to the second how long it would take. Even so, he was still impatient and wanted the journey to end. He looked at a young man, probably in his early twenties that sat and chatted to two women at the other end of the viewing area. They were all watching in awe as they travelled through the Rift in space. It was old hat to Spartan. Little did any of them know how instrumental this one man's military victories had been in allowing the creation of what was now known as the Network.

Spartan was unlike anybody on the ship, however. Years of trouble had led him to a life of illegal pit fighting on the stations of Prometheus. The many fights and contests had toned his body and toughened his mind into that of a modern day gladiator. He had spent ten years in the military, with the first three taken up with the events of the Great Uprising that had led to a major civil war. Only the total defeat of the Echidna rebels and their hordes of Biomech creatures had averted the colonies from total disaster. He considered the great gulf of time that had passed since those bloody days, and in some ways missed the simplicity of the battles.

Not that my security work is exactly safe, he thought to himself with a wry grin.

In walked two Alliance Agents, one of whom he instantly recognized.

"Johnson? What are you doing here?" he asked.

The two men moved towards him, but only Johnson

put on any attempt of pleasantries.

"Spartan, nice to see you again," he said, reaching out to shake his hand. The two had worked on a good number of operations both on Prometheus and Hyperion during and after the War. Johnson looked both pleased to see him but also concerned.

"This is my partner for this operation, Agent Stefan Hammacher."

Spartan nodded to them both but concentrated on his old friend.

"Why are you here? I thought you were in charge of Special Operation on Kerberos now? Aren't you a bit old for fieldwork?" asked Spartan mischievously.

Johnson nodded and chose to ignore his barb.

"I am, but the rumors I've been hearing about Jack are worrying. I have selected the capture team myself. They are all reliable, skilled and understand the mission. We have to bring him in, ideally without violence."

Spartan raised an eyebrow at the last point.

"You think he'll come in without a fight? You do understand he's a son of mine? I know we go back a long way, Johnson, but I'm no ally against my own blood. If you are thinking of taking him, why are you telling me? Are you looking for a fight?"

Johnson smiled, but Agent Hammacher maintained a completely straight expression on his face.

Johnson spoke to his partner for a few seconds until

stopping and nodding to him. Hammacher stepped away and moved closer to the door, about twenty meters from where Spartan and Johnson were stood.

"That was just posturing in front of Hammacher. About Jack, I know he's barely eighteen now, but his list of offences keeps growing. At this rate, he'll end up spending most, if not all of his adult life in prison. Maybe he'll be given the same choice as you?"

Spartan shook his head.

"No, the Alliance doesn't do that anymore. I don't understand what happened with him. He was doing well at school, and Teresa and I have been spending more and more time with him at our new home, as much time as we can both spare. Okay, it's mainly her, but still, he has a good life."

Johnson nodded.

"True, but that last incident on the transport over Terra Nova left three men dead. He just doesn't have any respect for authority and keeps getting into trouble. I've pushed enough off my desk already, but this current line of attack is getting a lot of attention. Either I came or somebody else would have."

"Hey, you know that was an attempted hijack of a Jötnar supply ship. Seven of them were murdered before he killed one of them and helped space the rest of them. It was judged a justifiable homicide if I remember correctly. So quite how does Jack really necessitate the involvement of Alliance Intelligence?"

Johnson shook his head.

"You do know that isn't why I'm here, don't you? We both know what happened on the ship, and the Jötnar won't forget it either. That was a close run thing. The last situation the Alliance needs is a planet of angry Jötnar looking for some payback."

He touched Spartan's shoulder, moving him closer to the window where the flashing of energy marked their journey through the Rift. They were now a good distance from anybody else in the observation area.

"Your boy has dug up information on Epsilon Eridani that is causing quite a stir. I know you're heading back to work on this new contract, but I could really use an assist on this one. It's in your interest, Jack's and the Jötnar."

Spartan looked intrigued.

"What do you mean?"

"It's no secret that your boy has spent a few interesting vacations with the Jötnar on Hyperion. Hell, I'd say he prefers the Jötnar to those of his own kind."

"So? He's become good friends with the sons of Khan. He's not committed any crimes. Even if he had, Hyperion is Jötnar territory."

The Agent pulled out a secpad, a heavily improved and more secure version of the venerable datapad still used in the Alliance. It was the size of his fist and made from a toughened plastic. Spartan took it and placed his thumb on the side to activate the unit. It showed an image of Jack with two Jötnar climbing over a security fence. Although the Jötnar were the same age as his son, they were already the size of an adult man and much more strongly built. Originally a synthetic spinoff from the enemy's war efforts, the Jötnar had become an integral, if not volatile part of the Alliance.

"Your boy has been seen making contact with members of the Retribution movement."

Spartan looked surprised at the implication.

"The Retribution movement? We shut them down years ago. Why would he be involved with them?"

"That we don't know. You are well aware they have been conducting vigilante raids on those suspected of working with the Zealots in the War. My intelligence sources suggest they have altered their scope in the last six months. Now they are looking for anybody involved in the Biomech programs."

The ship shuddered violently, and the flashing colors of the Rift vanished to be replaced by the glowing orb of the new sun and the blue, watery planet below. Spartan looked out at the planet and allowed himself a short smile as he thought of his modest home on the surface. Epsilon Eridani was one of the newest star systems that had been colonized in the last five years, and with the construction of the bridge it had expanded at an incredible rate. It contained only one habitable world, but that was more than enough for dozens of companies to move in and start exploiting its many resources.

"Jack wouldn't be involved in that kind of crap and you know it," he replied, but truthfully Spartan just didn't know anymore. He saw his son infrequently, and when they did, they usually fought. Things had never been resolved since the incident with the woman on Kerberos. He tried to shake the memories for a moment and get back to business.

Johnson leaned in closer.

"Look, this is the official line. The truth? We have intel on potential threats to the Jötnar, and we have suspicions that Jack knows more than he is letting on. I came here because it is Jack. I won't risk him with any other agent."

Spartan looked over to the agent waiting impatiently at the end of the room.

"You don't have much faith in your own people?"

Johnson shrugged.

"The only person I trust is me, and I think I owe it to you to get this done properly."

Spartan nodded at this, thankful to have something that hopefully resembled the truth of the matter.

"Well, it looks like we'd better find Jack then. How many people have you brought?"

Agent Johnson looked back to his partner and indicated for him to come back. He then looked back to Spartan.

"Just the two of us. We will meet at your new office and

assess the information my units have established so far. I think we can end this before anybody gets hurt."

Spartan nodded, and the two agents moved back to the door. Spartan looked back out of the window, but now nothing but a dark cloud seemed to hang over his return. He'd been working away from home for four months, and it had been hard work getting the contract organized for his firm to take over the security of the colony base. He had set up the small firm now known as Alliance Protection Services after leaving the military. Teresa, his wife, managed most of the day-to-day operations, and in just a few years, they'd moved from running security on a number of commercial sites to becoming the most important security contractor in the Alliance. Much of this was down to the reputation of its two founders; both decorated and experienced marines with exemplary track records.

Spartan pulled out his own secpad from a pouch on his belt and held it in front of him. He tapped the button that connected him directly to his office on the surface. Almost immediately the face of Ashley Helsing appeared. She was one of his best assistants and ran parts of the office when he was away.

"Spartan, good to see you," she replied pleasantly.

"Is Teresa there?" asked Spartan.

She nodded while simultaneously connecting him through to her office. The image quickly shifted to that of a slightly darker room and the face of his wife and co-director of APS.

"Spartan," she said with a concerned look.

Spartan recognized the expression immediately. The two of them had been in the trenches on many occasions and seen some of the bloodiest action of the Uprising. His heart felt heavy as he expected the worst.

"I need you down here fast. There's been trouble at one of the refineries. Two men killed and the control crew are being held hostage. In the last two weeks, we've had a string of incidents. There's a lot of money moving down here, and some of the competition are trying to muscle in on some of the smaller industrial operators. It's getting hectic," she paused and then did her best to smile. "It's nice to see you."

Spartan nodded, but he was actually relieved the news wasn't about Jack. After seeing Johnson on the same ship as him, he was starting to worry that his troublesome son had somehow turned into one of the Alliance's most wanted individuals.

"What about Jack?"

Teresa sighed with the look of exasperation he'd seen so many times in the last few years. Jack was a skilled and intelligent boy, but had the fire and passion of Teresa, mixed with the stubbornness of Spartan. Individually, it was awkward but combined it became a lethal combination.

"I've grounded him until this farce with Gun's sons

is sorted out. Apparently, they were found at one of the mining complexes with people from a Kerberos crime family."

"What?" asked Spartan incredulously.

"That's what I thought. Jack said something about a movement on Kerberos that's working against the Biomechs, some kind of vigilante program. You know, one of the groups that wants to push them out of Alliance business and trade, the usual discrimination. I think this time it has got more serious. One of the Jötnar juveniles was found dead last week, and there are rumors they tried to sabotage one of the planetary Rift gateways."

"What? He wouldn't be involved with that. He's good friends with the Jötnar and the Biomechs."

Teresa nodded quickly.

"I know. He wouldn't consider lifting a finger against them. That's the problem I think though. He knew the Jötnar, and he is taking it hard, really hard. Not even the crime families from Kerberos are interested in this violence.

"Yeah," replied Spartan, "not good for business."

Teresa nodded slowly.

"Exactly, and it looks like Jack has been working on finding out all he can on this movement. I think Gun and his own intelligence teams have been helping. You know Jack. He's a big supporter of him and his people. I'm worried he'll find out more than is safe. He's hot headed, like somebody else I know."

"Yeah, don't remind me!" he replied, doing his best to make light of the situation.

He remembered the last time he'd visited Hyperion and the Jötnar with Jack. They participated in one of their violent but entertaining martial contests. Jack had managed to bring down a juvenile Jötnar, quite a feat for a teenager that had not reached manhood. The synthetic Jötnar had more in common with the trolls and ogres of myth than of modern man, and they had been created by the enemy for the war effort in the Uprising; but a large number had turned and fought for his side. Their reward had been the jungle world of Hyperion and full citizenship in the Alliance itself. The War may have ended seventeen years ago, but there were still thousands of people that had a bitter hatred of the creatures, some of whom had caused the deaths of so many citizens.

"There's something else. Intelligence Director Johnson is here with another agent. They want to see Jack. Apparently, it is something to do with this Jötnar Retribution movement."

Teresa leaned in closer to her camera.

"No, Jack would never be involved in that. I thought it fell apart years ago when Gun found out?"

Spartan recalled the great problems that had followed the Uprising and the bitterness and distrust on both sides. He was sure they had moved past the worst of it.

The Jötnar were busy rebuilding Hyperion into a place befitting of their people, and he doubted they had the time or interest in that kind of vendetta. Gun was committed to the future of his people and wouldn't risk it in some petty movement. But he did recall the murder of a Jötnar engineer on Prometheus in the previous year. The distrust and hatred was never far from the surface, it would seem.

"Well, either way we will all be meeting at the office in a few hours. Can you get all the information we have on these groups, and also make sure Jack is there? I want this cleared up fast."

Teresa nodded in agreement.

"Now, onto more pressing matters, how about the rest of the family? Are they settling in to life in the military? Last I heard was that your boys had both passed the entrance exams for enlistment in the Navy."

Teresa smiled. Her sons from her previous marriage were both grown up, and although they had met Spartan several times in the last few years, there was little they had in common. Their grandparents had brought them up while she repaid the debts she'd incurred, but since leaving home, it had been hard to get them all back together in one place. The only person any of them really had in common was Jack. Although the youngest, he had got on well with the two boys while he spent his infant years on Carthago. Spartan suspected that part of his anger might have come from removing him from the family group to be back with his parents at Epsilon Eridani.

"Yes, they are working on Terra Nova and hope to finish their training early next year. Impressive, don't you think? Not bad for local boys brought up on the troublesome backwater of the Alliance."

Spartan smiled at the mention of the old world. The last time he'd visited had been to meet with Teresa's grandparents. They had done good work bringing up the boys, and he'd offered to sort out accommodation at Epsilon Eridani. They weren't interested, and instead, Spartan arranged for Jack to spend as much of his holiday time with them.

"How are your grandparents?"

"The usual, complaining about the crumbling cities and crime is still rampant. Carthago always seems to be the last place to improve. It's been a ruin since I was a child."

Maybe that's because they are always the first to cause trouble, he thought, but kept it to himself.

"Will all passengers wishing to depart please head for departure Deck Four. Your shuttles are due to leave in forty-five minutes," said another pre-recorded message.

Forty-five minutes!

Spartan couldn't but be amused at the long delay before leaving the ship. He was used to having no more than a few minutes for departure in most situations. Even though he'd been out of the military for some time, he was often amazed at the slowness of civilian operations.

"I'd better be off, I will see you shortly..."

Teresa nodded happily.

"Yes, I'm looking forward to our reunion."

* * *

Spartan's arrival at the APS offices was the exact opposite of what he had expected. The small shuttle had deposited him and the two Alliance agents on the landing pad of his large, newly constructed facility. There was only one major settlement on the planet of Eridani Prime, known simply as City One. They stepped out, each wearing a sealed suit to protect them from the thin toxic atmosphere. The planet was far from the hospitable worlds in Alpha Centauri, but what it did benefit from was an abundance of metals, ore and a surprisingly stable if uncomfortable environment. The other six planets provided a rich collection of ice worlds, rock and Jovian planets. The perfect selection of worlds for exploitation by heavy industry, and with it the perfect place for gangs and organized crime to move into for a piece of the action.

A groundcar met the three of them from the shuttle, and they stepped the short distance to its door. Spartan could feel the chill air through his envirosuit, and it was a feeling that never left him feeling particularly comfortable. With an average temperature of just ten degrees Celsius, it was a chilling place. He was also well aware that at night it was possible for that to drop down to over minus seventy. A number of workers had been found frozen to death in just hours over the last year. Once inside the groundcar, the door hissed shut and flashing green indicators announced they were safe and out of the toxic air. Even so, they were unable to remove their suits until going through decontamination procedures at the main compound.

"Been here before?" asked Spartan, his voice slightly distorted by the respirator.

The two agents sat quietly, but only Johnson showed any interest in what Spartan had to say.

"No, and I have to say it hardly looks like the kind of place I'd want to visit."

Spartan laughed at the two men.

"It might not look like much, but the wealth dug up here in the last two months has already boosted our security profits by triple of last year's. There's a lot of money to be made out here."

"Yeah," replied Johnson, "that part I do know. We've tracked several groups here with the intention of raiding companies operating so far out of our main areas of control. With Alliance funds tied up in trade and planetary security, there isn't much capacity for the border worlds like this one."

"That's why we get paid," said Spartan stoically.

Johnson nodded.

"Private contractors like yours are doing well in this

climate. Tell me, how did you manage to secure this contract? I thought you had specialized in shipping protection? That's what your commercials always say, anyway!"

Spartan smiled at him, knowing that getting this particular contract had been a major coup; one that a dozen other firms were itching to get their hands on. It was much more than providing security at the doors of expensive buildings. The infrastructure on Eridani Prime was worth trillions of dollars, and that didn't include the value of the ore and resources being mined and refined.

"You do understand that reputation goes a long with this kind of business, don't you?" asked Spartan with a tone of feigned injury.

Agent Johnson grinned at the reply.

"Your reputation couldn't be any more concrete than if you were made from solid rock, Spartan. Military service, gladiatorial combat victories and one of the key saviors of the Alliance, what isn't there to know?" he said with more than a hint of sarcasm.

The vehicle slowed to a halt, and the door hissed open to reveal two fully armored men. Agent Johnson couldn't but be surprised at how similar they looked to the Alliance Marines. Their armor was reminiscent of the PDS (Personal Defense Suits) worn by Alliance troops, yet the plates and ribbing suggested something even more substantial.

"Nice gear, Alliance issue?"

Spartan shook his head but gave nothing away.

One of the guards leaned closely to Spartan and spoke directly through the encrypted suit-to-suit communications channel.

"Sir, something is going on in one of the storage areas. I've dispatched a security team, and they have the area isolated. It's on the route to the refinery with the hostages."

"What?" demanded Spartan.

"It's Jack, Sir. He managed to break out with two others. Half an hour later, we got the message of gunfire in this part of the facility."

The small group entered through the triple sealed entrance and into the decontamination area. Even as the steam and gases washed over them, they continued their conversation. Spartan thought for a moment.

"What's down there?"

"In the storage area? Well, no weapons but there are about fifty spare sets of cold weather gear and some armor. There's also a winterized Cobra."

The light switched to green and each of them was able to remove the outer layers from their envirosuits. Agent Johnson moved up to Spartan and the guard.

"I take it there's a problem?"

The guard said nothing, but Spartan decided to share something with him.

"There's trouble in one of the storage areas. Reports

of gunfire and possible theft of equipment and a Cobra transport."

"Interesting, but not really something I need to concern myself with. I'll let you get on with that. We'll make our way to Ms Morato and get on with our interview of Jack, if that's okay?"

Spartan nodded, indicating to one of the men behind the desk to approach them. The man stood up and moved towards them. He wore a smart suit and looked half of Spartan's age. Spartan introduced the new arrivals.

"This is Intelligence Director Johnson. Please escort him and his assistant to Ms Morato, and give him any assistance that he might require."

With that, Spartan left them and made for the nearest elevator. The armored guard returned to the entrance of the complex, and Spartan noted that he locked down the door system.

Dammit, I can never catch a break, can I?

He hit the button on the wall to select the floor to the storage level and then connected directly to his office. Teresa answered it almost immediately.

"Ms Morato."

"Teresa, I've just arrived. What's going on?"

"Spartan, Jack managed to get out and he's met up with some of his old friends. He said something about a cell working against the Alliance. It has something to do with this Biomech-hating organization we were talking about."

Spartan shook his head.

"Jack, what have you done now?" he said despairingly. "I'm away for a few months, and you're in trouble again."

"Spartan, there is a tactical team down there. I sent Lovett, and he's already secured the perimeter. Hurry, Jack said something about them trying to sabotage the Rift generator."

"What, how can they do that from down here?"

Teresa shook her head.

"I have no idea, Spartan. All I know is Jack said it was urgent, and he was going to stop them."

"Okay, good work. Johnson will be arriving at your office very soon. Stall him, and I'll deal with this problem."

"Good luck, Spartan. Get back in one piece."

The elevator continued downwards until it reached almost two hundred meters underground. The site of the city was inside one of the craters, but for safety reasons, the storage of valuable equipment was kept locked down under the main complex. With a low-pitched pulse, the doors slid open, revealing a debris-filled corridor with four armored men pinned down behind an improvised barricade. Spartan moved out and took cover behind the group. They spotted his arrival, but only one turned to him. It was James Lovett, his old friend and comrade from the War.

"Spartan, keep your head down," he said with a grim smile.

He needed no further encouragement and took cover in the corridor along with the armored men. Almost immediately a flurry of small caliber bullets hit near their position.

"What the hell is going on down here? This is an industrial outpost, not a goddamned warzone!"

Lovett took aim with his own sidearm and fired one shot before looking back.

"Spartan, best we can tell there is a group in the refinery control room. They were loading stolen ore from one of the refineries when one of my patrols spotted them. They opened fire and then set the transport on fire. In the confusion, they took maybe four or five hostages. They want a fuelled freighter to take them away."

Another shot ripped towards them, and Spartan flinched, now acutely aware he was wearing no armor other than the ballistic vest he always wore.

"What is this all about?"

"Your boy, he got in there and trouble started. Next thing we know, the hostages are out, but Jack is still missing. We've had them pinned down here since then. I think your boy is trying to take them apart one at a time, and this is the only way out of the control room."

Spartan ducked down lower and checked his pistol. He'd been in a hundred similar situations and was perfectly aware of how easily a stray round could cripple or end his life in an instant.

"Okay, fall back and give them an exit point. Let them use the emergency stairs."

"What?" cried Lovett, in surprise.

Spartan grabbed him by the shoulder.

"You know this. Think. If we corner them, they will have no choice but to fight. Instead, we give them a way out and then use that against them. Just make sure they think they've beaten us."

Lovett nodded, understanding only too well the military need to always ensure your opponent had a potential escape route. He almost kicked himself for going in so gung ho.

"Security Team Alpha, withdraw to point six and hold," he called on the intercom.

With precision, the small security unit moved back, each firing the odd shot to cover their retreat. Rather than use the elevator, they took the large double doors that led to the emergency staircase. Like all structures, it was imperative that there was an alternative to the power elevator in times of crisis, and this was certainly one of them. Once through the door, they moved up two levels and then paused. The team fanned out and trained their weapons back down the steps, while Lovett and Spartan planned their next move.

"Well?" asked Lovett.

"Now we wait. As you said, there is only one way out, and I've already disabled the elevator. Either Jack will

74

finish them all off, or he will fan them this way."

One of the guards, a new man that Spartan didn't recognize, looked unimpressed.

"He's just a kid, what if they kill him?"

Spartan tried his best not to laugh, and it was left to Lovett to explain.

"The kid is Jack, Spartan's son. You don't need to worry about..."

The doors kicked open, and a small group rushing in interrupted them. As they moved inside, a volley of well-aimed shots tore at them and forced them to cover. Spartan watched carefully, checking on both their numbers and their disposition. He wasn't impressed. Although they appeared well armored and equipped with heavy weapons, it was clear that not a single one of them had any kind of mask or helmet to protect them from shock or stun weapons. He leaned back and looked to Lovett.

"They're amateurs. Stun them and move in with batons. You shouldn't need firearms for this one," he said seriously.

Lovett flicked a button on the side of his weapon to deactivate it and slid the gun to his side, removing a baton from his belt. It looked like an ancient mace, but it actually stored a high-capacitance charge that could knock out a man with one strike.

"Hammand," whispered Lovett to one of the guards. The man crept over and took a stun grenade from him.

"On my signal, flash the place, then we go in. Got it?"

One of the men tossed a headset over to Spartan. It wasn't just for the communications, it was mainly the sound deadening and white noise generator built into its electronics. He pulled it on and felt an odd sensation as it activated, blocking out extraneous sounds, like enhanced noise-cancelling headphones.

The guards nodded in agreement. Spartan knew it was risky, especially being as the men at the bottom of the stairs were heavily armed and intent on causing damage. The armor and stun gear used by his company was the best, and they would be safe from most attacks, even at close range. The man lifted the grenade and activated the charge. With the nod from Lovett, he dropped it down the stairs. Its rubberized outer coating deadened the sound, unlike the metallic weapons usually used. It seemed to take an age for it to reach the bottom. Then it activated.

The flash lit up the entire staircase and was followed by a howl of energy. Spartan knew full well the cost and capabilities of the device. It had been developed for ATU tactical units and was designed to incapacitate groups of people much larger than the one waiting for them. The security team were already halfway down the stairs before he chased after them. Spartan may have been by far the most experienced, but he knew what was sensible; charging into battle with almost no armor was a big mistake. Only when they started swinging their maces, did he finally jump into the fray. The numbers were equal, and the security team had surprise on their side. Even so, Lovett was knocked backwards by something, and as Spartan arrived, he realized another two men had just come through the door and had avoided the blast of the weapon.

"Watch out!" he yelled and leapt from halfway up the bottom level of the staircase to crash into the two men. The pair fell to the floor before they were able to fire, with Spartan on top of them. One rolled out of the way, but Spartan was able to twist the right arm of the second all the way behind his back into a classic lock. With the smallest amount of pressure, he could exert massive pain. The rest were either cuffed or unconscious, apart from the final man who had evaded Spartan's grasp. The man stood up and pointed his weapon directly at Spartan.

"Let him go, or I'll blow a hole in your chest!" he barked.

Spartan wore a smart suit, and there was little chance they would know he was wearing ballistic armor beneath it. Even so, he didn't want to chance the penetration level in anything other than a controlled training scenario. The door swung open, and the dark shapes of two more men arrived, each pointing weapons at the man with the shotgun.

"Do that, and I'll spread your brain across the wall!" said the shorter of the two.

The man looked about nervously and back to Spartan. Something in his face told him this man was trouble. The lines about his cheeks tensed, and Spartan knew exactly what was coming. A loud roar ripped through the room, and the man snapped back, a bullet hole directly into his forehead. He smashed into the wall and dropped to the floor.

"Spartan?" asked the new arrival as he held his smoking firearm.

Spartan's heart was pounding as the form of a young man, and at what looked like a thick set and well-built ogre, entered the room. The form of a Jötnar was unmistakable, but it was the young man that surprised him. He moved closer and stood in front of Spartan. He wore close-fitting armor of a type he was unfamiliar with and carried a modified Jötnar weapon that had much in common with the prototype coilguns he had seen on Terra Nova. Professional interest almost took him to the gun first, but it was his son Jack after all. Spartan lowered his weapon and exhaled slowly, glad the ordeal was over.

"What the hell are you doing here, Jack?"

His son looked back at him with a grim expression. Though barely eighteen, his aged face gave him the look of somebody almost ten years older. He was almost two meters tall, black haired and sported a rough looking scar that ran from his neck up to his ear. He moved ahead and examined each of the men before returning to Spartan, evidently more concerned with his job than speaking with Spartan.

"These aren't the ones we need. This is just an intelligence cell."

Spartan reached out and grabbed him.

"Jack, what is going on?"

He looked up.

"There's a plan to bring down the Network by the anti-Biomech groups, and these guys are part of it."

The Jötnar rolled over the body of the fallen man and then joined Jack and Spartan. He reached inside his armored chest protector and brought out a leather package. It looked about the size and shape of an old book. He extended his hand to Spartan and gave him the object.

"I am Wictred. This is from my father, Khan of the Jötnar. He said you would understand."

Spartan took it and looked at the worn and marked leather before moving closer so that nobody else could hear. He spoke directly into Jack's ear.

"Director Johnson is here from Alliance Intelligence. He wants to speak to you about this."

The Jötnar smiled at the news and even Jack seemed to grin. Their attitude took Spartan completely by surprise. Jack finally spoke, breaking their confused silence.

"Good, he said he'd find a way to meet face to face, so this must be it."

Jack and Wictred then walked to the staircase and started to move up. As they reached the next level, Jack turned back to look at his father.

"Well, are you coming?"

CHAPTER FOUR

The ground combat that took place at the battle of New Carlos in the later years of the War saw some of the largest battles of the War. Both the Marine Corps and the Army fought a series of desperate last stands until aided by the improvised engineers from the Marine Corps. The heavy armor and weapons proved vital in stemming the tide against the Biomech attacks and established the reputation of the Corps on a dozen worlds. This reputation continued on to the newly formed Alliance Marine Corp that was formed following the victory at Terra Nova.

Great Battles of the Confederate Marine Corps

ANS Beagle drifted a short distance from its arrival point as the crew and engineers worked against time to get the system ready. Captain Raikes supervised the myriad of tasks; but ultimately, it was down to the volunteer crew to return all the systems back to full capacity. He looked at his management console and noted that over seventy percent of systems were now operational. It was an improvement, but he was still unsure they would actually be ready in time for the reconnection to the bridge. There was a fixed time slot that had been pre-arranged with the engineers back at the Prometheus Seven Trading Post. When the Rift reappeared, they would have the time and power to do one of two things. Either they created their own spherical shell of energy at Orion to balance the bridge, or they would have to travel back through before the link became untenable and collapsed. He wiped his brow and looked over to the clock.

Fifty-one minutes left, this is going to be close.

"Captain, I'm detecting several fluctuations in the power levels of the habitation assembly," said one of the technicians just a short distance from him.

Captain Raikes had only a limited number of crew on the ship, and it was essential that he prioritized them for the connection.

"Is it serious?" he asked impatiently.

"It is within tolerable limits but will have to be resolved in the next forty-eight hours."

The Captain nodded quickly and moved back to his display.

"Understood, it can join the list of a hundred other things to do when this is sorted out. Let me know if it changes in the meantime."

On his main screen, the percentage of active systems increased yet again, and for the briefest of moments, he thought it might actually work. They had less than an hour to go before the designated time. A beeping sound caught his attention. It was coming from the desk where the Chief Engineer sat. The man turned to look at him.

"Good news, Sir. I've stopped work on all non-essential systems, and the Rift generator gear is now ready to start activation," he explained, his face slightly red from the stresses of getting the system ready.

Captain Raikes glanced at his display and noted the system status of all the major components of the station. Every single one showed up in green, and even he found it difficult to disguise the look of surprise on his face.

"Excellent work, I didn't doubt you for a second!"

The Chief Engineer did his best to smile, but was well aware the doubts the Captain had about getting the damaged system up and running. More importantly, he was surprised they'd got so far. Captain Raikes checked the diagnostic summaries himself before speaking again. He was normally a calm and collected individual, but the worries of this mission had revealed his deeply hidden insecurities of failure. In the past, he had managed an almost completely perfect career with just a single black mark on his file. It was his rush to create the first one-way Rift over a decade ago that had left a crippled station and a lost ship. Only the data from Hyperion had put his career back on track. Even so, the loss of so many people, and his fly by the seat of his pants nature, had won him both friends and enemies in the scientific and naval community. He lifted his eyes from the system and back to the Chief Engineer.

"We don't have a moment to waste. Start up the main systems, and let's get the preliminary work on the connection to Prometheus active ASAP," he said happily. "We need to be ready the minute the Rift opens."

It had been almost half a day since they'd arrived, and not a minute went by with him pondering the chance that they could end up trapped in the Orion Nebula, over a thousand light years from home. The automated drone was only a short distance from the moon now, but even that seemed low priority to him right now. They would have days, weeks, probably years to chase around the planets, but not if the Rift failed to work correctly.

The activation sequence was already well underway, and he watched with pride as his expert team rerouted the power from their powerplants to capacitors in readiness to establish the link. It would use nearly three-quarters of their reserves to activate the Spacebridge, but once running, it would use a fraction of the power to maintain the link. This assumed that the same was taking place on the other side, of course.

Let's just hope they are ready to complete the link!

"How long do we have until the sequence starts?" he asked.

"Forty-three minutes, Sir," came back a quick reply from the engineer monitoring the computing system for the bridge.

Captain Raikes was looking at his screen when an odd feeling of nausea ran through his head. A loud crunching sound hammered through the metal plating, and he found himself drifting out of his chair as if the vessel had just struck something. He reached out and grabbed a computer console, but only just in time. A number of technicians flew past him, their bodies spinning uncontrollably.

Gravity is off!

He pulled himself close to the computer in time for the lights to all flicker and cut out through the CIC. Only the dull red glow of the emergency lights gave any break from the eerie blackness of the interior as they activated. Shouting and screams echoed inside, and he was forced to bellow at the top of his voice.

"Calm down, and find out what the hell is going on!"

Captain Raikes was already adjusting to the low-level red lighting, and he could already identify two people that were not moving. He assumed they were unconscious, but there was no easy way to tell from his current position. A technician managed to get part of his diagnostic system active, but the main systems were still down.

"Sir, the power units are offline. Somebody has shut

them down."

"What?" responded the Captain, now furious that his vessel had been disabled.

"How is that even possible?"

The Chief Engineer nodded in agreement at the information from his technician. Although his own display was out of action, there wasn't a part of the ship he wasn't familiar with.

"That sounds right. If the habitation ring suffers a catastrophic failure, the main drives and engine units are shut down. It's a safety mechanism to ensure power isn't routed to the heavy engineering, especially the motors. I'd say we have a saboteur on board, and whoever it is, they have a thorough knowledge of our systems."

Captain Raikes lowered his head into his right hand; the weight of the problems was bearing down on him, and he was running out of ideas. He glanced about briefly, but most of the systems were still offline.

"Sir, there is only one part of the ship where the habitation controls and powerplant conduits come close to each other. There's a good chance the damage was caused there."

"And that's where we might find our saboteur. In the meantime, get me comms. I need to speak with Admiral Anderson. If we cannot get our systems active again fast, we will have to start a general evacuation to the Rift."

"Already on it, give me a moment."

Lieutenant Davies pulled himself along until he reached the Captain. He had gone through zero-g training like most marines and moved through the craft quickly and efficiently. He drifted at head height and was forced to shout for the Captain to even spot him.

"Sir, my marine comms system is independent of the ship's. My entire platoon has checked in, apart from one group near the habitation control station. I think it might..."

The Captain lifted his hand and nodded.

"Yes, that is where the problem is. Lieutenant, how soon can you have a team there?"

The young marine paused for a few seconds as he visualized the route in his head. It wasn't a long distance and normally required the use of the elevators to descend to the correct level. With no gravity, he could simply drift there.

"About four, maybe five minutes, Sir."

"Good, get on it. I suspect you will find our saboteur there. Trust nobody and stay in contact."

The marine saluted and turned to move away before the Captain grabbed his arm.

"Leave a squad here. There's a chance they might try and take the CIC."

Lieutenant Davies nodded and then kicked away from the wall to push himself towards the entrance to the CIC. Captain Raikes watched in surprise as the man made quick progress and faded into the blackness of the ship. He looked back to his crew.

"Where are my comms?" he demanded.

Out in the corridor, the small unit of marines were already using the grab handles to pull themselves at a good rate along the walls and ceiling. To any of the crew watching them move past, it must have looked as if the ship had been infested with creatures of some kind. In just two minutes, they were at the service elevator shaft and opening the access hatch. Lieutenant Davies was first inside, closely followed by more than a dozen of his comrades, who had assembled near the CIC before the incident.

"Follow me. We need to secure the habitation control station. Potential hostiles in the area, so keep your eyes open."

With those few words, they disappeared into the blackness of the tunnel. Most activated their suit-mounted lamps to send beams of yellow through the dusty environment. The shaft led from the command decks down past the many engineering levels. It seemed to take an age for the silent and motionless group to reach the platform to the side that was marked up as a service entrance. Lieutenant Davies helped the rest of his team reach the same spot before checking his weapon. Like all Alliance marines, he carried the L52 Mark II Assault Carbine, the most advanced weapon in the arsenal. It had replaced the previous L48 rifle in the last decade, and its flexibility and variable fire modes made it perfect for use in space, on land or on board ships. A simple silent operation mode could be selected by twisting the barrel. It reduced the energy to the coils and reduced the velocity to subsonic speeds. This also reduced the noise, but more importantly, the depth of penetration, a vital requirement for operations where a projectile tearing through the hull could kill them all.

With just a nod, the Sergeant of the platoon, a gruff old marine called Tex, activated the door and used the bypass to open the metal mechanism. It slid open to reveal nothing other than yet another dark room. Lieutenant Davies tilted his head and motioned with his left hand for them to enter. The first three moved inside and into the open lobby type room. There would normally be a dozen people moving about, but with the loss of power and gravity, it was deserted.

"The crew will be at their stations or waiting near the evacuation points in case the order is given by the Captain," he explained.

The young Lieutenant made it just a few meters from the entrance when a fusillade of thermal rounds struck their position. The weapons were archaic, and the kind normally used by smugglers and criminal gangs. Nonetheless, the marines were forced to pull themselves to cover as the super-heated scatter shot embedded itself around their position. One marine was hit in the shoulder and spun out of control back through the doorway. More flickers of light gave away the enemy positions, and Lieutenant Davies was forced to pull himself behind a narrow bulkhead to avoid being hit. He tapped his comms gear and connected directly with Captain Raikes.

"Captain, we've arrived at the service entrance and come under fire."

Another burst struck a marine as he returned fire with his carbine. The difference in weapons was apparent in both report and effect. Each time the shotguns fired, they sent a low velocity burst of molten metal that struck armor and glass and burned through. The metal projectile fired from the carbines, on the other hand, was designed to squash but not shatter on impact.

"Marines, push them back! We need the control station!"

With that order, the surviving marines pulled themselves into cover and fired back, each taking aim at the two muzzle flashes from the enemy. It was difficult to tell if they'd hit them, but in less than a minute, the shotguns ceased firing. The marines were able to push ahead nearly twenty meters to reach the station. Tex made it to the station first and pulled open the security panel.

"Lieutenant, the system has been deactivated."

Lieutenant Davies pulled himself along the right-hand wall and around the flank of the system. The control station was large, easily the size of a man, and consisted of three large displays and a rather antiquated looking computer system. It was, of course, all heavily ruggedized and intended to operate even after the effects of a major electromagnetic attack. Advanced systems were not required for this part of the ship, just simple and reliable electrical and mechanical systems. The Lieutenant reached out to touch the system to activate it, but the Sergeant grabbed his hand and stopped him at the last moment.

"Sir, they've probably booby trapped it. Let Arnauld have a look first."

Lieutenant Davies nodded in agreement, secretly kicking himself that he'd almost made such a rookie mistake. It was common knowledge in most of the military units that the non-commissioned officers were the ones with the experience, and that the junior officers were green and couldn't be trusted. He'd tried hard to avoid the stereotype, but it was small things like this that seemed to prove the rule once more. He nodded at his Sergeant and stepped away to ensure the site was secure. There was a red stain on the wall, presumably from one of the two that had been shooting at them.

"Sir, we've secured the station. There are at least two assailants, and they've moved back into the service areas," he explained on his radio.

"Good work. Can you get the system back online?"

He glanced over to the Sergeant and spotted Corporal Arnauld pulling out one of the boards and removing cabling. It was a surprisingly quick operation, and in just a few more seconds, the man reached up and hit a button that powered up the system. The operating system was based on the solid-state chips that had been used for hundreds of years and allowed it to activate and start managing systems in less than three seconds. Systems like this were built to run parallel to the main networked system in case of attack or damage.

"Well, she's up and ready. Looks like whoever did this knew where to hurt us. They've cut all computer control to the systems from elsewhere in the ship. I'm directing the starting charge to the powerplants, and they should fire up right away."

He glanced back to his commander, looking for the signal to continue.

"Is there any reason why we shouldn't do this?" he asked as a glimmer of doubt entered his mind.

"Well, it will restart all the main systems, including air filtration, habitation rotation and fuel management to the engines. There is nowhere else on the ship outside of the CIC where so much control exists. Like I said, they knew what they were doing."

Lieutenant Davies shook his head slowly.

"Yeah, that's what worries me. Don't you think they'd have disabled this system?"

His internal comms gear activated, surprising him by the noise in the near silence.

"Lieutenant, we're running out of time. What the hell is keeping you down there?"

He swallowed before replying. "The computer management system is ready. I was about to start the power sequence."

"Then do it and send your men to hunt them down!" barked the Captain.

Once again the young Lieutenant hesitated, but another order shouted down and into his helmet finally forced his hand. He looked to Corporal Arnauld and nodded for him to proceed.

* * *

The first indication things were finally returning to normal, was when the lights came back on. It was a simple matter, but the bright white lights instantly transformed the interior of the CIC, revealing the extent of the panic and injuries caused by the lack of gravity and light.

Dammit, thought Captain Raikes. *I should have been prepared for this kind of thing.*

There wasn't time to worry though as Lieutenant Rob Davis, the Communications Officer, received an urgent message.

"Sir, Lieutenant Davies reports the main generators are back online."

To emphasise the moment, the majority of the

computer displays activated, as well as the artificial gravity and air circulation system. Captain Raikes allowed himself a brief moment's relaxation, checking the status of each item as one by one the main systems restarted.

"How long do we have?"

There was no time to answer as on the main screen a bright flickering shape indicated the arrival of the Rift. It flashed and shook like water being dropped into a beaker of water before settling down.

"We're too far away. What is the distance to the Rift?" he asked.

"Uh...three point two kilometers, Sir," explained the navigator.

"I see. Plot a course correction and get us into position. We only have a few minutes."

If any of the crew had checked, they would have quickly spotted the propulsion sensor flag that indicated failures at two points in the main engines. It was the worry about the main power units and the Rift generator that had diverted their attention away from something as mundane, but also as critical, as the ability to move through space. The problem was with both the primary heat exchanger and the secondary turbo pump. The incorrect mixture pushed out into the propulsion chamber and exploded when ignited. Rather than pushing the craft forward, the fuel ignited and destroyed the already damaged heat exchanger, instantly cutting the flow of fuel and tearing a chunk of the engine assembly off and into space. Red lights flashed inside the CIC, and Captain Raikes watched in horror as the propulsion alarms sounded. The Chief Engineer looked at him aghast.

"Sir, we've got a problem!"

* * *

Admiral Anderson waited patiently as the countdown was read out. It felt like a week since they'd started up the system the first time and sent ANS Beagle through on its maiden voyage. Though it should have been no different to the last time, the system was activated, he was well aware that there was nothing normal about creating a Spacebridge. The fact that the large rifts were created in space rather than on planets was obvious to them all now. But even in space, the forces unleashed by the equipment on the station could vaporize everything within a hundred kilometers. The memories of the Rift Incident on Euryale, was a reminder to them all about what could happen if even the simplest mistake was made.

"Five...four...three...two...one...activate!" called out the senior engineer.

Admiral Anderson held his breath as the countdown reached its climax. On the main screen, the image of the energy field appeared that marked the opening of the Rift in space. As before, the entrance to the tunnel was created, and to the cheers of approval of those around him, the second one-way Spacebridge in history to be created was established. One of the technicians started the clock that gave them no more than twenty-two minutes until they would run out of power and need to shut down the system, and therefore the bridge. That would give them a safe margin of error with the power systems, and also enough redundant power to operate if any of the generators suffered problems while keeping the Rift open. It was another benefit of having a larger Rift in space, rather than on a planet, in that the cold, airless vacuum of space provided the perfect cooling system for such advanced and extremely hot machinery.

Well, at least it worked, he thought happily, but his nerves still felt frayed.

Though nicknamed a Rift, it was technically a type of traversable wormhole held open by a spherical shell of exotic matter often known as a Morris-Thorne wormhole. The design had much in common with the theories postulated by the late twentieth century scientists, Kip Thorne and Mike Morris. Not that most people realized it, but the solution had ultimately required additional information for it to work properly. Detailed analysis of the ruins around the Anomaly Spacebridge, as well as the intelligence recovered from Hyperion, had been vital in their rapid and reliable construction.

"Excellent work," he announced in a calm and collected

tone. He turned to his communications officer.

"Now get me in touch with Captain Raikes. We need to perform the link, and fast."

* * *

"One second, Sir, almost there," said the Chief Engineer. To everyone's surprise a number of the computer displays lit up, and then some of the main lights activated.

"Right, comms are back, and I've isolated three network nodes in the CIC. There's enough power stored on this level to power comms and orientation thrusters. The rest should be coming online about...now."

He had no time to thank him as the mainscreen lit up and showed the interior of an Alliance station. It was Admiral Anderson. More lights flickered, and each of the systems started to power up as if there had been nothing more than a power cut on ANS Beagle.

"Captain, what's happening?" he asked in a concerned tone.

"Sabotage, Sir! We lost our main power. The habitation ring is down, and our powerplants were offline. Systems are coming back online, but it will take time. We've got another problem though. Our primary propulsion system has been destroyed."

"What? Can you get into position to reconnect to the bridge?"

"Working on it, Sir. How long can you keep the bridge open?"

The Admiral turned to his staff for a few seconds, and he could see two engineers having a heated argument. Finally, he turned back to the camera.

"If we push our systems to breaking point, I can keep her open for thirty-two minutes. Anymore, and the power units on this station will hit critical. I am sending in a rescue party, and they will be at your position in four minutes. It is up to you, Captain. Either get your power system online and complete the connection, or get your people off the ship and back through the Rift. Commodore Lewis is commanding the relief effort. He has escorts that can assist in towing you into position. Whatever happens, you must do one or the other before the clock runs out. Stay in touch."

Captain Raikes nodded, and the screen changed back to an external view of the space station in orbit around Prometheus. Anderson was worried, and there was little he could now do other than send in more ships.

"Can't we connect to her from her current location?" he asked.

The two nearest engineers shook their heads.

"No, Sir," said the first. "The connection window is very small, just under a kilometer. The only other option is for us to shutdown and create a new Rift."

"But we don't have the power for that now for almost a

day, right?" he asked, but deep down he already knew the answer. The man nodded in agreement.

* * *

Commodore Lewis watched the approach of the Rift from the main display in the CIC of ANS Dragon. The ship was the most technologically advanced ship in the fleet, but even her thick armor and strong internal structure failed to instill confidence in him. He'd seen firsthand what happened when a warship entered an unstable spacebridge in the past. Even a minor power fluctuation could cause the space-based anomaly to tear his vessel apart in the blink of an eye.

At least it will be quick, he thought half-heartedly.

Stood next to him was a fully armored marine, wearing the insignia of a senior Captain. He waited patiently while the Commodore saw to the rest of the small force as it moved through the Rift. They reached a distance of just a few meters away before he turned to the marine.

"I'm sending in the two frigates to work as tugs to get this bridge open. Your job is going to be to root out these saboteurs. Information from the Beagle says there are at least two on board with thorough knowledge of the vessel and her systems."

"Sir," answered Captain Tim Howell. "Do we have any information on their weapons and capabilities?"

"Just two things. First, they're using thermal shotguns. Second, they've already injured two and killed one marine. Be careful when you get inside, they have knowledge and experience of the ship."

"Understood, Sir, I'll bring them in."

He saluted and walked away from the CIC to meet the rest of his team. Commodore Lewis watched him leave before the proximity alarms sounded and brought his attention back to the Rift.

"Sir, we're entering the Spacebridge...now," said the helmsman.

He held his breath; the doubts and concerns over the experimental Rift now starting to surface. The last thing he wanted was to be stretched and ripped apart over thousands of lights years of space. It was almost like his previous encounters with the rifts in space, but this one was a little more violent. Even so, ANS Dragon moved through and reappeared at their new destination without a scratch on her thick exterior. The entire crew fell silent as each watched the nearest display for their first view of the Orion Nebula. The sight of a new sun and planets was something to behold, but he knew full well he had a job to do.

"What is our status?"

Each of the crew reported back, and to his pleasant surprise there were no issues with either the ship or the crew. Two of the frigates appeared a short distance behind him and accelerated away as soon as they were clear of the exit Rift. Though barely half the size of his ship, they were still powerful vessels, and each easily capable of securing a colony or planet against the threats of pirates or criminal gangs using modified civilian transports.

"Sir, we're ready to commence boarding operations on ANS Beagle," said Captain Howell.

The Commodore picked up the intercom unit from its position on the console in front of him and lifted it to his mouth. It was old technology, but the simplicity and privacy it offered were vital in combat situations.

"Good, I will inform her Captain of your imminent arrival."

He then looked to his communications officer, who was busy scanning their immediate area for anything useful.

"Lieutenant," he called. The young man looked back at his commander.

"Sir?"

"Get me through to Captain Raikes on the Beagle."

"Yes, Sir."

The Lieutenant looked back to his own console and moved his hands about as he made contact with the massive ship waiting a short distance away. Commodore Lewis watched the vessel and couldn't fail to be impressed by the great bulk of her shape. She was part ship and part station, and with the rough finish, gantries and hundreds of crew that went with such a pioneering project. The image on the main screen changed to show the bustling interior of ANS Beagle. Captain Raikes approached the camera, but it must have been bumped during the crisis as it was tilted by almost thirty degrees.

"Commodore Lewis, glad to see you," he said with genuine pleasure in his voice.

The Commodore tapped a button that sent over details of Captain Howell.

"This is the commander of my marine detachment. I have a reduced strength of three companies on board. As we speak, one of them is approaching your vessel and will board near the last sightings of your saboteurs. I suggest you withdraw your own marines to secure the key parts of the Rift equipment."

"Sir?" he replied in confusion. "My marines have already secured the station and are performing a full sweep of the ship. They know this ship better than any other combat unit."

Commodore Lewis considered his comments for a moment. While he would much rather give his men free rein in the vessel, he was under no illusions as to the time limits available to his forces or the intricacies of the innards of ANS Beagle.

"Very well, Captain. Inform your marines to hold their fire. My men will be there shortly. It is imperative that we get the Beagle into position, and with her Rift generator functioning normally within the next fifteen minutes."

"Yes, Sir," replied the Captain. The image faded to black. Before the Commodore could move, it quickly changed to the inside of one of the landing craft. The interior of the vessel was very different to that of ANS Beagle. It was a large, heavily armed craft that could land a fully equipped marine force directly into battle while under direct fire. Captain Howell looked into the camera, but it wasn't obvious who it was due to the reflection on his visor.

"Sir, we're approaching the lower levels. Landing craft is attached and boarding skirt has linked. We're ready to board her."

The Commodore didn't hesitate in his response.

"Good work, Captain. Permission granted, get back to me as soon as you make contact with the enemy. Oh, and try not to shoot anything valuable!"

CHAPTER FIVE

The homeworld of the Jötnar had been transformed from a deserted jungle planet into a thriving yet violent community. Wooden compounds and structures filled the islands and tens of thousands of Biomechs farmed, built and traded. Unlike any other part of the Alliance, all Biomechs that were sent to Hyperion were given a chance of a new life. Most chose to join the Jötnar but some refused, instead wanting to strike out on their own. These rebels fought in the Jötnar Mutiny that resulted in the deaths of many Jötnar.

The downfall of Hyperion

With the artificial gravity now fully operational, Lieutenant Davies was able to assess the situation. His team had so far discovered two booby-traps that had been left behind to cover the escape of whoever had tried to cause so much damage to ANS Beagle. According to Sergeant

Tex, if they'd been another ten minutes, the redundant systems would have also been put out of action, therefore rendering the entire Rift generating hardware irrelevant. One squad stayed to protect the control station, and the rest of the platoon moved out to cover five separate areas that controlled the power levels to the Rift generator. Lieutenant Davies led three marines to the nearest evacuation platform. It was a small area that functioned as both an emergency shelter and a lifeboat.

"LT, why didn't they just hit the engines to start with?" asked Private Martok.

The group of four had already reached the platform, and as expected, it was deserted. Lieutenant Davies checked the control-panel next to the airlock leading to the lifeboat.

"Looks okay," he said, turning to Martok.

"Good question. Well, I suppose they wanted to cut the habitation system to make it harder for us to reach it before they disabled the engines."

"True, Sir, but we still lost the engines. What's their game plan?"

That was a question he really couldn't answer. None of it made any sense to him. First, they must have sabotaged the engines, then they cut the power and habitation systems, so they had to come down to investigate. After that, they restarted the system.

Yes, that's it!

"How else would they force a shipside restart and powering up of the engines? Without the habitation unit going offline, the powerplants would have simply shifted power. It must have been the surge of power and fuel that destroyed the engines."

Tex glanced inside the lifeboat and then to his Lieutenant.

"Could be, but if that's true, it means the saboteurs are members of the crew. What would they have to gain by doing this? All we're doing is..."

A gentle click caught their attention from ten meters away. All four marines lifted their weapons, but it was already too late. From out of the shadows emerged the shape of Jensen. None of them recognized the crewman, but his blood-splattered overalls marked him out as either one of their saboteurs or a crewmember that may have been caught up in the fighting. It was the belt of gas canisters running around his body like a bandolier of shells that stopped any of them firing.

"One move and I detonate the whole lot!" he snapped. In his right hand he held a pair of wires with the stripped ends held apart by no more than a centimeter.

"Easy now!" said Lieutenant Davies in as calm a voice as he could manage. "Tell us what it is you want."

Jensen looked at each of them in turn before extending his left arm to show a military tattoo. He was at least a decade older than all of them, other than Tex. The

Sergeant instantly recognized the marking.

"What do you care what I want?" he spat out.

Tex nodded as he looked at the man's arm.

"You're one of the survivors from the Santa Maria. You must have been there at the Battle of the Rift?" he asked with genuine interest, forgetting for a moment that the man was wearing a suicide vest and threatening them all with a potentially horrific end. Even now, it was only just occurring to Lieutenant Davies that they were positioned only a short distance from the outer skin of ANS Beagle.

"Uh...ah!" he cried and inched the two frayed wires slightly closer.

"That's it, stay there."

Lieutenant Davies looked to his side but could see nothing he could immediately use to improve their situation. The door to the lifeboat was shut, and this man could easily kill them before they could move even a meter away. The man looked at a device on his arm and smiled to himself.

"Soon...not long now."

"Hey, man, we don't want trouble. Just tell us what your grievance is. You know the Alliance Navy, they look after their own," said Martok.

Those last words appeared to grate with Jenson more than anything else any of them had said. While they continued talking, Lieutenant Davies whispered into his suit's intercom.

"This is Lieutenant Davies," he began. "We're trapped on Level Four at the secondary lifeboat station. Saboteur is here and armed with an..."

"Silence!" called out Jenson. He took a step forward and moved the cables even closer.

"If one of you speaks again, I will detonate this belt," he shouted and looked down at the many containers strapped to his body.

"This has nothing to do with me. This is for all of humanity and for our brothers and sisters that died at the hands of Echidna and her unholy monsters. You fools will consign us to history if you keep pursuing the demon Echidna and her children."

Off to one side, the shape of a woman appeared. She wore Navy overalls and looked like any one of the hundreds of crew that roamed the great vessel. She moved closely to the man and pulled a thermal shotgun out from beneath her jacket, pointing it directly at the marines.

"Hey, you're Ensign Christy. You are on the sick list," exclaimed Lieutenant Davies.

He'd checked the list before the start of the mission and had been keeping a close eye on those that came and left ANS Beagle prior to the operation.

She must have hidden on board before we left over a week ago.

He's right, you know," she said with a sickening smile. "Too many good people died to give us this technology, and for what? We come to Orion, to the source of the

Demon. They'll destroy us all."

A hiss to their right announced the arrival of one of the boarding parties from ANS Dragon. A group of four armored warriors clambered inside with their weapons raised and pointing at the two enemies. They moved in and took up positions near one of the exposed bulkheads, and another shape appeared. It was the commander of the unit, Captain Howell. The imposing figure of the marine entered the space and lifted his visor.

"My name is Captain..."

That was all he was able to say before Jenson touched the two ends of the wire together. There was a flicker of a spark between the two contacts, but it was enough time for Lieutenant Davies to leap forward. The woman opened fire but missed him and instead, struck Tex in the forehead. The thermal slugs penetrated the visor and sent his lifeless corpse crashing into the wall. The Lieutenant smashed into the shape of Jenson, and the two staggered and crashed back further into the ship. As they hit the ground, the canisters detonated. The blast created a superhot breach in the ship that instantly killed everyone within thirty meters of the blast. The entire section was filled with blood, fractured metal and debris, but incredibly, the outer hull remained intact.

* * *

The violence of the blast shook ANS Beagle right to her core. Even on the CIC, the vibrations could be felt. A number of alarms were triggered, but it was nothing like when the engines themselves had been detonated. Even so, it appeared the vessel had sustained yet another setback. Captain Raikes shook his head, fearful of even contemplating what might have happened.

"What was that?" he called out.

"Blast on Level Four at the secondary lifeboat station. Internal fire fighting system is in action."

One of the marines from the corridor entered the CIC.

"Captain, it's our marines. We just lost contact with a squad at the lifeboat station. Lieutenant Davies isn't responding."

The Chief Engineer altered the main display to bring up the status indicators of each of the ship's sections. He pointed to the damaged lifeboat station.

"Here, Sir. Looks like there was a blast. It took out one of the maneuvering thrusters and a backup generator. Nothing we can manage without, so it seems we were lucky.

"Sir, I have Sergeant Travis from ANS Dragon on comms. He says his team has boarded the lower levels and are inside the damaged section."

Captain Raikes nodded, but deep down he didn't want to know what had happened.

"Put him on loud speaker."

"There are bodies everywhere. Looks like there was a blast down here..." the audio cracked for a moment before returning, "bodies of marines...bloody hell, the Captain is here. Send Medevac now. There's blood everywhere!"

Captain Raikes knew deep down that he'd just suffered major casualties, but the only good news was that the engineering appeared sound. There would be time to mourn their losses later, for now he had one thing to worry about, getting that Rift open.

"Understood, Sergeant." He indicated with his right hand for the standby teams to be sent. "Teams are on the way."

He then turned to the helmsman who was working closely with the two frigates that had been maneuvering them into position.

"How are we doing on the positioning?"

The man looked back to him with a hint of a smile.

"Sir, we're there. Only a few meters for optimum range."

Thank the Gods! Now, will this thing work? He thought nervously.

The Chief Engineer already had the primary displays showing the Rift and the status of all the main components of ANS Beagle. Every item that was required to create the connection had been double and triple checked to ensure the activation would go to plan. He turned to the Captain and nodded.

"Sir, everything is ready. Distance is correct, and we

have enough power to start the capacitors."

Captain Raikes rubbed his forehead nervously. He had a terrible feeling that once the system was started, they would hit another problem. With the massive levels of energy being created, an attack of some kind could have terrible consequences for both the Rift and ANS Beagle. He reached out and grabbed the intercom microphone.

"Commodore Lewis, we are in position and ready to start the sequence. Are your frigates at a safe distance?"

"Good work, Captain. Yes, they are in formation with my flagship. Proceed with haste. Good luck."

He tapped a button on the console and switched the system to a ship-wide transmission.

"This is the Captain. We are starting the Rift generation sequence. If this works, we will have created the first stable Spacebridge that can reach out this far. Double-check your stations, and if any of you are believers, pray now!"

He replaced the handset, and for a second contemplated the odd idea of praying to a deity in this day and age. It always amazed him how people found God under the direst of circumstances. Not that he did, but at that very moment, he wished he did. He took a final deep breath and nodded to the Chief Engineer.

"Okay, it's now or never. Activate the bridge."

With no more than a nod, the man started up the rift generator sequence. It was the first time the equipment had been used to do this, and it would require almost all the stored energy of the vessel to create the energy capsule at the entrance point. It took just seconds for the generators to reach their peak efficiency and start building up the Rift capacitors.

"Ten seconds till activation!"

A low hum reverberated through the structure of the vessel as the capacitors quickly reached their full capacity. It was a short time, but for Captain Raikes it seemed like an eternity. Only when the counter reached zero did he exhale. A great pulse of energy burst from the vessel, and no more than a flash outside indicated the generator had done its job. Captain Raikes watched the indicators on his computer display as the sensors confirmed the Rift's stability and the status of the Spacebridge itself. His Chief Engineer looked over to him, but it was clear from the expression on the man's face that all had worked correctly.

"Sir, the Proxima Centauri-Orion Nebula Spacebridge is fully operational."

Captain Raikes settled back into his chair, a feeling of relief and euphoria kicking in to his body like a drug. He barely noticed the clapping and cheering from the others in the CIC as his body calmed down with the relief.

So here it is then, we have our bridge to Orion. What next? He wondered.

As he considered that question, he was reminded of two things. First there was the issue of casualties from the attack on the ship and second, there was the unusual transmission they had come across when they first arrived. With the bridge in action, they finally had a secure route, and these new potential problems seemed procedural by comparison.

"Sir, there's a message from the rescue team. We have a total of seven dead and twelve wounded," called out the communications officer.

Captain Raikes lowered his chin into his hands as he thought of the losses.

The War is over, so what the hell is going on?

"There's something else, Sir. They've found a few body parts from the saboteurs, but one of them is missing."

"What?" he demanded as he grabbed the intercom himself and connected directly to the Lieutenant in charge of the rescue party.

"Lieutenant, what's going on down there?"

There was a short pause before the slightly dulled sound of the marine's voice replied.

"Captain, the lifeboat was blown out, but the computer system is fragged. No way to tell if it was the force of the blast or if somebody released it. We have some part of the bomber, a male. Not a lot left, but I've sent the remains for analysis. Sir, one of the marine survivors says there was a woman. There's no sign of her in the danger zone. Either she escaped in the lifeboat, or she's still on board."

"Understood, Lieutenant, I'm sending two more teams to assist you. If she's on board, I want her, and fast!"

* * *

Commodore Lewis relaxed a little in his cabin as he recalled the sight of ANS Beagle finally securing access to the Spacebridge. In less than a minute, the anomaly had settled down and a stable route had been established back home. It was a major feat for the Alliance in terms of both logistics and engineering, but at a surprising cost in lives. As he lay back and rested, he worried about the troubling news of the saboteurs. With the defeat of the religious fanatics and their allies back during the Uprising, there had been nothing of this level of violence on board Navy vessels for years. In the vicious fighting with the Zealots, it had been common knowledge that they had infiltrated both military and civilian high command. New vetting procedures were in place to ensure the stability, reliability and honesty of all recruits in the military.

All that effort and still somebody slipped through.

Even more troubling was the rumor that it was a loyal faction trying to spare them from taking foolhardy steps into the unknown. He reached over for his secpad and brought up the latest scans from the moons around the nearest gas giant. He'd turned his attention away from the Spacebridge, now that more engineering teams and patrol vessels had arrived to secure the area of space around ANS Beagle. This meant his small taskforce was free to explore the immediate system, planets and moons for anything of note. Thinking of ANS Beagle, reminded him of his own losses in the suicide attack. As always, military requirements trumped social niceties. He'd already arranged for the dead and wounded to be shipped back to Prometheus, where they were receiving expert medical attention, and he fully intended to return for their internment ceremonies and subsequent investigation. It concerned him that he had been unable to return with them, but he was also well aware of the importance of this operation. The secpad started flashing, gently at first and then increasing in intensity. It was a video call from his XO.

Great, what is it now? He wondered before hitting the receive button. In his experience, he was only contacted when there was bad news, and so far he'd had quite enough of deaths, attacks and equipment failure.

"Sir, sorry to interrupt you. We've just regained contact with the reconnaissance drone. It is in position and starting its scan of the surface. We are approximately four hours from making orbit."

"Very good. Keep me informed of its progress."

"Sir."

The image of his executive officer faded away, and the details of the moon returned. He was due to return to the CIC in the next two hours, and this was likely to be the only chance for a short break for at least a day. He had no doubt that if they found anything of note on or near the moon, he and his forces would have their work cut out for them. He closed his eyes, but the image of the moon kept appearing to him, and instead, he sat back up and pulled the secpad to his face. The long distance scans were speculative, and according to his engineers, there was a high margin of error. What intrigued him was that of the large number of planets and moons in this system, surprising numbers showed viable atmospheres. The star system was based around a red subgiant with a size of almost three times that of the Sun back in Earth's Solar System. The planet they were approaching appeared to contain at least thirty small moons and eight large moons, one of which was still transmitting some kind of signal. He tapped the image of the moon in question and stared at its glowing outline.

What are the odds we find a moon with a potentially stable atmosphere?

Of course, there was nothing random about their arrival, but few outside of the Alliance High Command knew where the data on the Orion expedition had originated. Thoughts of the bridge reminded him of his new mission. With the Spacebridge secure, the maintenance and security of the site had been handed over to Admiral Anderson, and that had now freed up his own force for other missions. His own orders had changed to reconnaissance and consolidation of the Star System, provisionally known as Orion Major.

It was imperative that he set up a wide perimeter so that a long-term presence could be established in this sector. His briefing with High Command via video link to Terra Nova had been clear. The Alliance intended on creating a permanent link to the system and would build a supply and research outpost within three months. Parts were already being sent through, to what many back home considered to be the future for humanity. As he looked at his secpad, he doubted their faith in something they knew so little about. He tapped the image of the fourth plant, and it enlarged to fill the screen with long distance imaging and statistics, low gravity, small iron and silicate structure, and a thin corrosive atmosphere.

Sounds like hell, he thought half-heartedly. *If the people back home could see it, I don't think they'd be quite so excited.*

The other planets were less interesting, most of them rocky or ice planets with no usable atmosphere. Two asteroid belts split the planets up into three main groups with the single gas giant being closer to the central star. He placed the secpad back down on his bedside unit and looked over to the clock.

I'll take an hour's break, and then its nose to the grindstone time.

* * *

Spartan paced about his briefing room with the look of a man that was losing patience. He'd only been in the room for a few minutes, but his list of virtues had never included patience. The room itself was simply decorated with a number of paintings hanging on the wall, depicting various periods of history. From imagery of the Ancient Greeks in their battles with Persian hordes, up through to more recent battles in the Uprising. Most people tended to avoid discussing events of the last decades, but as CEO of the company, Spartan had wanted his people to confront issues straight on. A long oval table filled the middle of the room, and a model of the Alliance was projected directly above it. The door finally opened, and in walked his wife Teresa and his son.

"About time!" he said before instantly regretting his outburst. Teresa moved quickly towards him and threw her arms around his upper body, while Jack moved towards the wall, saying nothing.

"You've been gone a long time, Spartan. I thought you'd gone on one of your adventures with Gun again!" she said with relief.

Teresa was now in her late forties, yet her constant physical training and slight build gave her the youth and looks of a woman in her early thirties. Her black hair ran down even longer than when they had been in the Marine Corps together. Behind them appeared Intelligence Director Johnson, but the absence of his assistant, Agent Hammacher, was unexpected.

"Spartan...Jack, we need to talk," he said, motioning for

them to sit around the table. They complied, but Teresa remained on her feet and blocked his path.

"Johnson, what the hell is going on here? This is my family we're talking about!"

For a second, it looked as though she would strike him, but his body language remained relaxed, and he move back a few inches to give ground.

"Teresa, I know that none of your family would be involved in anything of detriment to the Alliance. That isn't why I am here. For official purposes, I am looking into some of your son's more interesting adventures. But in reality, there is something much more worrying going on."

He turned from Teresa and to the table.

"Isn't there, Jack?"

The young man looked at Johnson and then to his father. The two had a troubled history, with Jack frequently getting into trouble, and Spartan doing his utmost to get him to calm down. Jack, on this occasion, seemed much calmer than normal and simply nodded at Spartan before looking back to Johnson.

"Yes, Wictred and I have been tracking one of the sources Gun put out for the hunters."

"Hunters?" retorted Spartan. "They are angry juveniles looking to bag their first kill. I thought you'd stopped running with them?"

Jack shook his head and continued, doing his best to

ignore his father.

"There have been rumors about this new isolationist movement. We were following a group that have been trying to obtain technical specification for specifically, the control mechanisms."

"What?" Spartan snapped.

Teresa reached out and touched his arm.

"Spartan, let him explain...please."

He sighed but said no more, for now.

"The group here was just one of three that we have intel on. We thought they were going to try and send something through a Rift and then bring the entire system down from the inside. Looks like we were wrong, but we found this instead."

Jack pulled out a battered looking datapad, a model that hadn't been manufactured for well over ten years and slid it across to Johnson. With a quick tap, he activated the device and ran through the images.

"You found this here, in the colony?"

Jack nodded.

Johnson examined them for a few more seconds before passing it to Spartan and Teresa. Spartan wasn't entirely sure what he was looking at, but Teresa recognized the gate structure almost instantly.

"These are schematics for the Rift generator that was destroyed on Hyperion, aren't they?"

"What?" Spartan barked. "I thought all information on

Hyperion was either destroyed or taken over by Alliance Intelligence?"

Johnson laced both of his hands on the table and sighed.

"Yes, that is what we suspected. We've had more than a good decade in the Alliance, and a lot of it down to people like you and Teresa. The War is over, and the enemy are beaten, but there are still people out there who disagree with our plans. The Network is the greatest achievement in the last five hundred years, and it is forcing our colonies together, not apart. But there are some, even in military circles, who have long-term concerns about the technology."

Spartan shook his head.

"I don't understand. The Network has been proven safe...I should know, I've used it enough. We can travel between colonies in an instant, and it means trade and communications from here to Prometheus, and even back to Earth, are now possible in hours and days. Why would anybody not want that?"

Jack looked away from Spartan in irritation, but it wasn't exactly clear why.

"What?" Spartan demanded.

Jack looked around the room until fixing on Johnson who nodded at him.

"There are three groups that have big issues with the Network. First are those in the less official markets; traders, black marketers, pirates and smugglers. With all trade using the Network, it has become much more difficult to run illegal operations. Second, the military."

"What?" exclaimed Johnson in surprise.

Spartan lifted his hand.

"You started this." He then looked to his son. "Go on Jack, explain."

"The use of the Network has reduced the importance of the long-distance ships and the transports and troops that go with them. No world is more than a few hours from a Network Rift, so why have so many ships and facilities? You could have just one large naval base with a dozen ships to protect the entire Alliance."

"Really?" asked Spartan in feigned surprise. "And what is the third?"

"Combat veterans. There are some that think the use of this technology is hubris. By using this technology, something that we found rather than created, we are creating reliance upon it, and also dabbling into things that could bring back the rumors of Hyperion."

A tap at the door stopped their discussion for a moment. Teresa stood up and walked to the door. She stepped outside for a moment and was gone for almost a minute before returning and closing it behind her. Rather than speaking, she walked over to the computer system on the wall. She tapped it and brought up a projection of the Prometheus-Orion Spacebridge. It was an unfamiliar sight to Spartan, who had spent most of the last eighteen months organizing the security systems of a dozen ships and four different colonies; the Network was closely guarded by Alliance personnel only, and he was quite happy it stayed that way.

"This is the experimental Spacebridge that Admiral Anderson is working on. Very few people outside of this room and the staff working on it know that the data used to construct it and the coordinates for its exit point were discovered at the Hyperion dig site. The bridge has been created, and ANS Beagle has gone through and established a stable path back to Prometheus. It will be going public shortly, but not until an issue is resolved."

Jack looked at the others in surprise but noticed they seemed unfazed.

"What the hell is this? Why didn't I..."

Spartan grinned at him.

"Because you never needed to know."

He then looked to Teresa and the image.

"What is it?"

A device on Director Johnson's wrist started to beep, and he lifted his hand to be excused for a moment. He looked down, and in just a few seconds, his face turned ashen from whatever news he had just heard. He looked up to Teresa.

"I must commend your intelligence network Ms Morato. It appears you beat my own department."

He stood up and walked to the model.

"May I?" he asked.

Teresa nodded and stepped to the side. Johnson zoomed in on the image of ANS Beagle, that was now far away in the Orion Nebula.

"A short time ago, a terrorist unit set off a device aboard the main vessel, killing a number of people. Information coming in says it was Lieutenant Jenson, an officer that had previously served on your old ship, the Santa Maria. I've been recalled to Prometheus to head up the investigation, and to assist the Admiral with the security of this new territory."

He paused for a few seconds as he considered his next move.

"Look, I know this is a little unorthodox, but I have doubts about almost everybody. Hell, that's my job, right now. We have an entirely new region of space with planets, moons and stations to consolidate. I could do with an independent eye on this one. Help with establishing security procedures, personnel and patrols, but more importantly, I need somebody outside of the system to help with this investigation. Who knows how far it could go? Your company is already providing security for Alliance facilities, is it not?"

The room fell silent at this last point. Johnson could sense they weren't quite sure how to respond to his request.

"I also have a request from the Admiral. He wants you

and your company here to assist. It looks like our presence in Orion is going to be long-term."

"Isn't that what Alliance military forces are designed for?" asked a suspicious Jack.

Johnson smiled.

"Of course, and who was instrumental in helping create the Alliance Marine Corps? There are times where private security is preferable to the installation of permanent military garrisons. If nothing else, something tells me that Orion is going to become the new frontier, and one that is ripe for exploitation. If you don't go, I can assure you there are others, like Terra Corps that will jump at the chance. Not interested?"

Spartan looked to Teresa who smiled right back at him.

"If it's a chance to get away from Epsilon Eridani, then you can count me in. I've already had enough of this place."

Director Johnson smiled at her response.

"Good. Get a small team together, and meet me at the spaceport."

With that last message, he was gone.

Spartan looked at his young son and his wife, both who seemed excited and a little confused at what had just happened.

"Well, you'd better pack your bags because we have work to do, and it looks like it might take us to a new star system."

Jack stood up and headed for the door. Spartan reached out to grab him.

"Keep this between us now, okay?" he said seriously.

"What about Wictred? He's been helping me with this. He could help."

Spartan nodded.

"I have no doubt about that. Let me speak with Gun first. We have things to discuss. Until then not a word to anybody, and that includes Wictred. Understood?"

Jack agreed, but it wasn't without protest. Once he'd left the room, it was just Spartan and Teresa left. She walked up to the door and hit the internal electronic lock mechanism. It clicked shut with a dull thud, locking them both in the room. She turned back to face him with a look on his face that she knew all too well.

"We should be getting ready to leave," he said as firmly as he could muster.

Teresa moved closer and then pushed him back to the table.

"Not just yet, we have a little time, don't we?"

Without waiting for an answer, she leaned over his prone body and placed her lips on his.

* * *

The fleet of five ships moved into a high orbit over the largest moon. Two of the frigates had stayed behind to guard the numerous civilian ships and engineer teams coming through the Spacebridge. This left just two Crusader class cruisers and three frigates to continue on to start a preliminary investigation into the gas giant, its moons and the unusual signal that had been detected when ANS Beagle had first arrived. Before leaving the Spacebridge, the two cruisers had been reinforced with more crew to bring their complements up to full strength.

Inside the CIC of ANS Dragon, and in front of the tactical display, stood Commodore Lewis, two of his science officers and Colonel Daniels, the newly arrived commander of Alliance Marine Corps. A detailed model of the moon lay in front of them, as well as lines that indicated the paths of the scores of other moons and debris circling the great planet. The moons were dwarfed by the great bulk of the planet gas giant, of whose diameter exceeded an entire astronomical unit.

"Explain that to me again?" asked the Commodore.

The most senior of the science team, Commander Garret Blackford altered the image, to show the shapes on the surface of the moon.

"The surface shows an artificial construction near this region of craters. The reconnaissance drone isolated the source of the radio signal to be coming directly from the centre of this shape."

The dark collection of shapes expanded until just one hexagonal looking site filled the screen. It was grainy, and substantial noise had obliterated much of what they were looking at.

"Well, that's great. All I'm seeing are shapes on the surface, and you're telling me that some, if not all, of this site is artificial?"

"It is more than that, Sir," explained the second of the two men. "We have faint traces of expelled fuel on a landing trajectory with the body. Somebody has been there, and in the last day."

Commodore Lewis looked intrigued at this information. Commander Blackford continued his briefing.

"It isn't just the surface of the moon. Of this Star System, we've established the following information. There are eight planets orbiting this red subgiant and there is a distant companion star, an orange main sequence star approximately three hundred astronomical units away. The nearest planet to the sun is the gas giant we are approaching. The remaining planets are an odd mixture of mainly ice planets, including a heavily volcanic world, and one that seems to have methane oceans. There are also three rock worlds with potentially interesting properties for establishing refining operations. The jewel though is the fourth planet, already named by the AANC (Alliance Astronomical Naming Commission) as Luthien. It has a thin but corrosive atmosphere, point seven Earth gravity, iron silicate structure and...

"Commander, we appreciate your interested in

the rest of this system, but for now we have a specific mission around the first planet...this moon, no matter how insignificant it might appear." He explained with an almost disappointed tone to his voice. It was perfectly understandable though. There were a number of more interesting targets to visit, but while exploratory drones and science vessels moved into the system to explore, he had been given the role of investigating the signal from a mere satellite, a moon of the gas giant.

The Commodore examined each of the planets on the display, but apart from mild interest, he appeared less than excited at the information.

"Is this what we travelled over a thousand light years for?"

Commander Blackford grinned at his comment. *Wait till he hears this, then.*

"That is just window dressing, Sir. Look at this."

He pointed to an image of dark shapes in space.

"We've also found traces of debris in orbit around the moon. The recon drone is moving towards the largest of the objects, but our best guess is that they are the remains of something that was built out here. There are low-level traces of radiation from several segments. We need to perform detailed scans, but our first assessment is that they are the remnants of a vessel of some kind."

Commodore Lewis leaned back slightly with a skeptical look on his face.

"You do understand that we have never been here before? This is new territory, ripe for exploration and exploitation. We built this Spacebridge to explore a new, virgin territory, and you're telling me there are signs of a derelict vessel here?"

"Well, Sir, we did select these coordinates based on the Hyperion Rift data. Is it that far-fetched that we would discover something, other than this?"

Commodore Lewis didn't really want to answer the question. Like many military people, he had wondered at the reasoning behind establishing their very first long-distance Spacebridge into the unknown. There were star systems mere light years away with known planets that would have made better sense in every way. Yet the word from Alliance Central Command was that establishing a connection to Orion was of the highest priority. He tapped the image of the moon and turned to the rest of his crew.

"Look, the assumption with this transmission is that it is something to do with the arrival of ANS Beagle and possibly her own saboteurs. We are missing one of the pair, and there is a chance, however unlikely, she may have escaped to the moon and is broadcasting a distress signal."

Commander Blackford shook his head.

"No, Sir. My best guess is that this site below is a derelict station or post of some kind. With the distance to the surface, and the relatively thick atmosphere of the moon, it isn't going to be easy to understand much more."

Colonel Daniels tapped the screen and zoomed the image back out.

"I don't see the problem here. This territory is being officially claimed by the Alliance. If we want this place for our own, then we need to establish a presence at any potentially useful site. I have two ships' worth of marines, nearly a thousand marines at my command, and they are ready to perform any operations deemed necessary by Alliance High Command. On board ANS Dragon, I have Vanguards, mules and drone carriers. Our armor is proof against pretty much any environment. I can drop a small recon team in, get your recce done, and secure the site for further evaluation."

Commander Blackford lifted his hands in the air as protest. Though he was part of the Alliance military, his primary job was physical science in the advanced research programs on Prometheus.

"Sir, is it really necessary to deploy ground forces? All we have so far is a repeating signal on a moon and some orbital debris. My recommendation is to release more drones into the system. Until we have more to go on, it might be unwise to risk sending people to the surface."

Commodore Lewis paused and looked back around the CiC. Only the senior officers were present, and every one of them was busy scanning and analyzing the data coming directly to the flagship. He looked back to the main display and the image of the debris field.

"Look, nobody expected to find a signal here, let alone any other kind of artificial construction. I need information, and I need it fast. Get every drone and reconnaissance vessel we have into space and scanning. I want the derelict investigated thoroughly, but more importantly, I need to know about the source of the signal."

He then turned to Colonel Daniels.

"I've been given full authority to secure Orion. Colonel, I want you to send a small team to the surface to perform a full surface scan. I need this information fast. If anybody has been here before us, we are going to need to make decisions before things could potentially escalate."

Colonel Daniels looked a little surprised at his order.

"Anybody? You think there could be signs of life down there?"

Commodore Lewis smiled at him.

"Colonel, we've seen Biomechs, artificial creatures that can talk and machines powered by AI cores. I'm leaving nothing off the table. If life exists on seven star systems in the Alliance, and we can create life ourselves, then why not somewhere else? Hell, knowing our luck, we'll find an Echidna Union facility waiting for us."

CHAPTER SIX

With the contract won at Epsilon Eridani, the APS Corporation finally supplanted Alpha Company as the most profitable security and paramilitary company in the Alliance. With their purchase of the four ex-Confederate Navy frigates, a civilian transport ship and a squadron of landing craft and shuttles, they offered a military capability second only to the Alliance Navy and Marine Corps.

Private Security Directory

The Senate was in full session, but this happened to be one of the rare occasions when cameras were not allowed. Most sessions held in this ancient and impressive structure were now broadcast in real-time by making use of the Interstellar Network. It allowed citizens in the many disparate parts of the Alliance to watch their representatives on Terra Nova and feel they had a part to play in their democracy. Though similar to the previous Confederacy, the new Alliance was based upon firmer ties between the colonies and greater central control from the centre. Stood on the raised podium was the lithe form of the aged Maria Hobbs, President of the Centauri Alliance and the supreme commander of all her citizens. She waited patiently as the Council Magistrate called the session to order.

Senator Broby Ramir watched the proceedings with interest from his position in the second row directly opposite the President. As one of the newest senators, he was still getting used to the system and ever watchful for information that could help his own citizens back on Centauri Prime. His career had included a stint as a soldier with the New Carlos Militia in the War, and it had been his impeccable service record that had helped to propel him so far into this arena. He was a young man in his later forties and well below the median age for senators. Even so, after six months of being in office, it was only his third visit to the Senate Building and now, as on the previous occasions, he wondered if he was the right man to be listening and making such momentous decisions.

It took several seconds before the chattering and complaining settled down. Even though this was an emergency closed session, it seemed to do little to encourage those senators present to act with even a little decorum. Broby watched with a mixture of dismay and apprehension as each of the senators returned their attention to their elected leader. Once satisfied, The President nodded and then spoke.

"Senators of the House. In the last hour, a confidential newsflash has arrived from Admiral Anderson, the commander of Prometheus Research Station and leader of our experimental Rift generator project. You may have heard rumors, but so far nothing has been confirmed or denied. The press will be informed within three hours; however, and the news is momentous."

She paused for a few moments to ensure she had the attention of every single senator in the House.

"With the construction of our Interstellar Network, we have enjoyed a period of fruitful peace and trade, the like of which hasn't been seen since the early decades of colonization. Just three days ago, the Rift generator experiment at Prometheus was activated. I know this is probably the worst kept secret in the Alliance, but behind this lays a hidden truth. By a stroke of luck and ingenuity, our engineers have managed to create a stable Spacebridge to the Orion Nebula and have sent both equipment and people through!"

The senators could no longer contain themselves, and a great crescendo of sound rippled though the building. The President lifted her hands to the air as if appealing to some great deity. Some stopped but most continued talking.

"Senators, please keep quiet, there is more and time is limited!"

The noises abated enough for her to continue.

"The Spacebridge has by some miracle, created an exit point near a resource rich star system of ten planets. Several have atmospheres, but all are within our grasp. I have already issued orders to our military and scientific departments to start a complete and thorough examination of the system, with a view to settlement, mining and exploitation. Senators of the Centauri Alliance, today we are no longer a people of seven stars. We have moved on from the Solar System to include Proxima Centauri, these twin stars of Alpha Centauri and our three most recent acquisitions, the research and mining operations at Epsilon Eridani, Gliese 876 and now Procyon."

Senator Broby Ramir's secpad lit up with a series of documents from the office of the President. Her words had indeed sounded fine, but he knew only too well that of those stars, only the two-dozen worlds orbiting the triple stars of Alpha and Proxima Centauri had any real significance. The three new stars were nothing more than outposts and mining stations. Useful as they were, they were nothing compared to the core planets. Even Sol, the old solar system, from which they had all originated, was little but a charred shell of its former self. For some reason, a Spacebridge had only recently been constructed that led directly to the red planet of Mars. The over mined and heavily polluted Earth was slowly being reintegrated into the community of planets, but few wanted to trade or even travel there anymore.

This Orion could be very interesting though.

He thumbed through the details while the President continued her plans for the star system. As he looked through, he couldn't help but feel a little suspicious at the destination. He was no scientist, but he knew the odds of pinpointing a star at random were almost impossible, let alone one with planets. He could only assume the Alliance scientists had been able to isolate or lock onto something at that great distance. He looked up and listened to the end of her speech.

"With this news will come many opportunities for our citizens. Work for industry, the sciences and even for yourselves. Orion is the new frontier, and it is my intention to open it up to any of our people that wish to go."

A cheer of approval rose in volume, but Broby was well aware something was missing. They wouldn't have been recalled unless they were required to debate and vote on something. The President had the authority to make short-term decisions, but ultimately, these decisions had to be ratified by the Senate.

What does she want our support on?

"But before a single civilian can take a ship into this new land, it will be necessary for the House to read, digest and vote upon my actions. Even now, our military and science vessels are exploring the near moons and planets of the star, that the astronomical society has named New Charon, in honor of the ancient ferryman of Hades, and in honor of the many that have lost their lives in pursuit of this technology."

The mention of the military reminded him of the decision the Senate had taken whilst he was still serving. He had seen at firsthand the disbanding of the colonial militias and even the abolition of the Army. To replace it came an enlarged Marine Corps, though still smaller than the earlier numbers of ground troops available in total. All regular troops were now based on ships or stations, and no units were allowed to remain on the colonies for more than six months. It was a vast change, but even then it had required a unanimous vote from the Senate to push it through.

"Senators..." she called out one last time, "I call upon you to ratify my intention to designate New Charon as the eighth star system of the Alliance. By doing this, we are announcing our intentions to secure the star, its neighboring world and its limitless resources to the benefit of our people."

The sound of chattering senators once more filled the House, but Broby was left with a hollow feeling. It wasn't the exploitation of something so recently found that bothered him. No, it was the language she was using. Quite why the Alliance needed to announce anything seemed absurd to him. They were the only sentient beings discovered other than the most primate of microbes and planet life; such as those found on worlds like Terra Nova and Hyperion so many hundreds of years earlier. He shook his head and stood up, much to the surprise of the other senators and the President.

"President Hobbs, I have one question regarding Orion!" he called out over the din.

She lifted her hands for silence as before, and the sound dropped as they spotted him standing. It was against protocol to interrupt an announcement, particularly when it was the President. Even so, she nodded but remained standing.

"Very well, Senator, one question."

Broby cleared his voice and turned to see so many pairs of eyes staring at him with a mixture of interest, irritation and boredom.

"We are the only sentient beings ever discovered. Quite why do we need to declare this territory for the Alliance? In the past, we have simply sent ships to an area and then exploited it in whichever way we felt was necessary."

The President said nothing for a few seconds, and this short pause caused a reaction like that of an electric shock through the senators. Like most politicians, each was keen to watch their own backs, and the mere hint that something was being kept from them finally grabbed their attention.

"President, has something been found on New

Charon?"

The look on her face answered the question, and what had started as a loud outburst, turned into shouting and even screaming in the great building. Broby watched in surprise as the formal facade of the Senate Building turned into nothing more than a common crowd. It took almost a minute for the senators to quiet down, and for the President to indicate for him to sit back down. He could feel the anger emanated from her eyes and wondered if perhaps he should have kept quiet.

"Senators, I have just received information from the Defense Secretary that a small number of our ships are investigating a moon orbiting the second planet in New Charon. The information is subject to more work, but initial signs indicate that it has been inhabited at some point in the past. I can confirm to you all that Alliance military forces have encountered the signs of sentient life almost fourteen hundred light years from Prometheus."

* * *

Spartan's family arrival at the Prometheus Seven Trading Post was less auspicious than he might have hoped. They stepped onto the station to find only their own APS representative waiting for them. Angela Brevik had served in the Marine Corps a decade before the struggles with the Zealots. Though now slightly overweight, and with more than a few grey hairs, she was both quick minded and physically strong. On more than one occasion in the last year, she had been forced to rely on her own martial skills.

"Spartan, Ms Morato," she said politely and then looked past them both.

"Where is Jack Morato? I understood he was coming as well."

Spartan moved up closer to her and shook her hand.

"Ms Brevik, good to see you again. Jack will be joining us shortly, but he has business to attend to with..." he noticed Teresa twisting her head discreetly at him.

"...the station's security chief."

Teresa then shook her hand and indicated for them to move inside the station.

"Where are the Alliance security forces? We expected to be met by them."

Ms Brevik glanced around and motioned for them to continue inside to the main corridor. It was a wide space, and its sides filled with glass. A number of civilians moved about, but every one of them looked like they were in a rush. They moved a little further until reaching the main foyer area.

"Ah, this takes me back," Teresa said to Spartan.

He smiled at her, remembering that her only ever visit to this station had been back in the War when he had been a prisoner on the planet below. Teresa and a small team had come to the station seeking information.

"I seem to recall you had a little fun on your last visit?"

Teresa tilted her head as they moved out into the open area. It was massive with a circular floor and mighty marble staircases moving up to the higher levels. In the centre was a great sculpture of a man digging into the ground. It all brought back memories of the place, few actually being ones she wanted to remember, especially the arms fair they had come to infiltrate. The thought reminded her of Bishop and Kowalski, her old friends that she'd worked with.

"Not quite the way I remember it," she said seriously.

Scores of people moved about, and most wore suits or uniforms, a far cry from the mercenaries and traders that used to inhabit the site. Spartan looked about the vast open area and recalled the plans he'd seen when discussing the security arrangements with Alliance security several years earlier. APS weren't providing station protection like they usually did, but they were involved in ship loading security, as well as personal protection on the site itself. Both he and Teresa had pushed Admiral Anderson, the man in charge of the station, for a larger contract, but this was the best he could manage. They took a few more steps before a man in naval uniform appeared from one of the side doors and intercepted them both. He stopped and saluted.

"Sir, Lieutenant Commander Sanlav Erdeniz. I've been sent by the Admiral to bring you down to the research lab.

He requests your assistance with a pressing issue."

His name meant nothing to Spartan, but Teresa appeared to recognize something about him.

"Erdeniz? Aren't you the young officer that worked with Special Agent Johnson on Kerberos?"

Sanlav looked at her in surprise.

"Yes, Ma'am, you know him?"

Teresa nodded but said no more.

The Naval officer indicated for them to follow him to one of the doorways guarded by two armored marines. They stepped inside but stopped when Angela Brevik tried to enter.

"Sorry, this is for cleared personnel only," said the taller of the two marines.

Spartan looked to the Lieutenant Commander, but he shook his head apologetically.

"Sorry, Sir, you know how it works."

Spartan sighed and stepped back to Ms Brevik.

"This won't take long, so get a video conference ready in one hour. I'll need to speak with all company directors."

Ms Brevik nodded and made to turn, but Spartan stepped in closer.

"Get me in touch with Governor Gun on Hyperion. It's time we had a chat again."

"Understood," she replied and moved away and into the crowd.

They followed the Lieutenant Commander further into

the naval part of the station and past a number of secure laboratories. Spartan noted the number of marine guards stationed at different points, quickly working out that this was one of the most secure sites he'd seen in some months. They reached a final open space, behind which lay two large glass doors. The officer stopped and looked back at Teresa.

"How is Johnson? I've not seen him since the rebuilding of Kerberos, and that was more than a decade ago. He's the Director of Alliance Intelligence, isn't he?"

"Yes, he is," answered a firm voice as the door opened.

Intelligence Director Johnson appeared, along with Admiral Anderson and a small group of high-ranking military officers. For the briefest of moments, the man forgot military procedure and stepped forward to shake Johnson's hand. An agent moved quickly between then to block his path. Johnson waved him off and took his own step closer to shake his hand.

"Sanlav, it's been a long time. Slightly nicer setting than the Kerberos Underground, don't you think?"

The Naval officer smiled but quickly stepped back, remembering military protocol. The Admiral indicated for them to step inside the room, where a projected model of part of ANS Beagle filled the room. All along the one side was a massively reinforced window that gave them a perfect view of the entry point to the Spacebridge. The Admiral indicated to the object. Spartan spotted a group of Marine

Corps officers, and he was sure he recognized one before the Admiral caught his eye. He looked impatient and a little irritated by the wandering eye of Spartan.

"As you can see, we have activated the Spacebridge to Orion Major. It is the provisional name given by the Senate to this newly discovered region of space. There are already rumors in the media about this project, but nothing concrete has been issued...yet."

He looked back from the Rift and to the projected model of ANS Beagle.

"We were in the middle of this discussion when I heard you had arrived, Spartan. If you are interested, I have some work on the other side of the Rift?"

He gave him no time to answer before he moved over to Teresa.

"It's been some time, hasn't it, Ms Morato? I take it you're still watching his back? Remember, don't let him and the General go off on one of their adventures!"

Teresa grinned at his comment. It was well known that the two of them had been part of the rescue party involved in freeing untold numbers of prisoners and slaves on Prometheus.

"Your timing is fortuitous, if not because things are developing in Orion at a much faster rate than we expected. I have been authorized to use this station as a research and command centre for the entire Orion sector, as we continue to explore, expand and exploit the region.

To facilitate this, I will need military, civilian and private sector involvement. We've already discovered a number of very interesting moons and artifacts that I think we can all benefit from."

As they considered his words, he indicated to the group of marines.

"I think you've all met the General."

From the corner of the group, the form of the battle-hardened General approached. Spartan hadn't seen the man for some time, and the years had certainly taken their toll on him. Even so, he was still physically fit and commanded a presence in the room that even the Admiral couldn't match.

"Admiral, I've just received the report from Colonel Daniels. Have you seen it?" said the General, without even acknowledging the others present. He handed over his secpad and waited patiently. Admiral Anderson examined it for what seemed like an age before finally speaking.

"Well, this is incredible. Colonel Daniels has landed a company of marines onto the largest of the moons...and they've...found something."

General Rivers looked at the group briefly and laid his eyes on Spartan. His expression changed instantly to pleasure, and he stepped forward and embraced him as only two men that had faced the rigors of war together could.

"Spartan, I thought you'd retired from all of this?"

"Yeah, me too."

"General, I requested the assistance of Spartan's APS Corporation in the Orion sector. We have military forces, but the protection of facilities and personnel is a task APS is well suited for," explained Admiral Anderson.

The General laughed at his words.

"I think you'll find that in reality what you mean is you've found something, and sending in private security will double our numbers in the field, without having to redeploy most of the fleet and Marine Corps!"

Admiral Anderson shook his head.

"Well, that is one way to look at it. Anyway, you have all been cleared for this project, and I would remind you that anything you hear in this station is classified. Only the senior members of the Senate, the Defense Committee and our senior military commanders know all the details, and that is the way it will stay. If anybody doesn't want to go further, please state this now."

There was a short pause, but not a soul moved.

"Very well, then. I asked you all here to finalize the initial stages of exploration and exploitation. This news from the moon doesn't change anything, other than increase our need to establish a strong presence in Orion."

He walked over to one of the many computer displays and hit a button. Most of the assembled personnel turned their attention to a civilian heavy transport that was entering the Rift entrance of the Spacebridge. It distorted and then vanished as though it had never existed. Admiral Anderson spotted their interest; noting that even the General was intrigued.

"Yes, even as we watch, more ships are travelling through. Commodore Lewis already has access to a small taskforce, and seven civilian vessels are in the vicinity of the bridge to enlarge ANS Beagle to provide a longer term exit point."

"So the plan is no longer a short-term exploration mission of six months? What's changed, and why do you need civilian security involvement?" asked Spartan.

The video display changed to an encrypted data stream direct from the CIC of ANS Dragon. It showed helmet footage from a squad of marines as they waited inside a shuttle.

"I think this video will explain things more clearly. Let's just say that Orion has many secrets, some good and some, well...less so," said the Admiral. "It was packaged and sent directly from Commodore Lewis less than an hour ago."

The view took Spartan back to his days in the Marine Corps, and he couldn't help but feel a pang of disappointment to not be there with the marines. The side door opened, and it took a few seconds for the exposure unit of the cameras to adjust to the bright light as opposed to the darkness inside the shuttle. The marines stepped out and looked around the landing area. It was a small open space, much like a crater, and perfect for the safe landing of people. Two of them moved out of camera shot, and it took a moment for the blurred feed to stabilize as the marine turned around. A large series of mountainous structures filled the screen, but it wasn't the geography that drew a gasp from the assembled military and scientific personnel. It was the fact that as the image became clearer, they could see that the formations were actually shaped and carved directly into the rock.

"Are you seeing this, Sarge?" asked the marine in the video.

"Keep moving, marine!" came back the gruff reply.

A calmer voice appeared, and Spartan quickly recognized it as coming from Colonel Daniels; a man with whom he'd also served with in the past.

"1st Squad stay with the shuttle, 2nd and 3rd Squads with me. We need to reach the source of the transmission."

They continued forwards, along what looked like a dry riverbed. The ground and hills around them were colorless, much like the surface of many moons, but the bright glow of the gas giant in the sky overshadowed everything, even the distant sun. Their movement was confusing to all of those other than the marines present. It was a classic low gravity world, and the marines were forced to use the odd skipping movement to make quick and safe progress. A few more minutes, and they came to an obstruction; much like a wall, but this was a natural barrier like a dam. The Colonel appeared, and his lightly armored PDS suit, with its unique striped camouflage, looked odd against the dull grey background. He bent his knees and jumped up, easily reaching three meters before grabbing at the barrier and pulling himself up.

"What are they looking for?" asked Teresa.

None of them could tear their eyes from the screen as the display shook violently. When it settled down, it was clear the marine must have jumped to join his commander. He looked up and over the ridge to see something that shocked the assembled group. A large group of thickly armored buildings littered the ground. Many were damaged with holes in their walls or roofs.

"How did we not see this on the way down?" asked the marine.

"Look at the angles. You can only see this part of the terrain if you approach down this riverbed," said Colonel Daniels.

The marine continued to turn his head slowly, panning across the skyline and taking in the site of the damaged structures. It was then that he fixed his gaze on something metallic that was broken up across the ground.

"Sarge, is that what I think it is?" he asked.

In the pause before anybody else spoke, the marine tapped a button and the camera shook. The optics shifted, and the depth of field changed as the lens zoomed into the object. It was massive, probably a hundred meters long, dark grey, metallic and smashed beyond recognition.

He fixed on something hanging out of one of the holes. It was about two meters tall and a similar color to the vessel. Then it moved. He gasped with excitement and horror as he recognized what he was seeing.

"It's alive! Sarge, there's somebody down there!"

The camera shook again, and the man and the other marines broke out into a fast hop over the broken ground. The images became confused as they bounced over the ground, but it was clear enough for those watching, to make out the shapes of the small bunkers and buildings.

"Is it me, or do they look like long abandoned military fortifications?" asked Spartan.

General Rivers nodded in agreement.

"Not abandoned though. Look at the damage. I'd say there's been fighting here."

The marines were over half way to the debris when the moving shape vanished into cover, and the object itself vanished in a bright flash. It forced the exposure control of the camera to change, and the image turned bright white. When it returned, the image was sideways and facing away from the object. In the background were the sounds of shouting.

"Marines, fall back!" shouted the Colonel in a cool and dispassionate tone.

The image was now stationary and gave a clear view of the ground and one of the bunkers. Two marines ran past the camera and off to the right.

"To the shuttle!" shouted the Sergeant.

A blurred shape of an armored man came from the left. His armor was thicker than the marines but beautifully crafted with no exposed cabling, wiring or connections. The armored head was shaped almost like a bug with a pair of antennae pushed up from the back. A dark black visor ran where the eyes should be. He ran up to the camera and bent down to look at the lens, turned his head and raised his right arm. A double-barreled weapon system seemed integrated into the armor. As the warrior lifted the weapon, a dark shape smashed down into him. It must have been massive because it filled the screen. Gunfire crackled in the background, and in less than a few seconds, the dark object lifted up out of view to show the crushed and broken body of the armored man, and then the feed went dead. The image froze on the last still as if somebody had deliberately paused it. Admiral Anderson turned back to the group.

"What the hell was all of that?" asked Spartan.

General Rivers shook his head in dismay. He had already stepped up to the display and reversed the video to the section showing the debris in the open area prior to the blast.

"It looks clear to me. There are a number of people already on this moon. Look, they are the same height and build as us, but this armor and the weapons are not Alliance. Maybe somebody else got a Rift generator working before us?

"Maybe, but I doubt it," replied the Admiral. "Those fortifications looked old, at least a few decades, maybe more."

"Well, we did start this operation based on intelligence recovered from Hyperion. Didn't you see legions of Biomechs on the other side of the Rift before it was destroyed?" asked Intelligence Director Johnson, directly to Spartan.

The question took Spartan back to the last battle of the War. The fighting had occurred around a secret archaeological site from which a massive Rift generator had been sited. Unfamiliar Biomechs and war machines had arrived through the Rift, and though it had been destroyed, he had seen what was on the other side. Few believed what he and his comrade Kowalski had seen, but he knew it to be true. On the other side was a great cavern filled with enemy warriors.

"Surely this isn't related to the enemy of Hyperion? They were destroyed."

"Well, why do you think this region of space was selected to start with? We have known for some time that the Rifts generators, the Anomaly in space, the Zealots and ultimately the Biomechs are all intimately linked. There is no way they could have built up such a massive and successful infrastructure on their own, without us knowing about it. What if what we're seeing on this moon is part of the puzzle? Maybe there are others out there, and they have been behind the Zealots and their Uprising?" asked Johnson.

His question was the one none of them had wanted to ask, but it needed to be answered. There were many questions left unanswered from the War, and few had answers that seemed helpful. Admiral Anderson shrugged at his question.

"The simple answer is, we don't know. These people could be from ANS Beagle or less likely from another Rift that has been built. Until we know more, this is all speculation. I think you can see the gravity of the situation though. In a matter of days, we have both discovered a new star system ripe for exploitation and also made contact with an unknown people. Who are they, and why are they on this moon? Do they have any connection with us or the Biomechs?"

"But I have another question, Admiral?" asked Spartan. "Well?"

"That armored man, assuming it is a man, was running from something, and it wasn't our marines. What the hell was it that crushed him and why?"

General Rivers turned from the feed and to the group.

"That is for us to find out. One thing I do know is that the Senate has already voted on making this system part of the Alliance. We need land for our people and resources. New Charon is the greatest planetary discovery since we first colonized Alpha Centauri. That means we have carte blanche to explore and secure every site in the sector. If we want this territory, then there is a chance we will have to exert our authority here.

"General, if there are already people on the moon, doesn't that mean it's already been claimed?" asked Teresa.

Admiral Anderson shook his head in disagreement.

"It doesn't really matter now. Either way, they know we are there now, and the official policy of the Senate is that we have no interest in giving up this discovery. I have been ordered to secure several sites and to make first contact with these people. We will try to establish some form of communication with them, but be under no illusions, New Charon is now part of the Alliance."

Spartan looked over to Teresa, and he knew instantly that she was uncomfortable with the situation. He looked at the video display and the group of military people around him with both pride and confusion.

We've arrived in a new world that may already belong to somebody else. Has anybody even thought about whether we should even be here? He thought.

"What about Daniels and his marines? Have you heard back from him? What about Commodore Lewis and his ships?"

This caught the attention of General Rivers, and he spoke before anybody else could interject.

"That was the first thing I thought, Spartan," he said

while looking at the others with barely concealed contempt.

"The Commodore detected a vessel on approach to the moon and withdrew his vessels to one of the thick debris fields orbiting the moon, prior to the action we've just seen. That was the last we heard from either the ships or the ground troops."

He paused for a moment, but Spartan was instantly reminded of the missing ships at Hyperion. He couldn't see anything positive about this situation.

"I have redirected ANS Devastation, as she only recently entered through the bridge. She will be here soon and will stop at the station to pick me up. Interested in coming along? I could do with an experienced eye, and knowing our luck, Daniels and Lewis will have ended up is a shitstorm, as usual!" he laughed in a way only the senior military commanders seemed to be able to get away with.

"I'm not military anymore, General," Spartan answered.

The General shrugged.

"So what? You're military cleared, and you run security services for the Alliance, don't you?"

Spartan nodded slowly, but he knew where this was going.

"Good, then consider your Corporation hired to provide auxiliary services for the Marine Corps. I think you'll find there is going to be plenty of work to go around in Orion."

Spartan turned to Teresa, and she quickly nodded.

"It's Daniels, if anybody can get him out of this mess, it will be you two. At least this way we get a foot through the door, and help out Daniels at the same time."

Spartan looked back to the General and shook his hand.

"Good, get your kit, we'll be leaving within the hour."

General Rivers left the two of them and started speaking with the Admiral. It was clear they were having a difference of opinion, and as Spartan watched, he was secretly pleased it was something he no longer had to be involved in. Looking about, it was clear from those in the room that exploration and exploitation was the number one priority, even at the possible expense of another people. Maybe he was wrong, but the fate of the small group of marines seemed far from any of their minds. While the others talked excitedly about what was happening, Teresa moved close to Spartan.

"What are we doing here?"

Spartan looked at her and thought back to the planets he'd landed on and the enemies he'd faced in the past. First were the Zealots, the religious fanatics who'd resorted to suicide bombings and terrorist attacks through to the Echidna Union and their biomechanical creatures. Nothing had ever prepared him for the potential of meeting a new species on another world. His gut instinct told him this had something to do with the War, and if that were true, then who knows what they might find.

"I don't know, but something tells me we'll be seeing

a lot more of Orion soon. If we're going to expand into this territory, then APS is going to be there. If we don't go, then somebody else will."

Teresa sighed at his comments. They both looked at the Admiral, the General and the host of other senior officers. It was clear something big was about to happen, and for even just a moment, they both wondered if they were actually the good guys this time. Spartan looked at her and smiled.

"Hey, whichever way it goes, they're gonna need a lot of security out there, and we are the best."

Another ship, this time one of the Crusader class warships moved through the Rift, but only Spartan and Teresa seemed to notice it this time. She looked back at him.

"That's what I'm afraid of."

CHAPTER SEVEN

Prior to the Great Uprising the common disposition of fleets was heavy warships, including warbarges and battleships with fast cruiser squadrons as escorts. Frigates and light cruisers were used in smaller taskforces or to provide skirmish screens in major actions. The transition to multirole ships in the Alliance reduced the requirement for such a diversity of ships and increased the importance of fighter wings and marine detachments. The single weakness of this new philosophy would be if Alliance vessels were ever again required to fight major ship on ship action.

Naval Cadet's Handbook

The private space for APS staff was less impressive than Spartan had expected. Although the office on the Prometheus Seven Trading Post was modest, he hadn't expected their space on ANS Beagle to be even smaller.

In a matter of days, the spacecraft had been turned from a space-going craft into a combined space station and Rift generator, exactly what she had been built for. Living space on any ship was at a premium, but the three small rooms, including this cramped canteen area was starting to irritate Spartan. It was as sterile as a storeroom and interrupted by the constant drone of machinery that pervaded through the metal of the ship. The only real upside was the view, and that was more due to accident than design. A window of almost two meters in length ran along the left-hand side to provide access to a now removed lifeboat. It gave him the perfect view of the Rift.

Some might wonder why he and Teresa were in Orion rather than their other operatives, but that simply betrayed their lack of understanding about the company. Though the two had founded the corporation some years ago, they now had a board of directors to respond to, as well as hundreds of employees and even more operatives throughout the Alliance. Both had relinquished their positions at the top years ago, but were still senior members of the board and with the controlling stakes in the company. Of all their top people, there were none more qualified or better suited to tackling the unknown than Spartan and Teresa Morato.

Not that it was particularly important right now; the news coming from Orion was becoming more intriguing by the hour. Another message arrived with new facts and figures from the official Alliance media channel. It was filtered, of course, but that was fine. Spartan needed to know the public mood, just as much as what was actually happening. As he chewed on the piece of steak he'd just been served, he watched a number of vessels maneuver away from the exit point of the Rift.

"How many is that now?" he asked.

Teresa took a sip from a tall glass of wine before replying.

"Seven ships in the last hour. Pretty soon this system is going to start to run out of space!"

They seemed calm, but the opposite was true of Jack. He sat next to Teresa but had managed to eat nothing and was more interested in watching the queue of ships waiting to return through the Rift. Some of the vessels had now made the trip back and forth more than a dozen times as they brought people, supplies and equipment into the system.

Spartan looked back down at the reports laid out on his secpad. More drones had been sent out, and so far, information was coming back on two of the ice worlds and a number of moons. What was getting the most attention was the number of derelicts found using long-range sensors in the massive asteroid belt. It was too soon to be certain, but the press was already having a field day with the news. Rumors were flying that ranged from Alliance separatists found at the asteroid belt through to

Alien spaceships discovered. But it was all irrelevant until the first of the recon drones passed through the belt in a week's time. Until then, they had to manage with the images from the telescope mounts.

If they knew about this one, there would be ructions. He thought as he moved to the next report.

He had to provide both a thumb and retina scan before the secpad would even grant him access. It was the latest information on the missing marines on the gas giant's moon and could not under any circumstances be made public. He leaned in closer as he checked the information. It seemed that contact had been made with the marines, and a team was being sent to reinforce their position.

Now that is somewhere I should be.

Spartan had that feeling everybody felt when somebody was looking at him. His pulse changed slightly, and he lifted his eyes to see Jack looking directly at him. Spartan lifted one eyebrow as if in question.

"What did Gun say, then? Has he found out any more on this underground movement?"

Spartan chewed another piece of steak before lowering his knife and fork.

"Jack, whatever they were planning, it failed."

Jack stood up and moved back to the window where he could watch the arrival of more ships. Off to the side of the Rift were two massive platforms, each surrounded by workers in spacesuits and remote drones. It looked like a giant construction site, but it was being worked on while vessels continued to come through.

Spartan looked at Teresa who pointed him back to Jack with just her eyes. They'd known each other for two decades and understood each other without even speaking. A very useful benefit in some of the tense situations they'd found themselves both when in the Marine Corps and afterwards. He considered what had happened prior to their arrival and nodded.

"You were right, though. There was a plan to bring down the Interstellar Network, but this Jenson character was killed on ANS Beagle. Since then, all leads from there have dried up other than the missing lifeboat. Whatever they were planning, either died with him, or is still a potential threat right here in this system. Knowing our luck, I would say there is at least one more of them left, and they are waiting for the right moment."

Jack moved away from the window.

"Yeah, but what about the guy we found back on Epsilon Eridani? I think it's about time Wictred and I went back to see what we could find."

"Alliance Intelligence is still working on him. Look, Son, it's out of our hands now, and you're neither Alliance Intelligence nor military. We have our own problems to work on, and right now that is focused on Orion. You saw the last report from the moon and the drones they've been sending out. There are all kinds of ruins and artifacts out there, and their value is incalculable."

Jack walked up to the window and looked out to the ships. He watched yet another vessel entering the Rift and looked back at his parents.

"You don't need me there. I've spent the last two years helping Gun and the others with stopping these people. I've learnt my skills with you and the Jötnar since I was a boy. You don't need people like me interfering with your business. Since I've been here, my sources have dried up. They're either dead or gone to ground. What am I supposed to do now?"

Teresa looked to Spartan and then to Jack.

"It isn't over. Johnson is convinced that access to Orion and its secrets will just be another reason for these people to attack us. The War might be long gone, but there are still people out there who will use violence to their own ends."

Spartan nodded in agreement.

"True, and in this case, they probably believe what they are doing is for all our benefits."

Teresa waited for a moment. She evidently wanted to say something, and it had been down to what she and Spartan had been discussing for several days now.

"We are leaving for Orion tomorrow, along with several teams from the company. Alliance science teams are already establishing a temporary facility on the moon, and more will be built in the next three months. You've seen the plan, haven't you? Outposts are to be built on three of the planets and a dozen more on the most suitable moons. All of this will happen fast. We want you to work for the company in Orion."

Jack looked at the two of them with a mixture of annoyance and confusion.

"Why? What do I know about military and security operations?"

Spartan slid his secpad across the table. It showed three dossiers of men. Jack lifted it and placed it back on the table.

"These men all served at Hyperion, what about them?"

Spartan took a long breath as if he was building up to something.

"Johnson passed this information on to me. He thought it might be useful. Two weeks ago they escaped from a medical facility on Terra Nova. They are connected with Jensen from their time in the military, the man that triggered the blast on the Beagle and almost destroyed the Spacebridge."

Jack nodded, now understanding.

"And you think they might have an interest in continuing his work? So this is moving on from anti-Biomech activity and on to stopping us moving to Orion? Why?"

Teresa looked disappointed at his question.

"Why? Isn't it obvious? Orion was chosen because of information found at the archaeological site at Hyperion.

You know what we saw back on that planet, the same horrors that Gun and his people have been hunting there ever since. It can't be a coincidence that the people that hate Biomechs would seek to stop us travelling to and therefore exposing us to a potential Biomech threat."

Jack looked confused and turned to Spartan who simply nodded in agreement.

"They must believe that Orion and the Biomechs are linked. In their own way, they are trying to protect us from ourselves."

Teresa stood up.

"By attacking us? They are no friends of ours. It is one thing to lobby for change, but when you turn on your own people, you make yourself an enemy. Now, if you come with us, we could use you for intelligence operations with the company. It's a new frontier out here, and it's a place you could make a name in. Gun is sending a team over to assist, and I'm sure you'll want to help with that. They are due to arrive in the next few hours."

Jack's face lit up at the mention of Gun, but he still seemed unconvinced.

"Why is Gun sending people?"

Spartan simply laughed in reply.

"Because I asked him to send me a dozen volunteers to help with security. Nothing stops violence like a group of loyal Jötnar. They've worked with us before, and they are damned useful. Remember the hostage situation on

Carthago? They cleaned that up quickly before Alliance forces could even reach the planet. There is a reason we have so many on the APS payroll."

Still Jack seemed confused at the option before him. Teresa stood and walked to where he waited.

"I know you have a fondness for them, all three of us do. They've been loyal friends since our meeting on Prometheus. That's why we're planning on setting up a special taskforce in this sector. It will be made up of our best units to provide security and training for personnel in this area. The Alliance military force has been run down since the War. They might be well equipped and trained, but they can't be everywhere. Corporations like us are vital to provide the military backbone so they can retain their mobility. There are also plenty of operations where private units are preferable to Alliance involvement. You're already cleared for executive work in APS. We arranged that years ago. This would be something much bigger though. How would you feel about joining the special taskforce? Your skills would come in handy, and we need help in shutting down this group of saboteurs."

"What about Wictred? He's still on the station. Will he be coming as well?"

"Why not? I hear Khan is coming anyway, and I'm sure he'd rather see his son in action at Orion rather than wasting away here."

Jack smiled at his father for the first time in years.

"So I get to explore new moons, hunt down the enemies of the Alliance, and get a decent paycheck in for the bargain?" he asked with more than a hint of sarcasm.

Most parents might worry about the offer they were giving but not Spartan. He was well aware that that Orion was hardly a safe place, but deep down he was content to know that his son would be nearby, and with the full resources of his company and people behind him. The fact that Jack had sought the difficult road when a choice was given to him simply made him feel even better. He reached out and grabbed him.

"Good. You'd better finish your food because I need to introduce you to the rest of the team before we board ANS Devastation. A shuttle is collecting us within the next twenty minutes, and I know Khan is very keen to look inside a Crusader class warship."

He placed his hand on his son's shoulder and looked out at two frigates maneuvering around the Spacebridge.

"We have places to visit and weapons to test, and if things go badly, you'll get a chance to shoot a few guns. From the documents I've seen, this sector is going to make Proxima Centauri seemed like a backwater. We have man-made structures, derelict objects that are possibly ships in space, and resource-heavy planets and moons. The Alliance isn't leaving this place in a hurry."

Jack grinned at the suggestion, but even he found it hard to hide his excitement at both meeting Khan and the rest of the Jötnar, as well as standing on board one of the Alliance's newest and most advanced ships.

"Where exactly are we going, anyway?" he asked, his mind now away from meeting his friends and back to the potential mission.

Teresa walked to the window and pointed at a group of ships that had just appeared from the right-hand side. There were a number of small ships, but it was the great hulk of ANS Devastation she was singularly interested in. The ship was big, with only ANS Beagle and her extended gantries taking up more space.

"There they are. Devastation was supposed to be leading a science team to explore some of the space borne debris when they received the call from this station. APS is providing military and intelligence assistance to the Alliance, under the authority of General Rivers. I am staying here to liaise with the company back in Centauri space. We have a lot of work to do here. You two will be meeting up with the marines, General Rivers and our Jötnar friends."

"Why? What's happened?"

Spartan interrupted.

"Jack, you'll have to wait till we're on board the ship. Needless to say, that as of now, you're an executive officer of APS. We need to go over the agreements we have with the Alliance, and you're going to need to go through verification and vetting. It'll take a few hours, but it can all be done on our trip."

Jack was becoming more and more impatient.

"Without the specifics, what the hell is this trip?"

"It's a rescue mission, that's all we can say."

On perfect cue, Spartan's secpad lit up with an urgent video communication. Spartan picked it up and glanced over to Teresa.

"It's him."

He then placed the device in front of him and hit the connection button. The image of General Rivers appeared almost instantly.

"Spartan, good, the shuttle will be there in three minutes. I'll see you and your command team in the briefing room when you arrive. Khan is already here, and he has some interesting observations."

"Understood, General, but there's one other thing."

"Which is?" came back the short reply.

"Jack, our son, has just joined the company. He'll be working with our unit and liaising with the Jötnar contingent. He's the man that tracked down a number of the saboteurs, and he has information on others."

The General lifted his hand to quiet him.

"Spartan, if he has been cleared by you, then I'm happy. Just get aboard fast. Things are moving quickly, and we have work to do."

* * *

Another powerful blast shook the surface of the moon and with it, sent large chunks of sharp debris over the retreating marines. Since leaving the scene of the first blast, only half of the platoon was still on their feet, and most had sustained injuries. Colonel Daniels was the only man of any rank remaining, and he slid behind a series of rocks before checking behind them. The thin, ragged line of dust covered marines staggered on, but all that he could see of their attacker was a great cloud of dust; it was as though some ethereal creature was pursuing them. That was when he spotted the flashing indicator on the heads up display in his armored suit.

That doesn't make sense.

"Corporal, can you get a lock on quadrant seventeen, above that ridge?" he shouted even though it was unnecessary, through the digital intercom gear.

Colonel Daniels had fought a great number of different enemies on many worlds, but one thing he'd never had to face was an enemy he was unable to detect. His suit had detected a low level signature, but there were no identifiable IFF signals coming from it.

"Sir, I've got something. It's low but accelerating and coming this way. No signals, she's not ours."

Two of the marines ran over to him as fast as their tired bodies and the low gravity world would allow. Between them, they pulled their wounded Sergeant into cover before checking they weren't being followed. The small group of survivors were almost a kilometer away from the blast radius.

"Crap! It's coming this way!" cried the Corporal.

Daniels immediately pulled himself low and used hand signals to the rest of them. Like a well-oiled machine, they each dropped down and moved away from line of sight from above. Luckily, the ridges and impact craters provided perfect cover from any direction other than directly above.

"Thirty seconds blackout!" he snapped, hitting the button on his suit. It was almost instantaneous, as each part of his suit from the powerplant down through to the communications, optics and life-support system shutoff. It was a dangerous move, as there was never a guarantee that all systems would restart after such a drastic shutdown. Even so, it was also the sure-fire way of not emitting electronic or radiation signatures that could be picked up by the most common of sensors. Even the suits built-in cooling system would keep them hidden, but only for a few minutes. After that, the heat from the marines' bodies would start to alter their thermal reading.

A loud noise like that of a banshee screamed overhead, and it reminded him of he sounds he'd come across in the reports of the fighting at Hyperion. There wasn't time to consider it any longer; the sound was getting louder. He lifted his head slightly and watched as the dark mechanical shape emerged from the dust cloud. At first, he thought it was a creature like some of the horrors he'd seen previously, but the shape extended out until it had more in common with a warship than a creature. But it was nothing like any ship he'd seen before. Its engines glowed blue, and the underside was filled with ridges from which hung dark shapes. Mountings along the side moved continually, and he was convinced they were turrets of some type. As it moved past their position, he was sure a burst of fire would strike them down as they waited.

What the hell have we found out here?

Then the vessel lifted up higher and vanished up through the thin atmosphere and into space. Colonel Daniels watched with a mixture of shock and apprehension as it disappeared from view. He started to move his muscles, but then he spotted dark shapes in the thick clouds. Around the shapes flashed bright colors, much like that of an electrical storm. Then the vessel reappeared, but this time it was trailing smoke and heading in a death spin towards the ground. It didn't take long for the devastated vessel to strike a mountainous region almost a kilometer from their current position. The shockwave was powerful, and the marines were forced to grab onto anything they could find, for fear of being blasted a great distance on the low gravity moon. He lifted his head and watched the red hot fires burning around the wreckage of the craft. The flashing in the clouds had stopped, and there were no more explosions or signs of danger, other than the burning wreckage.

I need backup!

He tapped his intercom on his helmet, desperate to reach somebody.

"This is Colonel Daniels, is there anybody out there? I repeat, Colonel Daniels of the Alliance Marine Corps. We've been hit by a major blast, have casualties and need immediate evac."

He was greeted with total silence, the kind that was rarely encountered by marines in the field. He looked back at the marines near him, and especially the wounded man the other two had been carrying. They were too busy attending him to notice their commanding officer looking at them. That was when the crackle of a broken audio message made its way into his helmet.

"Sergeant Arkos, are there any survivors out there? I repeat. This is Sergeant Arkos, 1ˢᵗ Squad."

Colonel Daniels could barely conceal his relief at the news from the marine.

"Arkos, Daniels here. What's your status?"

The next few words were slightly broken before the signal came in clearly.

"Shuttle is down, three casualties. Something came over our position and bombarded the LZ. We were lucky nobody was killed. I've pulled the unit back and into the cover of the nearby craters."

Daniels nodded at the news, satisfied that things were starting to return to his control. He'd worried that the rest of the unit had been wiped out in the attack, and the news that 1st Squad was intact meant there was a chance that at least half of the platoon had survived. It was still not perfect, but much better than he had expected just a minute earlier.

"Good work, Sergeant. We have a number of dead and wounded in 2nd and 3rd Squads. Did you get a look at your attacker?"

"Negative, Sir, it just flashed over us and in the clouds. Next thing, we detected devices coming down. By the time we were in cover, the shuttle was gone. I did have time to send an emergency distress signal to the fleet. Either they are hiding or that thing took them out."

He glanced back and spotted three more marines emerging from cover and helping to carry one of the supply crates. As the men approached, he noticed the damage to their armor. Luckily the improved PDS armor was tough and able to absorb severe damage before rupturing or spreading heat or damage to the marine inside. What really caught his eye was the front of one man's helmet that was badly cracked and slightly fused by heat. It was almost as if he had been hit at long range by the blast of a thermal weapon like the low-tech thermal shotguns. He shook his head. He knew he needed to concentrate on the mission right now, not the fate of individual marines.

"Okay, we need to keep low in case there are any more of these things and meet at the Charlie LZ. Understood?"

"Sir!" barked the young Sergeant.

Colonel Daniels crawled over to the group of marines. As he moved, he was forced to slow down due to the dust cloud he was kicking up.

"I've just made contact with 1st Squad. Looks like they made it, but the shuttle has gone. What do we have here?"

The marines looked about as they checked the salvaged gear the small number of men and women had recovered during their rushed escape. Apart from the crate, there were just four spare rifles and a partially damaged scanning unit.

"The crate, is that the support unit?" he asked.

Corporal Handel nodded quickly.

"Yes, Sir, it's the remote drone unit, one craft and two spare propulsion modules. Should be fully functioning."

"Good work. We need to get to the…"

He was interrupted by a new transmission. His suit confirmed the source and decoded it using the standard Alliance Marine Corps ciphers. The computer displayed the ship confirmation code that matched the signature of ANS Devastation."

What is she doing out here?

The computer had one last stage to complete before the link was established and the audio feed began.

"To all Marine Corps units, this is General Rivers.

We are bringing in reinforcements within twelve hours. Your landing zone is flagged as compromised. If you are able to respond, send a code IFF burst packet with your pickup point. Find yourselves some shelter and conserve your power. Under no circumstances are you to travel and investigate any other parts of the moon."

"Thank the Gods," he whispered to himself with a calmness that disguised his almost panic at being abandoned on the moon.

* * *

Spartan and Jack entered the port landing bay of ANS Devastation to the pomp and ceremony expected for an arriving dignitary. Jack looked out of his depth, but Spartan recognized the joke for what it was. No sooner had they moved into the shelter of the ship than Khan of the Jötnar appeared. He was flanked by five more of his kin, each of them armored in their new style armor, but unusually they carried no heavy weapons. Even so, Spartan could see the blades built into at least two parts of the arms and the thick plating around the neck and chest.

"Khan, I see you've brought some muscle with you for a change."

This brought a guffaw from the old warrior who stepped forward and thumped Spartan on the shoulder.

"It's been a long time, Spartan. These are my brothers,

hunters from Hyperion and all itching to taste some combat."

"Jötnar without combat experience?" asked Jack, finally stepping forward to examine them. Compared to their great hulk, he looked like a schoolchild, but each of them was well aware of his background and experience. All Jötnar knew the good reputation of Spartan and his family, especially his exploits in fighting for them and for their protection. Without Spartan and Teresa in their corner, there was a good chance the Jötnar would no longer exist as a race.

"Trust me, they've got the experience, but only on Hyperion. They want to taste off-world blood."

Spartan grinned and indicated forward with his hand.

"The briefing room?"

Khan nodded with a grin and turned to his comrades.

"You see. Spartan is all action. On the ship for less than thirty seconds, and he wants to know the mission. I told you this was the place for you. Give it a week, and I promise you, each of you will have a belt of kills."

They walked down the corridor, and Spartan noticed Jack was grinning from ear to ear. He leaned over just enough so that nobody else could hear him.

"Careful at the briefing, these things tend to get political and fast, especially with the Jötnar on board."

Jack nodded and said no more. The corridor was longer than he would have expected and much lower. Whether this was down to the ship's new design, he couldn't tell. The gravity generators were technology he still didn't fully understand. Khan moved to his left so that the two men and the Jötnar were walking three abreast. It left no room for anybody else, and the small number of naval personnel in the same part of the ship was forced to move to the extremes to avoid being bumped into.

"Spartan, is it true about this place?" asked Khan.

"What do you mean?"

Khan grinned, but his oversized head and muscled neck made it look more like he was growling at him.

"Gun told me before we left, that artifacts had been found out here. That maybe Orion isn't the wasteland the press have been announcing."

"Did he now? Seems Gun is getting more information than any of us!"

They approached the double door that led into the briefing room. Two marine guards nodded rather than saluted, and the doors hissed open at their arrival.

"Go in," said the first marine.

The three stepped inside, but the marines blocked access to the rest of the Jötnar. Khan turned back, blocking the doorway with his vast bulk.

"What's going on here?" he demanded.

"Orders. Only command staff or APS executives are allowed in the briefing room," said the marine without even a hint of emotion to his voice. Khan exhaled and prepared to start shouting, but Spartan intervened.

"We're here at the request of the General. Now let them in," he said firmly.

The marine guard looked at Spartan and moved his eyes back to his front. Khan looked to the marine and then to Spartan. His look took him right back to their many violent escapades, and Spartan new immediately that Khan meant business.

"Your temper hasn't calmed with time, has it?" he said humorlessly.

As Khan reached for the marine, he was sure he could see a grin on his face. Rather than leave his friend at the risk of being shot, he jumped forward and at the second marine. Jack stood there silently, dumbfounded by the speed and violence from the two of them.

Way to go, Father. Get us all kicked off the ship in the first ten minutes! He thought with a mixture of humor and pride.

CHAPTER EIGHT

Like all racial units throughout history, the Jötnar encountered racism, abuse and discrimination from the first days of their use in war. Their track record during the Uprising was exemplary, and many were killed in the fighting on multiple fronts. Not one Jötnar unit was ever recorded as having refused orders or ever breaking or retreating under fire. Their steadfast nature, coupled with unswerving loyalty to the Confederacy, only worsened the blow when the Alliance disbanded all ground forces other than reserves or regular Marine Corps troops. Overnight, the 1st Jötnar Battalion was relegated to nothing more than a training unit for part-time warriors and was disbanded within a month. This lack of foresight would be dearly felt when they would be needed once more following the Orion Incident.

The 1st Jötnar Battalion

From inside the briefing room, business was put on pause as the sound of a struggle took precedence. It was short, but noisy, and resulted in a number of the marine officers standing from their seats and moving to the entrance. None were armed with more than military issue sidearms, but they were all clear that the General was on board. Apart from being of senior rank, he was also one of the most highly decorated and experienced officers of the last quarter of a century. The door burst open, and Spartan and Khan entered the briefing room, followed by the five Jötnar.

"Apologies," said Khan, "we were delayed by security."

Jack grinned at his father, who nursed a bruised cheek, as he moved up to his son. Khan, on the other hand, seemed to have avoided taking even a scratch and was holding the weapon carried by one of the marines from outside. The room was of modest size and mainly taken up with seating that faced a raise platform. General Rivers turned from speaking with the ship's XO and CAG, who both stood to the side of the raised section. A dozen other marine officers and naval crew waited patiently for their briefing to continue.

"Spartan…Khan, I see you've made your entrance."

A group of armored marines burst in through the door with their weapons leveled at the Jötnar. At the head of the group was an angry faced Asian Captain. Unlike the others, his helmet was off, and he shouted loudly at

Spartan.

"Get on the floor, now!"

Spartan turned to face him with both his arms raised to defend himself.

"Stop this!" roared the General, with a booming voice that even surprised Spartan.

The marines stood their ground but dared not come even a footstep closer into the briefing room. The Captain looked up to the even angrier looking General Rivers.

"Sir, these unauthorized civilians assaulted my men. They have no business here, and they must answer to my authority!"

"Your men, Captain?" The General retorted. "Every marine on this ship answers to me! This group, under the command of Spartan, has all been personally cleared and invited by my staff to assist in this operation. Their paperwork went through nearly an hour ago, Captain. They are to be treated with the respect due any marine and navy crewman on this ship. Both Khan and Spartan have long, exemplary records with the Corps. I requested his entire party to be brought here for this briefing. I suggest you find out who screwed up and sanction him or her properly. Understood, Marine?"

The Captain stared with piercing eyes at Spartan and looked back to the General.

"Sir!" he called out.

The General then looked to Khan, doing his best not

to smile.

"If you could send your retinue with the Captain here, he will show them to your quarters. It is mainly the two of you I need to see. In the meantime, we have things to discuss."

Khan looked back to his people and said nothing. He simply nodded slowly. Spartan was dismayed to see the lack of trust now held between marines and Jötnar. In his time, they had fought side by side on planets and ships, but now it seemed there was a whole new generation with little or no respect for their brothers in arms. They filed out of the room until just Spartan, Jack and Khan remained of their group. After the door had shut, the General continued speaking.

"Khan, it is to my deepest regret that the Alliance saw to the disbanding of the Jötnar Battalion. I argued against it, but you of all people will understand the whims of politicians. We fought some tough battles to get where we are now. Perhaps the three of you from the APS Corporation would listen in on this briefing?"

Khan nodded politely, and Spartan noted that his manners had improved massively since the last time they'd met. The Jötnar glanced to Spartan.

"We get to do more fighting with Spartan's company anyway...and we get paid better! If we didn't do that, then we'd end up spending our time hunting on Hyperion," he laughed and squeezed himself in next to Spartan and Jack.

The seats were large but still not suited to the oversized frame and muscles of a nearly three-meter tall Jötnar. General Rivers grinned at his words. He was well aware that numbers of Jötnar had served with APS teams throughout the Alliance and had achieved some staggering victories against criminal gangs, thieves and even the odd insurrection. It amused him that most there would think Khan referred to the hunting of docile beasts on Hyperion. He was, of course, referring to hunting down the surviving Biomechs that still roamed the jungles and mountains of the mist-covered planet. Their numbers were apparently under control, only just though.

"I have no doubt about that." He then indicated to those around him.

"Let me introduce you to some of the command staff of the ship. This is the XO, Commander Jane Parker."

The tall woman wore her uniform without a single regulation crease showing on her uniform. Her neatly cropped reddish hair was pulled back, and her blue eyes seemed to almost glow at him. She nodded but said nothing. The General moved along to a short man wearing his navy uniform and with the rank of lieutenant showing.

"Devastations Tactical Officer, Lieutenant Jesse Powalk, his father fought at Euryale in the Uprising."

"I heard you were there, Sir," said the young officer to the seated Spartan. "My father spoke of your ground troops and the Jötnar. He always said they should have been mixed with the rest of the Corps. I think he was right. Your people are an asset to the Alliance."

General Rivers looked to Spartan and back to the Lieutenant, but the XO interrupted him.

"He's a civilian now, Lieutenant," she said sternly. "You will refer to him as Mr. Sir is reserved for officers in the Alliance Military."

General Rivers looked to her and shook his head. He had spent only a short time on the ship, but it was clear the XO was a stickler for the rules and would make it her mission to hold him back, or at the very least to hold back anybody not part of her crew. He was well aware of the antagonism towards private companies in the military, but it was an evil they happily made use of. The PMCs fought, bled and worked just as hard, sometimes even harder than the regular units they helped or replaced.

"Actually, no, Commander. As you are no doubt aware, under the articles of the Alliance, all military forces, whether regular, militia or private will fall under the same rules and regulations as the regular military. Any military-type operation requires clear chain of command, and this also necessitates a formal rank to be applied to all members of a private unit. This was introduced to ensure private companies operate under the same laws and restrictions as regular military."

He looked to Spartan. "Can you explain to the Commander?"

Spartan nodded and stood up.

"Of course, General. At this level, our combat forces are based on small units with the same size and capabilities as Marine Corps squads and platoons. You'll find almost all of our operatives are ex-military, mainly ASOG and Marine Corps. They are led by Team Leaders, roughly the equivalent of a sergeant in the Corps. Our equivalent of private is Operative, though they are normally known as ATLs or Assistant Team Leaders and use code letters instead of ranks or names. Leadership for these units, when in theatre, is by Security Managers, such as myself. This position in our Corporation carries a similar level of responsibility as a company commander such as a Captain. We are held accountable to the same rules and laws as you, and report directly to our assigned commander, in this case General Rivers."

The XO was having none of it, and she glared at Spartan while replying.

"Yes, Spartan, I'm well aware of the rules governing Private Contractors in military theatres. You are still a civilian though. You gave up your commission in the Corps a long time ago."

General Rivers shook his head in annoyance.

"Spartan and Khan are both senior members of APS and will be given the same respect and authority given to Marine Corps ranks of an equivalent seniority."

The General came to Jack and sized him up. He had

a great deal of experience with Teresa and Spartan, but he'd only met the boy a few times. He knew little about him, other than the dossier he'd scanned briefly while transferring over to the ship.

"Son, you have no formal military training, do you?"

The young man was of a similar height to Spartan but much less broad, and with dark hair and a darker complexion, no doubt due to his Hispanic mother. Even so, his face was hard edged, and he looked a good deal older than he actually was.

"No, Sir, but I've plenty of experience with the Jötnar, and with company special operations."

"I see. Well, according to my paperwork that still makes you an operative for APS. You are granted the same privileges as any Marine Corps private and that goes for any of your other... Assistant Team Leaders," he looked over to Spartan, "...or whatever you call them!"

The General took a step back and checked the rest of those he had requested were present. He looked a little confused, but the door opened and in walked two more officers. One wore in Marine Corps overalls and the other the smart uniform of a Navy Captain.

"General, apologies, we've been supervising the transfer of spares from ANS Beagle," said the Marine Officer.

General Rivers looked less than impressed with her response.

"You are?"

The young woman stopped and saluted, immediately recognizing the seriousness of the situation. Her tunic was only half tucked in, and it looked like she must have run all the way there.

"Lieutenant Colonel Maria Barnett, I'm the senior commander of the two embarked Marine Corps companies."

"And you?" General Rivers continued as he looked at the Navy officer.

"Captain Vinson, General. Commander of Devastation's air wing."

"So you're the CAG?"

"Sir!"

The General took a deep breath before speaking.

"Captain Thomas has already laid in the course to our destination, and we are underway. We will be meeting with Commodore Lewis and the rest of the Orion Taskforce for a rescue mission. I will pass on the exact details when we are closer to the objective. For now, all we have is that a Marine Corps platoon has been scattered, and there are casualties on one of the moons. It looks like they were hit by an explosion of some kind."

The XO looked at him with one slightly raised eyebrow, as if questioning him.

"There is more, though. Our scout drones are returning images and details that are well, quite frankly - they are astounding. Long abandoned settlements have now been found on two of the planets, and we suspect we will find more. The debris fields we detected upon arrival seem to be the remains of constructions, presumably man-made. It is clear to me that people of unknown origin have already beaten us to this place. The good news is it seems they left. The bad is that something is still here, and it attacked our marine unit."

He brought up a static image of part of the moon. It showed a cratered surface, as well as the outline of the craft the marines had taken to the surface.

"These images were taken by the last shuttle down. Within an hour, this entire area was subjected to an orbital bombardment that covered over a square kilometer."

A murmur spread amongst those in the small group watching the briefing. General Rivers took a few paces in front of them and continued.

"That's right. We're talking firepower that is equal to the entire arsenal of Commodore Lewis' taskforce. There is a chance this was nothing more than a meteor storm or impact, but in the meantime, Commodore Lewis has withdrawn his flotilla at the request of Admiral Anderson until we can fully assess the situation. His ships were already spread out when the attack happened, as they were conducting scout operations. He has launched drones to scout the area of space around the moon itself, but will not be close enough to start a rescue for another seven hours. I have been in touch with the marines, and they are making their way to a secure LZ, prior to their evacuation."

The General paused and let that information sink in. As he waited, the XO nodded, and she continued the briefing.

"As you can see, this is one of those great days in history, and the one many of us have wondered or dreamed about."

She then pointed to the image of the planets in the New Charon system.

"It is true that we have discovered the remains of intelligent life on another world. Is it from our own species? My opinion is this is probably something to do with our early colony ships sent from Earth hundreds of years ago. Who knows, though? That is for the scientists to discover, and right now is of little concern to us. You are Alliance Military, and you all have a job to do."

General Rivers was still slightly surprised at her abrupt nature but said nothing. Although he was in overall command of the operation, it wasn't his ship, and he was well aware of the subtle differences between ships and their crews in the Navy. It was important he disassociated himself from the day-to-day running of a warship and concentrated on the strategy for this mission. He lifted a hand to indicate he wanted to continue, and the XO moved back, but not without looking more than a little displeased at being interrupted mid-flow.

"Thank you, Commander," he said politely and turned to the rest of those in the room.

"Our ETA is in twenty-six hours, so there is a chance

all of this could be over by the time we get there. Even so, we will be ready for any and all eventualities, both on the ground and in space. I will need three platoons of marines, ground support and air cover for the operation. Spartan and his APS team will be coming with us."

Lieutenant Colonel Barnett took immediate exception to this.

"Sir, I don't understand. Why are..."

General Rivers lifted his hand.

"Spartan and his team have decades of experience, including trench time in the Marine Corps. You would be well advised to listen to what he and his Jötnar friends have to say. They might be civvies now, but they are equal of any units in the fleet. Use them, and use their knowledge."

He then spread his gaze around the group.

"We don't have much time, so check your secpads. I've pre-planned the entire operation, but there is time to make modifications if any of you have useful suggestions. We will meet on the stern landing ninety minutes prior to the operation. That is all for now, to your stations."

As quickly as Spartan and Khan had arrived, the room seemed to empty incredibly fast. In less than thirty seconds, it was just Spartan, Khan, Jack and the General remaining. A number of Marine Corps officers had quickly left; much to the surprise of Spartan who thought they might want to speak with him. Jack moved a little closer to Spartan, now unsure what was to happen next.

"Jack, go and speak with the marines outside and find the others. They already know you are being put in charge of the Team. Get them ready, and make sure they have everything they need."

Jack looked at him and then to Khan who bared one of his oversized teeth at him. He considered asking more, but with the General around, it seemed prudent to leave. As he reached the door, Lieutenant Colonel Barnett walked back into the room. He watched her with a great deal more than a passing interest, until he was outside and the door closed. Barnett glanced in his direction as the door shut the last few centimeters and then proceeded forwards to the three men.

"General, Spartan," she said almost apologetically to each of them.

"I recall both of your actions in the Corps. I just wanted to let you know I've cleared you for operations on our landing craft. All of your APS team have been given equivalent status to the marine platoons. You have access to our equipment and systems, and that of course goes for your Jötnar as well."

Spartan nodded politely.

"Thank you, Colonel, it is appreciated."

She saluted the General and left the room.

Once satisfied they were alone, the General beckoned for them to come to the front where he laid out a larger secpad.

"As you know, we lost contact with the Colonel on this moon. We now have contact but are still unsure as to what exactly is happening out there. The Defense Secretary has stated that this moon and its artifacts are to be secured as soon as possible."

"I thought this was a rescue mission?" Spartan asked.

General Rivers nodded as he displayed a surface map of the moon.

"It is. We cannot start any work on the moon until it is safe, secure and under our control. I intend on landing rescue parties at their location to start evacuating our wounded. We will then conduct a thorough sweep of the area. The Corps of Engineers is already in the process of bringing habitation modules through the Rift."

"They found something?" asked Khan.

General Rivers tapped a button that showed a heavily cratered surface. Dust and smoke still drifted about as if a major battle or storm had just been fought. In the middle of the site and amongst the many craters was a sharply pointed object. It stuck up at least four meters.

"What the hell is that?" asked Spartan.

"That we do not know. The video feed came directly from the recon drones carried by the Colonel. Johnson and his people have looked over the data and confirm it isn't ours. Best we can tell is that it is buried under the surface and is not natural."

Khan scratched his head in confusion.

"I thought a ship tried to bombard the site? Why would it bomb its own people?"

General Rivers closed the device and looked at them both seriously.

"Now that is the real question."

* * *

Spartan walked along the narrow corridor inside ANS Devastation and try as he might, he just didn't feel part of the ship's complement. It didn't make sense, of course. His unit had been given the same privileges as the embarked marines, but there was still something different. The first thing was that nobody saluted him. He'd left the Marine Corps as a Captain. It wasn't a high rank, not after a decade's service, but his outspoken nature and more than a few enemies, made it certain he would never move any higher. Bizarrely, by forcing his hand, he was now higher placed than many of the officers he'd fallen out with in his time with the Corps.

Something isn't right. He thought as he continued the long walk to his designated quarters.

It was the gravity, he was convinced of it. No matter how advanced the technology, it just never seemed the same as when he was on solid ground. He spotted movement up ahead, and his eyes were instantly drawn to two Jötnar and a marine sergeant, who they seemed to be having an argument with. He increased his pace and moved directly alongside the three of them. The Sergeant was bruised down the side of his face, and he also seemed to be wearing a bandage on his left elbow. Spartan sighed. It looked like the Jötnar had been in trouble again.

"What the hell is going on here?" he demanded.

The marine lifted his hand and spoke first.

"Hey, there's no problem here. We just went two for two in the training hall with one of your boys here. I was just handing over their prize," he said, with evident annoyance at having lost some kind of a bet.

Spartan looked at the Jötnar, who although twice his bulk, seemed nervous at his gaze. They had good reason to be nervous. Spartan had fought their kin back in the War when all Biomechs had been the blood-enemies of humanity. It was rumored he'd even defeated at least two of them with his bare hands.

"A bet, have you been looking for a fight again?" he said angrily.

I spent all this time and effort getting them here, and then they screw me over with their usual antics. This is going to have to stop.

Two more marines arrived and moved quickly to the group. One of them extended a hand to the Jötnar and shook their great paws with obvious pleasure.

"Holy crap, you two, I've never seen combat like that before. Is that how you train back on Hyperion?" asked one of the corporals before noticing the suit-wearing

Spartan.

The Corporal ignored him, and then something clicked. He looked back at Spartan, pointing his finger at him.

"Hey, you're Captain Spartan, right? The officer that led the assault on Terra Nova."

Spartan nodded but said nothing. The last thing he wanted was the adulation of rookie marines. Right now, he wanted respect and professionalism, no more and no less.

"Enjoy your chat, try and keep out of trouble. We have a big operation coming up soon. Understood?"

The Jötnar nodded and bizarrely to Spartan, so did the marines. He did his best not to laugh and stepped inside the quarters put aside for his team. It was bigger than the usual marine quarters, and easily capable of holding forty marines. But the space was necessary, as the Jötnar took up twice the space of most people. He spotted Jack sat towards the end of the room, speaking to somebody on the video comms unit. Jack heard his approach and turned to face him.

"It's mother. She's got news for us...from Hyperion."

Spartan moved closer until he could see Teresa's face on the display.

"Spartan," she said happily, "I was just explaining to Jack about the new developments. Have you seen the news?"

Spartan shook his head.

"No, we've only just finished a short briefing with General Rivers for this op. What's happening there, problems?"

Spartan noticed that Teresa was no longer in the room they had organized on ANS Beagle. In fact, he was sure he recognized the signing on the wall as being back on the station orbiting Prometheus.

"I thought you might have been busy. Our share price has just gone through the roof with the news. That's why I've come back to the Prometheus offices. We need to bring in recruits, and fast."

Jack looked to Spartan concerned. Spartan, however was still none the wiser.

"I don't understand, what's happening?"

Teresa nodded and then reached for something. Her image vanished, but she continued to speak as a live feed from the Alliance Network News came through.

"Here, just listen to the headlines."

The video cut to an anchorman with images of a dark shape drifting in space. In the background, a diagram showed the layout of the star system that he instantly recognized as New Charon. The scrolling ticker line at the bottom said something about science teams were already on the way.

"Jack, what is it?"

He was answered by the voice of the anchorman.

"For those of you that have just joined us, this is a

momentous day for mankind. In the last few minutes, we've received images from the successful Rift experiment being conducted somewhere near Prometheus. If this information is correct, we are seeing our first looks at planets in a star cluster over a thousand light years away. The breaking news, however, is even greater. Alliance scientists have already located the remains of what appears to be a derelict spacecraft."

The image moved in much closer to the cockpit view of a Navy fighter. Spartan suspected it was a lightning fighter, but he couldn't be certain. The pilot was speaking, but it was too quiet and muffled to be heard. From the man's cockpit, the derelict structure seemed massive, at least the size of a Navy capital ship.

"How did this get out?"

"The Senate released the video feeds a few moments ago, and they're spreading like wildfire. Three mining companies who are sending exploratory vessels to the Rift within five days have already contacted me. Rumors of possible habitable moons and planets are getting a lot of interest, and one thing they all want is security."

"Why?"

Jack looked up at his father with a whimsical expression.

"The derelicts. They think that if there were people there before, then they might come back. That makes it dangerous, ergo, they need protection."

Teresa quipped in.

"True, but there is more to it than that, as always. With every company and contractor that wants some of the action in Orion, is another competitor. You remember the first incidents at Epsilon Eridani when the mining corporations arrived? It was violent."

Spartan nodded and then remembered Hyperion.

"What's happening with Gun and Hyperion? Are they okay?"

Teresa smiled.

"More than that, Gun and his High Council have been talking since you last chatted. Apparently, your news on the saboteurs trying to block off Orion, for fear of making contact with the enemy, got his attention. As always, he thinks it best to tackle any problem head on, and that's why his Council has decided that they want a stake in Orion as well."

Spartan shook his head at the news. Gun was an old friend and the first Biomech that had been freed from the mind control exerted on them by the Zealots and their allies, back in the Uprising. His name had come from his first meeting and violent struggle with Spartan on Prometheus, and the fact that the Biomech had been fitted out with a Gatling gun that was strapped to his arm. Now his old friend was the leader of tens of thousands of Jötnar, as well as an even larger number of freed Biomechs who had sworn loyalty to him and the Alliance.

"Somehow I don't think the Senate will be very happy

at the idea of Biomechs, even those we call Jötnar, looking to find new homes in Orion."

Teresa reappeared as the video stream closed down. She looked to her left as she checked her personal secpad. It only took a moment before she looked back up to the camera.

"The Senate has tried to block his travel, but their block has been vetoed by the Citizen's Tribune. As Alliance citizens, they are entitled to travel anywhere in Alliance space. The Senate has already decreed that New Charon is under Alliance jurisdiction and open for exploitation by any and all citizens. Either they must revoke its status, or remove the Jötnar's citizenship."

"What?" Jack demanded. He wasn't experienced in the world of politics, but even he knew that such a move would cause outrage amongst the Jötnar. It could even lead to a bloody civil war that would make the Uprising seem like a minor border war.

"Anyway, the information I have here from Gun is that he has chartered three ships and is leaving for the Rift tomorrow. He suggests that the Jötnar will be claiming a new world, and he'd like our assistance with security should the need arise. I need to go. I have urgent communiqués coming in from Terra Nova now. Both of you try and keep out of trouble. Love you," she said happily and cut the signal.

Spartan looked about the room until spotting his two

cases that had been brought along. One was very small, no bigger than one man could carry in a single hand. The second was much larger. He stepped closer and examined it carefully. Jack watched him as he walked around the large shape, easily as big as a bathtub.

"What is it?" he asked.

Spartan ignored his question and continued checking it. He finally stopped in front of the long edge and entered a code, followed by a thumb scan. The top hissed open gently, and Spartan leaned over to look inside. Jack walked over and gazed inside its darkened interior. It was heavily padded and included small boxes and a battered looking but well maintained coil weapon; standard Alliance Marine issue from what he could tell. There were a few changes to the sights, but underneath it was standard gear. What really caught his eye was the armored personal protection suit. It was the body armor worn by all marine units and provided a sealed system with protection against most small arms.

"You brought your old Marine armor with you?" asked Jack in surprise.

"No, this is second-hand ASOG gear that I bought at auction. It's had a tough life, but all works perfectly well."

He pointed to the end of the room where another crate stood up against the wall.

"What's that?" asked Jack.

Spartan grinned at him in a way only an old warrior could. "That's your armor!"

CHAPTER NINE

The Zealots took their initial teachings from the Church of Echidna, but where did the technological and military support come from? Most assumed that the destruction of the Rift at Hyperion also marked their destruction, but the reality was far more complex. Information retrieved from the ruins pointed to the Stars and to Orion. While the small number of Zealots continued to preach against the citizens of the Alliance, it became clear that without their support infrastructure, they were too weak and separated to continue more than a token resistance.

Origins of the Zealots

Agent Stefan Hammacher paced in front of his prisoner and then slammed his fists down onto the table. The man wore nothing but his issued overalls and dripped with sweat. It was a small room, with no windows and a single secured door at one side. Just two chairs and a table were all that broke the monotony of the space.

"Your brothers are dead, and your only friend in the world is your lady companion from the Beagle."

He noticed a faint glimmer of recognition on his face. It had taken some serious investigative work on behalf of the Intelligence community, but they had finally linked the attempted thefts on Epsilon Eridani, and now Prometheus, to the attempted sabotage on ANS Beagle. By all accounts the group was small, no more than a dozen people, possibly less. They weren't even related to the Zealots or any other religious faction. No, these people were all linked by just one thing, a connection to Hyperion seventeen years earlier.

Stefan knelt down to the side of the man so that his face was the same level.

"She's already offered to give up the rest of your cell. All she wants is confirmation that we have stopped exploratory work in Orion, which we have."

The man lifted his eyes slightly, instantly betraying doubt or interest in what Stefan was telling him.

"The coordinates used were a complete waste of time, so our efforts are being redoubled elsewhere. So the question is, why are you attacking the Alliance?"

The man looked up to him. "It doesn't matter. You'll reach her, and then we'll pay, all of us."

Stefan stood back up and sighed. It was the same answer, over and over.

"Who exactly do you think we'll reach?"

The man looked directly into his eyes, and Stefan knew immediately that it was fear he was staring directly into. He'd seen this look before, but only in the most dire of situations; when a parent knew their child was about to die, the moments before a car crash or the reliving of something as awful as a violent rape. It was the instinctive reaction of sheer terror and remembered past ordeals, that he'd seen a few times before.

"Echidna!" he hissed. "She is real, and she is coming. It doesn't matter where you point spacebridges. Eventually, you will make it easy for her. She wants to come back, and you are all making it happen."

Stefan stood up and walked to the door. It was his fifth visit to the man, and so far he'd established no more than the Alliance interrogators had. As he approached the door, it hissed open to a dark corridor. A guard in black clothing and armed with a cut down coil carbine watched him leave. A few meters along the corridor were a number of blackened glass doors. He entered the first and moved into a larger room that contained a number of video displays and two senior agents.

"Anything?" asked the first.

Stefan shook his head. "No change."

He walked up to the first screen and moved his hand

in front of it to select Director Johnson. It connected but placed him in a holding queue. As he waited, he looked over to the two men.

"How about you? Anything yet on the Euryale Cell?"

The first man looked back at his screen, but the second, a tall bald man with rounded glasses, nodded.

"Not much, but it is something to go on. They were tracked entering a datacenter in one of the research labs. Our agents stopped them but let them escape, so we could continue tracking them. Guess what we found?"

Stefan lifted an eyebrow inquisitively.

"This," said the agent, and he tapped a button to bring up a video feed. It showed the group of men moving to a parked groundcar. They opened the back and climbed inside. The camera zoomed in and managed to get a detailed view of the interior before it closed shut.

"What am I looking at?" he asked, unimpressed.

"The box on the bed of the car, Sir. We ran it through the system, and it matches the gear found two decades ago. Best we can tell it's one of those artificial intelligence hubs."

Stefan looked surprised.

"You mean the half-electronic, half-biological control units that we recovered in the Uprising? I thought they were all captured or destroyed?"

The bald man nodded.

"Apparently not, we have their vehicle bugged, and it's

being tracked. Maybe we'll get lucky."

A gentle tone from the display behind him reminded him the link to the Director was going through. He turned back to see the face of Director Johnson waiting patiently.

"Sir, the prisoner has confirmed the attacks are definitely a response to our exploration outside of our system. He believes by doing this we are inviting Echidna to attack us."

There was a short delay as the signal was routed through the Rift to the Director, who was now back on Terra Nova. Normally, it would have taken months for such a signal to work, but with the new Interstellar Network, trade and communications had been made almost instantaneous.

"I see. And by Echidna, we assume he is referring to some kind of Biomech leadership."

"Either that, or he thinks we have a God on our doorstep that wants payback."

Again there was a short delay before the grimfaced Director spoke again.

"The question is, which one is worse? I've passed the latest intelligence up through to the committee."

* * *

The dark grey hulk of ANS Devastation dwarfed the group of frigates as she rotated about in space, prior to reversing her engines. Like many vessels, she made use of her main engines as the means of both acceleration and deceleration. Few people outside of the Navy understood how ships covered wide distances in the time that they did. When not in a rush, a ship set its course, accelerated to its cruising speed and then coasted to the target. When near the destination, the engines would be used again to slow the craft down to avoid it sailing past the end point. This ship needed to travel much faster than that and had been accelerating at maximum power for half of the trip. By moving at 9.8 m/s^2, the ship would actually create the equivalent of Earth's gravity. The internal gravity generators were forced to counter this movement to avoid subjecting the crew to multiple forces. Devastation was equipped like all of the ships in her class, with substantial numbers of point defense turrets. The ship was the first of the Crusader Class to be equipped with a number of new technologies developed on Prometheus. The most significant of these was the modification of the bow to use a new weapons system. All her railgun batteries had been stripped out and replaced with experimental direct-energy particle beam technology, adopted from the enemy ships in the Uprising. The most obvious distinction was that two large emitters were now visibly protruding from her bow.

Inside her thickly armored hull waited the men and women of the embarked marine unit, as well as Spartan's APS Team. For most, this was their first actual combat landing, but for Spartan and his people it was something they'd done dozens, probably scores of times.

"Jack, you landed with marines before?" asked Khan loudly.

A number of the younger marines turned to listen in on the conversation, but Jack seemed unfazed by all the interest. The young man shook his head and looked down to his carbine to check it one last time.

Both he and Spartan wore the advanced PDS suits that his father had brought along. They were camouflaged in a mottled digital pattern that the APS Corporation had been working on, along with Alliance development teams. Stood next to them were the half a dozen Jötnar, with each of them using the crude looking and heavy armor. The look betrayed the complexity of the structure; the ability to absorb all but the heaviest of weapon impacts. Even the Jötnar's helmets were now completely sealed so that the creatures looked more like robotic ogres then living, breathing people.

"Don't worry, they aren't all as useless as you might have heard!" said Khan, followed by a great roar of laughter from the other Jötnar. One marine, a private with a spotless suit, moved towards them but was called back by his sergeant.

The landing bay of ANS Devastation was completely different to any previous Alliance starship. With the development of rudimentary artificial gravity, it was possible to land shuttles and craft onto the deck without having to transfer people from rotating sections, and thereby clearing up internal space. The aft of the ship included a single deck with additional storage above and below for more craft. There were currently four armored shuttles waiting to be loaded. Each was designed to carry a full twelve-man marine squad, and a number of marines were already filing inside the first. The shape of General Rivers and two Marine Guards appeared from the main access door and entered the deck. All those present saluted at his approach but not Spartan and his team. He stopped in the middle and called out with his booming voice.

"There has been a change of plan. Commodore Lewis confirms he has extracted Colonel Daniels and his platoon from the surface. The wounded are being taken care of while he sends down more marines to recce the area. His men have already found two entrances to a derelict structure of some type. Check your suits' internal secpads, and you'll see it resembles a spaceport of some kind, but most of it is now buried."

The General stopped and spoke to a nearby deck chief who rushed off and started barking orders at a group of Navy crewmen. It took only a few seconds for them to start dragging equipment from one of the many stowage areas. Spartan recognized a helmet being pulled out. He'd last seen it worn by the General in the middle of hand-to-hand combat.

The old fool, he's coming with us! Either there's trouble, or he thinks it's too important to leave to green recruits, maybe a bit of both? He wondered.

"Commodore Lewis already has two platoons on the surface, checking the remains for intel or technology. In the last hours, he's prepared another nine shuttles of marines, that's a full combat company of your comrades. We will be joining them to enter the facility. We have no idea what we might face down there, so check your gear, weapons and armor and keep this by the numbers. I don't want to lose a single marine on this rock, understood?"

"Yes, General!" came back the chorus of marine voices.

The marines returned to their preparation while the Deck Chief and his team arrived with the General's old equipment. One of his guards helped him into the main suit, and he waved over to Spartan and his team.

"I want your unit with us as well, Spartan. I could do with some experience and muscle down there in case things go pear shaped."

"You think there might be trouble?" asked Jack with an inquisitive tone.

"I always think there could be trouble."

General Rivers looked at the young man and was reminded of Spartan two decades earlier. Both had the hunger in their eyes, and in their formative years had witnessed violence and been involved in great struggles. Spartan's background was still blurred and little known until his time as an illegal pit fighter. The skills he learnt over that short career had helped hone him into the violent and courageous warrior he had become in the Marine Corps. Jack was an unknown to him, though. His track record on clandestine operations had been impressive, but he'd also broken a long list of local laws, and his criminal record already beat Spartan's. Although similar, there were still enough differences to tell them apart. Spartan was the rougher of the two, but he detected a streak of arrogance and violence in Jack that was all too familiar in young members of the Marine Corps. He stepped closer to Spartan.

"I want APS to take point when we land. You and your Jötnar have experience most of these marines can only dream of."

Spartan nodded and moved away to his waiting shuttle. It was crewed by marines and carried a four-man security detail but no passengers. The Jötnar filed aboard, each of them muttering as they went. As they moved, Spartan noticed the youngest of the group.

"Wictred? I wondered where you'd got to."

The young Jötnar glanced at him, but Khan pushed him inside without a word.

Odd, thought Spartan.

He'd known the Jötnar for decades now and was still learning new things about them. He was certainly familiar with their attitude to the young. Unlike other humans, they placed a greater value on their adult population. He recalled an argument he'd had with Gun back on Hyperion. A hunting party had been forced to leave three Jötnar behind in an ambush, and Gun had selected the youngest. He'd explained it simply, as they had so far not achieved work of note and had a lower value than the adults. Their potential was less important to him than the reality of the moment. It was a strange, even alien concept, but Spartan could understand his point of view. Osk, the first Jötnar female, had reminded him that it was easy enough to get more children. Adults, on the other hand, took a good many years to train and teach, now that the birthing chambers and equipment throughout the Alliance had been scrapped. Natural birth requires natural solutions to problems.

"Looks like Wictred will get to see the elephant, after all!" said Jack in a slightly despondent tone.

"Elephant?" asked a confused Spartan.

Jack grinned. "The animal with four legs and a trunk."

Spartan shook his head and indicated for him to climb inside the shuttle. The Jötnar were already fitting the magnetic clamps around their suits to keep them secure during flight. Once they left the innards of the warship, they would once again experience the unsettling sensation of weightlessness.

"Thank you, Jack, I'm well aware of the animal. What did you mean?"

Jack pulled on the straps before replying.

"It's a saying I heard used by some of the part-timers coming to Hyperion for training. You know, the camps Gun runs for them and the tourists. One of the scenarios is where a Jötnar would ambush them at close quarters. Most have never seen them or combat before. One of the officers told me that soldiers in the past would described it as 'meeting the elephant' for the first time. A man's first experience of war and combat."

Spartan now understood what he meant. Combat was certainly something he had plenty of experience of, but he was dubious his son was quite as experienced himself as he liked to think.

"Well, Jack, it's not just him, you know? This isn't a hunt or raid. There's a good chance this could escalate at some point, and in my experience, when marines get stuck into action, you find a lot of trouble."

The deck crew clamped the doors down shut, and an odd sucking sound indicated the internal pressure system was stabilizing, prior to leaving the ship. Spartan's suit showed the current pressure, temperature, and atmospheric readings as they quickly altered to match those on the surface below. Khan leaned over and shouted from inside his thickly armored helmet.

"Spartan, it will be like old times!"

Spartan smiled at his enthusiasm. He might now be forty-eight, but he was far from past his prime. Modern medicine, diet and fitness programs had allowed him to maintain the body of a man almost half his age and then some. What had changed were his attitudes and experience. The number of missions he'd gone in that had resulted in crashes, death and disaster were numerous, and he was tired of watching the deaths of so many. It was that spirit that had given the APS Corporation such a firm and solid reputation for integrity and professionalism in the industry. The video communications display lit up in his suit, just the same as for all the other marines and Jötnar. It was the face of General Rivers who was now in his full PDS body armor and stood aboard one of the other shuttles. Around him stood a group of marines, and they were all wearing the mottled grey and red camouflage pattern of his personal guard.

"This is it, people," he stated, and almost simultaneously, the shuttle lifted from its docking clamps and started moving on one of the pintle-mounted brackets to the flanks of the ship. They moved almost fifteen meters into the launch pod before a pair of reinforced shutters clamped behind them. There were four pods, two on each side of the stern for launching shuttles, fighters and landing craft.

"The marines from the rest of the Taskforce are in the air and waiting for us. Our platoon will be taking point on the landing with the APS Team providing recon for us. We land in forty-six minutes, be ready!"

Spartan looked to the others in his shuttle. The Jötnar looked both excited and serious, ever the professional soldiers. Jack, on the other hand, simply gazed out of the window and watched the shape of ANS Devastation as they drifted silently from her flank. As they moved further away, the clear glowing orb of the gas giant appeared like a monstrous star. Spartan had seen the planet type before, but there was something about this one, the way the light seemed to shimmer and reflect much further than normal. Jack noticed his interest.

"It's the composition of space around here."

Spartan didn't quite understand, but he was pleasantly surprised to see his son had taken some of his studies in, rather than just skills with weapons.

Maybe Teresa was right about him, after all!

"What do you mean? Isn't the space out here just the same as space anywhere else?"

Jack looked back out of the window and again before looking to his father.

"This star system is just one tiny part of the Orion Nebula, right? Well, you must have seen the photos of this place back from Proxima Centauri. It shows lots of clouds, many of them bright blue."

Jack was a little surprised his father was so unfamiliar with the basic science of space. He was well aware that Spartan's background was on the more physical side of space, but even so, he thought most knew of this.

"Well, there are massive amounts of gas and dust in the nebula. Some areas are more concentrated than others. There are massive bullets of gas that pierce hydrogen clouds. That's where the glowing blue streaks and orbs come from."

He looked back to the window.

"According to the news report I just watched, the Alliance astronomers are arguing about what started it. One idea is that something happened a thousand years or so ago to cause it."

Spartan scratched his chin.

"But aren't we seeing light on Prometheus that originated fourteen hundred years ago?"

Jack looked back to his father, intrigued that of all things he might pick out this one.

"Yes, so back home we are seeing events that have already happened. The event that caused this massive disruption was vast. It would have involved hundreds of stars, maybe thousands of them."

Spartan nodded as if a number of pieces were falling into place.

"And yet we get here and find clouds that are of a different composition to those we've seen from the past, and even weirder, we find remains of an unknown people."

Jack nodded at him, both pleased with his father but also dreading the inevitable conclusion that both of them must have been making at the same time. Jack spoke first.

"So something must have happened in the past, something massive, and it resulted in the destruction of entire colonies and ships?"

Spartan said nothing, but it was evident to him that something bad had happened.

"The question then is, what the hell happened out here?"

Khan must have heard them speaking because he look at them both and tilted his head to the enlarging moon to the right of the shuttle.

"I bet we'll find out what caused all of this down there."

All three of them looked through the window and the small disc of light as they hurtled closer to the moon. Around the shuttle were the rest of their formation, three more from Devastation and another nine from the Taskforce. Spartan hadn't been involved in such a large landing for years, and the thought of thirteen armored shuttles swooping down to an alien world started to get his blood moving around his body. He tapped Jack on the shoulder.

"Son, this is going to be interesting."

Wictred nodded happily at the two of them, completely ignoring the stern look from his father and the other senior Jötnar.

"More than interesting!" he laughed. "This mission is going to kick ass!"

Spartan looked to Khan and try as he might, he

couldn't hold back the laughter. Khan joined in, and before long the entire shuttle was shaking to the roaring of amusement from the entire team. Jack looked at them all with a mixture of disbelief and surprise.

* * *

Teresa walked along one of the many corridors of the Prometheus Seven Space Station, and she did her best to avoid bumping into any members of the media. This part of the station used to be where a large number of traders and black market sellers worked. Now it was being used by a much smaller array of independent stores that had been granted licenses by the Alliance to sell goods to the thousands of people stationed there; everything from food and clothing, to entertainment to amuse those out here on their own for months at a time.

Looks just a little less interesting than last time, she thought.

The stand to her right caught her eye, especially the odd shaped trinkets and artifacts that she had seen as a child on Carthago. She stopped at the stand and leaned over to pick up one of the small green carved figurines. It was about the size of her hand and shaped like a monster of ancient myth. The simple design betrayed exquisite skill in the working of the ebony; a skill rarely encountered anymore.

"You're from Carthago, right?" a scrawny man asked,

emerging from behind a loose hanging curtain.

He wore beige trousers and a poorly maintained jacket that was at least two decades out of fashion. Teresa noted the tattoos on his face, marking him out as from one of the unofficial Carthago militias that had been formed to try and help local police and Alliance units maintain control. The shape sent a shudder through her body as she recalled some of the rumors about them.

Like I'm talking about it with him.

"I've spent some time there with the military," she explained with a thinly disguised half-lie. There were enough problems on Carthago, without her stirring up more out here. Teresa still had a small number of relatives back there.

She lifted up a figurine that was towards the back of the stand. Like the others, it was green in color, but this one was more discolored than the rest and shaped into the body of a multi-headed dog.

"Kerberos," explained the man helpfully.

"Yes, I know, the three-headed dog that guarded the entrance to Hades. Not a common sight on Carthago, from what I've heard," she answered with a pleasant smile.

The man looked back at her with a look that reminded her of the scheming expressions she'd seen on hundreds of crooks, smugglers and Zealots. Her gut instinct told her she needed to speak to someone. Luckily for her, two of her APS associates arrived. Both wore the grey paramilitary uniforms that were the staple of all non-combat roles in the company. It had been Spartan's idea to keep a military feel to their company, apart from those in higher management. Both were about two meters tall, well built and carried themselves with the assertiveness common with the experienced military. They stopped alongside her and beckoned for her to move away from the stand. She moved several paces, and the nearest leaned in and spoke quietly.

"Ms Morato, we have an urgent message from Admiral Anderson."

Teresa looked at him. She couldn't remember his name, but she remembered he had worked with Spartan on an operation in the previous year. Like all their employees, they were background checked, and their loyalty was guaranteed by both their allegiance to the Alliance and more importantly, to the company's deep pockets. The cult of personality of the two founding members went a long way in establishing APS's reputation for ruthless efficiency and reliability.

"What's going on? Why didn't he contact me through the normal channels?" she asked suspiciously.

They were already walking back along the corridor, and the man spoke again.

"Our sources in customs indicate that three ships have just arrived. They are armored and claim to be here on official APS business. I checked the logs, and all three ships were bought by the Jötnar nearly two years ago."

Teresa shook her head in both annoyance and amusement.

Gun, you crazy bastard! What are you doing at Prometheus, and why have you brought three ships?

As she left the corridor, flanked by her two security professionals, she did her best to disguise a smile. The Jötnar were nothing if entertaining, but she did consider the possibility that Gun was here in person. If that were true, then it would confirm the information she'd seen from the Senate concerning the Jötnar being able to enter New Charon to establish colonies. Gun had been very clear that he would use any measures necessary to eliminate threats to his people. The new planets and territory discovered through the Spacebridge could represent a new future for the Jötnar.

It had better not be the start of another fight, though. She thought worryingly.

* * *

The formation of armored shuttles split up as they approached the atmosphere of the moon. Though thin, it was slightly corrosive, and as each of the craft skimmed the edge, they left a color wake behind them. Each streak indicated the high-speed orbital descent of a craft as it followed the most direct route to the target. Once at medium level, they started the normal deceleration procedure and dumped low-burn flares in case of ground-based defenses.

"Here we go again, Spartan!" barked Khan.

The battle-hardened Jötnar watched through the tiny windows as the color of the sky changed with every hundred meters lower. Spartan could see him grasping the hilt of his weapon.

Always looking for a fight. He thought wryly.

"Ninety seconds to the landing zone," said General Rivers over the suit's integral comms unit. It was a fast and efficient system, giving secured high speed data between all the ships and warriors in the Taskforce. The fully integrated digital battlespace system had only come into full use in the last ten years and was one of the few improvements that genuinely impressed Spartan.

"Understood, General, we're ready and awaiting the landing. Do we have any new intel on the ground?"

"Yes," was the simple reply, as a number of three dimensional models mapping the landing zone appeared. They instantly amalgamated with the two-dimensional maps already scanned by the previous landing.

"We're moving three hundred meters further to the west. There is more debris, but surface-penetrating radar indicates a number of passages underneath."

Spartan nodded. "Understood."

The small formation of shuttles deployed their

first-stage airbrakes to start the slowing down descent procedure. Spartan was the only person in his shuttle to look upwards and back to the direction they had arrived from. Directly above them, sat in high orbit above the shuttle waited the Taskforce, a dozen ship; including three of the latest and most technologically advanced warships in the Alliance. It was a modest affair, compared to the great fleets of the Uprising, but for this obscure moon, it was a sight to behold. The first three shuttles burst out through the fog of chemicals, swooping down low over craggy mountains.

"Father, look!" Jack called.

Spartan returned his gaze to the horizon as the flight of shuttles circled their landing zone. The surface was dry, ragged and unwelcoming, like many moons he had seen before. There appeared to be many lines and markings running along the surface, but he was well used to these illusions. They were frequently no more than natural phenomenon. What Jack was pointing to was a formation of mountains around a single point of rocks and rubble. Khan looked with interest back to Spartan and Jack.

"Does that remind you both of somewhere?" he asked.

Jack grinned.

"What? You mean the Rift archeological site on Hyperion that's situated between a series of mountain tops?"

He turned to Spartan. "No, it looks nothing like it."

"Ten seconds!" The pilot called out through the digital communications system.

Spartan grabbed the electromagnetic coupling that held him down. It was more complex than a simple set of straps, but it was stronger and could be locked and unlocked in a fraction of a second. Then, just as quickly as the word for their landing had arrived, they hit the ground. It was bumpy, but there appeared to be no signs of enemy activity.

"A safe landing and no reception committee? Is that a first?" laughed Khan, as he stood up from his seat and punched Spartan on the shoulder. The doors opened, and the group of Jötnar leapt out of the shuttle and onto the solid surface of the still unnamed moon. Jack glanced to his father who simply nodded for him to go.

Here we go again, he thought. Then stepped out behind him, his carbine ready for whatever the moon might throw at them.

CHAPTER TEN

The creation of the Centauri Alliance was the last stage in humanity's violent struggle to create a solid, stable and secure political system. Gone were the days of colony versus colony warfare, and instead, the gaze of most citizens turned to the great Orion Nebula and the seemingly limitless opportunities it offered; hundreds of thousands of stars with an even greater number of worlds orbiting them, each ripe for exploration and exploitation. How few even considered the possibility that somebody might have already beaten them to it?

Orion – The future?

The landing zone was almost three hundred meters in diameter and the perfect site from which to land additional men and materiel as required. In the first minute, advance scouts had pushed out and secured the site for the arrival of the rest of the unit. Four full platoons of marines plus the APS Team was a considerable force, with nearly a hundred and fifty heavily equipped warriors and their supporting equipment. The marines' first job was to establish a defensible landing zone and communication array so that contact could be maintained with the ships above. The men and women from ANS Dragon had already moved the armored array from one of the support shuttles and were in the process of powering it up by the time the last shuttle had landed. It was as big as a marine and equipped with two main antennae, the secondary specifically in case of malfunction or damage. It was all part of the enhanced digital battle-space system that all Alliance military equipment was now tied into.

As the squads of marines continued making the site safe, the APS team, led by Spartan and Khan, moved away from the safe area and into the until now unexplored parts of the moon. They had chosen to head towards what seemed to be an entrance, at least that was what the scanner had indicated. General Rivers had also sent out four small scout parties to recce the peripheries for anything of use while the APS team scouted the primary access point. There had been a minor disagreement as to who should go where, but the General would have none of it. Spartan's APS team had experience of similar sites, and their skills were never in doubt to him. He had twelve squads of a dozen marines plus Spartan's unit, and that gave him the manpower to conduct a wide sweep of the area. Three more units followed the routes of the more level ground while the fourth followed a winding path to the right.

That fourth group included both Wictred and Jack, much to the annoyance of the marines, who failed to appreciate why two juveniles were going with them. As they moved away, it appeared they were more interested in competing with each other to reach the objective while the single marine squad did its best to keep up. It didn't take long for this annoyance to turn to frustration.

"Kid, what's the hurry?" called out the shortest of the marines, who could have been barely a year older than Jack. The emphasis was on the 'kid', and it had an immediate effect.

Jack turned his head and shook it before jumping over a series of rocks, landing in a shallow depression to stand alongside Wictred. To the uninformed, it looked as if they were racing ahead for the sake of it. The reality was that Wictred had spotted something, and in their haste neither had informed the marines. At the implied insult, Jack spun around to face the small group of armored marines.

"Kid? You're not much older than me, you know. I've been on plenty of operations before, and this one is nothing special."

The Sergeant of the unit pushed up closer to him, shaking his head slowly.

"We're a unit, and if you were in the Corps, you'd know

that. I don't care if your Pa is some Corporation big shot, out here we play by the rules…or people get hurt."

He paused for a second to let that sink in.

"Now, why are you rushing ahead? If you find trouble, we'll be too far back to assist you."

Wictred laughed at the comment. Like most of his kin, he had a short temper and had no problem expressing himself. Unlike Khan and the first generation of Jötnar, he had yet to learn humility or empathy, not that it was a particularly common trait amongst any of them.

"Then stop lingering in the rear, marine!"

Jack saw the look on the marine's face, and though at first he almost enjoyed the man's discomfort, he could see the marine was right. They had moved almost a hundred and fifty meters from the shuttle, without even speaking to the rest of the unit. He looked over to Wictred who, compared to the rest of the group, simply towered over them.

"You're right, Sergeant, my mistake," he said, trying not to look at the crevice further ahead.

Even so, the more he tried to avoid it the more his eyes refused to shift away from it. It was about a meter tall, but what set it apart from anything else in sight was that the upper part appeared to be man-made. The lines were straight, and there were carved portions at intervals. The Sergeant was still trying to work out if the young man was being sarcastic or not when his interest in the subject finally got the better of him.

"What is it?" asked the Sergeant.

Wictred moved a few more meters and thrust his oversized arm into the gap. The rest of the squad moved out and into position, watching in a mixture of interest and surprise.

"Wictred?" asked Jack, now worried that he seemed to have got his armored forearm trapped inside the rock.

His friend groaned as he exerted himself, pulling hard at the rock. With a dull crump, the bottom part split and fell away to create an opening nearly two meters wide. Jack almost jumped forward, half expecting the entire thing to fall apart, but instead his friend did something even stranger. Wictred thrust his head inside before leaning back and looking at Jack and the Sergeant. He smiled in that wicked way that only his kind could.

"You're gonna want to see this!" he laughed and stuck his head back inside the gap.

The Sergeant looked to Jack. He just shrugged and clambered over the rocks to reach Wictred and find out himself.

* * *

When Teresa arrived on the main observation deck of the Prometheus Seven Space Station, it looked like something from an old Wild West novel. A dozen marines stood at the flanks of Admiral Anderson, along with a handful of Alliance dignitaries. Facing them was the battered, scarred and fully armored bulk of Gun and his small entourage of four Jötnar. As she entered the room, the Admiral saw her and sighed in relief.

"What's going on, Admiral?" she demanded.

Gun lifted his arm and blocked the Admiral, reaching out to grab her. She ducked sideways and yanked his arm only for him to go limp and kick out at her legs. He managed to clip her, but not before she ripped out his blade from his belt and leveled it at his belly. He started laughing loudly at her.

"So, time with Spartan hasn't slowed you down..." he leaned in closely, "yet!"

One of the marines made the display of camaraderie between her and the Jötnar as some kind of violence and lifted his weapon at Gun. One of his henchman, a slightly shorter juvenile Jötnar, smashed it aside and threw the man to the floor before stamping on his elbow, instantly snapping the bone like a dried out twig.

"Stop this!" cried out the Admiral with both hands in the air.

Gun looked similar to Khan, but his many scars and marks indicated he was one of the first of the Biomechs to be freed from the shackles of the Zealots' control. In fact, he and a small group had never been mentally conditioned, and from his first meeting with Spartan, he'd fought for whomever he thought deserved his help. Teresa stood alongside him, facing off against the Admiral and his party. The statement was both simple and clear; Teresa wasn't going to abandon the Jötnar.

"The only person stopping anybody is you, Anderson. I thought you were our ally? Our friend?" he said sternly.

Admiral Anderson pointed to the Rift, and the dozens of ships waiting to enter it and start their journey to the riches and prizes of New Charon and beyond. Most of the ships were civilian, along with a smattering of transports and the odd military escort.

"That Rift is taking us to a place that ten years ago was no more than a dot in the Orion Nebula. Now we have soldiers, miners, corporations and workers all heading out there to make their fortune. I have been given express orders that no paramilitary forces are to be granted access. Only Alliance forces have permission to enter with firearms."

Gun snorted under his breath and looked over to Teresa. She shook her head.

"Anderson, you know we never travel unarmed. Our race is attacked openly by Alliance citizens on planets and on ships."

The Admiral nodded as if well appreciating the problem.

"I know, Gun, trust me, I do. I have pushed the Defense Secretary to allow marine security units to accompany your transports if you still wish to travel. They can protect you from any possible dangers."

Oh, crap, he's done it now! Teresa thought.

One of the older looking Jötnar stepped towards the Admiral and opened his visor to reveal a hideous face with multiple cuts along one side of his face. He lifted his left hand and pointed to his injuries.

"I took these on the surface of Euryale, fighting for your people in the Uprising. My name is Olik, and I need no man or woman to defend me."

He moved closer to Gun, placing his hand on his leader's shoulder.

"Everything you said about this Anderson is wrong. You said he helped our people, our first females, and taught us engineering and industrial skills. Is this not the man?"

Gun grunted but said no more. Teresa looked back to the Admiral and noticed what seemed to almost be a smile on his face.

"Teresa, I understand your corporation has been busy in New Charon? Anything of note to report?"

Teresa seemed confused and shook her head slowly.

"No, nothing yet, why?"

Gun listened to them both, but he already recognized the scheming tone in the Admiral's voice. He'd encountered it many times in the past, when it seemed like this one man was the only official that seemed to have even a moment's thought or consideration for his people.

"Strange. I heard rumors that Alliance forces were spread thin and that more APS operators had been called for."

He paused, but Teresa still hadn't quite worked out what he was saying. For the first time, Gun reached the conclusion before she did.

"I think what the Admiral is trying to say is that you requested more people, and they have now arrived," he said, pointing his hands at his small group.

Teresa looked to Gun, and a slow grin started to form on his face. She looked back to the Admiral who was doing his best to give nothing away.

"That's right. Gun and his people have been deputized under the Private Military Contractors Bill. They are to provide area and ship-based security for non-military operations in New Charon."

Admiral Anderson looked disappointed.

"I see. Well, then I have no legal grounds to stop you from your legitimate business. I will leave you to it."

He turned, but Teresa caught a hint of a wink as he moved away, leaving just her and a group of bemused but happy-looking Jötnar. As soon as the door shut, Gun moved closer and brought his hands together with relish. He looked to the Rift and back to Teresa.

"You see. I knew Anderson wouldn't let us down. Now, let's get ready. I have three ships and a thousand Jötnar who are itching for some exploration. Do you have some work for us?"

Teresa nodded as she looked to the Rift.

"If the reports of the discoveries in New Charon are true, then everybody from Old Mars to Terra Nova will want in on the action. From today onwards, you and your ships are official APS Private Military Contractors."

Olik looked at them both and scratched his head.

"APS Corporation? Does that mean we get paid?" he asked hopefully.

Gun punched him in the chest and knocked him back almost a full meter.

"No, Olik. It means I get paid, and then I pass some of it back to whoever does their job. Understood?"

Olik nodded glumly. Teresa indicated for him to come closer. He bent down so his head was the same height as hers. She leaned in and whispered in his ear.

"I see you're running a tight ship here."

He stood up straight and roared loudly, looking to his group.

"All we need is to find Spartan and Khan, and somebody to fight, and it will be like the old days."

The Jötnar continued with their shouting and howling, but Teresa simply stared out into space and to the Rift. She knew that something unexpected had been found out there, and deep down her gut told her it wasn't going to be good.

* * *

The squads of Alliance marines were now all spread out and busy examining their preselected targets while being closely monitored by General Rivers. He stayed near the shuttles and communications array, protected by his two squads of marines. It wasn't that he was avoiding combat, quite the opposite in fact. He wanted to be ready the minute any of his people found something of note. In front of him were a number of devices that projected a three-dimensional map of the area, as well as each of the marines and their units. It provided him an improvised command and control site for his entire force. Information from the aborted landing seventy kilometers away by Colonel Daniels' force had showed a number of trails, each of them heading towards the new LZ. They were linked somehow, and he intended on finding out how. Stood next to him were two officers, both watching a pair of displays intently. They showed a top down view of the moon as it whisked passed slowly.

"Lieutenant, how are the drones doing?"

The officer, middle-aged with reddish hair, looked over to him.

"General, we're sixty seconds out from the Colonel's LZ. I have three birds in the air, and they will be circling from seven hundred meters and up."

General Rivers nodded and looked back to his own displays. He tapped the icons hovering over each of the squads to check on their status, but so far, only Jack's squad had uncovered anything more than ruins and rocks.

"Sergeant Ajax, Sitrep?"

An image of the man's face appeared on his system. It was being recorded directly from inside the man's PDS suit and showed a man that had been exerting himself, yet he was completely calm and collected.

"General. We're inside the structure located by the APS scouts. Proceeding inside."

"Very well, exercise care inside. I don't want any accidental discharges."

"Yes, Sir."

The image vanished, and General Rivers moved his hand over the three-dimensional terrain until reaching Spartan's own team. They were a different color to the others, yet each suit was broadcasting a clear IFF signal so that he could identify friend from foe. They had already covered more ground than any of the others but were now stationary. He tapped the icon above them to reveal the video feed of Spartan.

"Spartan, sitrep?"

The feed blurred for a second as Spartan turned his head. The video showed the team of Jötnar moving cautiously as though they expected some great beast to burst from the ground and attack them. Not that he could blame them; their own world of Hyperion was known to be one of the most dangerous places in the Alliance. Anybody venturing into the jungles with Jötnar guards, armor and weapons could expect to never return.

"General, we've reached what looks like a granite wall. It is covered in badly damaged glyphs and markings. Like this one, Sir," Spartan explained, completely forgetting he was not in the military. Old habits died hard with him.

The image on the camera was clear and showed images of planets and machines. General Rivers definitely recognized the style, if not the content itself. Spartan looked over to his second-in-command.

"General, Khan is convinced the markings are similar in style to the material he saw inside the ruins with the tech expedition seven years back on Hyperion. There is a section to the right that appears weakened, and we're planning on going in."

The General looked at the images of the glyphs that Khan and Spartan were sending him. He was no expert, but they were clearly no accident. Somebody or something had carved them directly into the rock.

"I see, how do you want to proceed?"

The image changed so that it displayed Spartan's point-of-view. Directly in front of him stood Khan and two other Jötnar. Each was carrying one of their glaives. The device was a common polearm weapon, consisting of a single-edged blade on the end of a pole; it was favored by the Jötnar for its simplicity and intimidation factor in battle. The metalworking skills taught to them by Confederate, and then Alliance engineers, had allowed them to incorporate the hardest alloys with fine edges that were tough enough to break even the strongest stone.

"Uh, Spartan, What are you doing?" he asked curiously.

Khan heard his message on the Team channel and looked into Spartan's visor and grinned. Spartan knew that Khan loved nothing more than violence and smashing things with tools and weapons, and the glaive was one of those tools that generally resulted in destruction.

"General, we are doing what we do best." He then spun around and lifted the weapon above his head. Spartan laughed.

"I think we know what happens next, General."

All three of the Jötnar smashed their weapons into the weakened section and tore open a space big enough for a Jötnar to enter. Before they could do any more damage another part of the wall collapsed with a great rumble. A chunk almost four meters tall collapsed to the right, leaving a gaping wound in the stone structure. Dust flooded out and covered the entire team.

"Talk to me, Spartan," said General Rivers.

Spartan waited patiently until the dust cleared to finally reveal a large open room. Specks of light in the tall ceiling sent shafts of yellow to the ground and highlighted dark shapes along the floor.

"What the hell?" he said, stepping into the breach and inside the open space. The rest of the team followed him inside and pushed on forward. It was still poorly lit, and they were forced to activate their lamps. As each one came on, it illuminated yet another long row of shapes. Spartan approached the nearest, bending down to examine it closer.

"They look like beds," said one of the Jötnar in surprise.

Spartan took a deep breath and brushed his armored hand across the dust-covered shape below. Underneath, through colored clothing, it showed the face of a woman. He almost fell over backwards, but Khan grabbed him as he lost his footing.

"Who are they?" asked the General over the comms system.

Spartan straightened up, took a deep breath and moved closer, pointing his lamp directly at his subject. The woman wore a dull red breastplate that was scored from a thermal impact of some kind. A symbol of a curved weapon, much like a scimitar, was barely visible directly in the centre. Her face was white, completely colorless. He moved his hand slowly and made contact, only to feel the hardness of her features.

"It's a casing, not alive," he said quietly, looking at the other shapes.

"What about them, are they the same?"

Khan was already checking the shape of a similarly

dressed man.

"Same here. It's like they have been turned into stone," he said in wonder.

Spartan wasn't convinced.

"Stone, or maybe these are just shells."

He pushed his hand to the face of the woman, and the outer layer cracked open like old porcelain to reveal the bones of a long dead woman. Spartan took a step back and lifted his head. The lamp on his armor also lifted, following his gaze as he scanned through the massive hall.

"There must be hundreds of them in here, each of them lying down and protected by these fragile coverings."

The other Jötnar spread out and checked the other bodies, but apart from physical size, they all followed the same pattern.

"General, they all have their armor and a pattern of a weapon. I'm sending you all the data now. I think we're going to need a research team down here."

"Understood. Can you see anything else?"

Spartan looked around again, but the wide-open space appeared to contain no more doorways, hatches or shafts. There was nothing but dust, rubble, the arched ceiling supports and the hundreds of encased bodies.

"Negative. General, this is it."

Khan tried to lift one of the figures, but it crackled and splintered in his armored forearms. He looked back to Spartan with a guilty expression.

"They've been here a long time."

Spartan nodded at him.

Yeah, I don't doubt it. What I want to know is who the hell are they?

* * *

Jack took the lead with the marines following in a loose column. Their suit-mounted lamps filled the derelict structure with dull orange streaks that emphasized the rocky outcrops with hard shadows. Once a few meters inside, he was able to perform a full three hundred and sixty degree turn to examine the inside.

Impressive.

Though most of it was now in ruins, there had clearly been a number of substantial arches, most of which now lay in heaps on the ground. Only a third of the area was traversable, as the rest had fallen in to create what looked more like a ribbed tunnel than a large domed interior.

"Jack, what have you got?" asked General Rivers over the comms link. Although the commanding officer was able to watch a video feed from each person there, it was still difficult to gauge depth and dimensions from such a small and grainy image.

"It's definitely man-made and old. Same kind of architectural structure as the stuff found on Hyperion, I'd say."

The Sergeant of his marine squad pushed forward to stand alongside Jack. He looked directly at the man-made sections of the area so that General Rivers could get a good view.

"I think I should take over from here," he said grimly.

Jack lifted his hands submissively.

"Sure, go ahead, I'm sure you're familiar with this kind of site."

The marine looked at him and moved ahead along the tunnel. He tapped the marine-wide audio band so that all the unit commanders could hear him.

"This is Sergeant Ajax. We're moving into the tunnel. Will advise."

"Understood, Sergeant, be careful down there," came back the General.

They pushed on forward, but this time there was no spare room for either Jack or Wictred to do any more than follow the rear of the squad. Wictred didn't really seem to care, but Jack was becoming more and more annoyed by the second. He pushed passed the last marine to speak, but Sergeant Ajax stopped and lifted his right hand in a fist. The entire squad dropped to their knees. With there now space to move, Jack pushed ahead and reached the Sergeant, who waited a short distance ahead of the others. Jack made to step past him when the Sergeant grabbed him.

"Watch your step, boy!" he snarled.

Jack ignored him and quickly felt a sickening sensation as his right foot moved out into the blackness and touched nothing but empty air. The Sergeant yanked him back, and he fell backwards and to the ground ungracefully. Wictred pulled himself forward, but upon reaching them both, he stopped and looked in the same direction as the Sergeant. Jack sat upright and shook his head, anger now starting to well up from inside. Wictred grabbed his arm and pulled him up, pointing ahead. Jack could see little at first, until the infrared imaging part of his armored suit adapted to the lighting conditions.

"Wow!" was all he could manage at the spectacle of the place. Gone was the small corridor, and instead, they were greeted by a vast open space like an ancient arena. The low level was a dust basin, and a number of galleries were cut into the walls, just like the one they were presently stood upon. Large metal shapes and craggy spikes littered the ground, but it was the shapes at the far end that intrigued Jack.

"What is it?" asked the Sergeant, seeing the look of recognition on his face.

"My father described a place like this, an assembly point for Biomech warriors and machines. He said it was buried deep inside Hyperion, but nobody ever found it."

Wictred nodded slowly and pointed to the shape in the distance.

"That is the same shape as the Orb on Hyperion."

They all looked at the large stone structure that had been blasted by something powerful. The stone around it had fused as if it had been superheated by some kind of terrible weapon. Marks along the ceiling and wall expanding outwards, and substantial damage had been caused. Wictred leaned over the edge and looked down.

"How far do you think?" asked Jack.

Wictred shrugged and dropped off the edge. Sergeant Ajax rushed to grab him, but instead watched the Jötnar drop at half the rate he'd expected.

Low gravity, he thought, hoping no one had realized his obvious error.

Wictred hit the ground with a gentle bump and crouched down to absorb the impact. He looked up to Jack.

"It isn't far, you should be able to make it."

Jack looked to Sergeant Ajax, who looked unimpressed at the idea. Rather than discuss it, he ran and leapt from the edge. The gravity was much lower than Earth standard, but it was still enough to make him feel more than a little nervous. He built up speed and covered nearly fifteen meters horizontally from the ledge before crashing ungracefully to the ground. The impact was hard, and his gut instinct said something had broken. Even so, when he stood up, there was little trouble other than a few more scratches and dents in his armor. Wictred stood his ground, simply throwing him a look that told him to follow him up to the devastated orb. Instead, he stopped next to a pile of twisted and smashed metal. It was covered in dust, but unlike the structure itself, it looked as if it had no more than a decade or two's worth of dust on it. He brushed the side of it with his hand to reveal dull and pitted metal.

"Uh, does that look like..." he started, but a thumping sound made him spin around. He lifted his carbine up to face the danger, but it was the Sergeant and the other marines who had dropped down to join them. All landed safely, other than the youngest corporal, who managed to hit a rock and fall over onto his back. He quickly lifted himself up and did his best to hide the embarrassment of such a messy landing.

"My sensors are picking up a decaying power source around that thing," said Sergeant Ajax. He lifted his left arm and activated the main sensors on his suit.

"Yeah, part of it is still active."

Wictred pulled at a slab of masonry, and with his final tug, it lifted and broke in two. As it dropped, it struck another piece that fell down and smashed. With a low rumble that seemed to shake the ground, many more pieces broke apart, like a great domino effect. It went on for almost thirty seconds before calm returned and the dust started to settle.

"Maybe next time, you don't touch anything," said Jack sarcastically to his old friend.

Wictred was about to respond when the dust finally cleared enough to reveal a number of badly smashed and damaged machines. Their shapes were hard to determine as they were covered with what appeared to be broken limbs.

"They must have been covered by the masonry," said Sergeant Ajax.

He looked up and lit the ceiling with his suit-mounted lamp.

"Yeah, look. Half the ceiling must have come down at some point and buried them down here."

Wictred, ever curious when finding new and unusual things, took a step nearer the closest of the damaged machines. He reached out and lifted one of the appendages, to the bemused expressions of the others. It was joined in multiple places and as thick as a man's leg. At the end nearest Wictred was a flat, hardened piece of metal, shaped much like a blade, but it was badly scored and chipped in places.

"Uh, is it me or does that thing look like a weapon?" asked the Corporal.

Sergeant Ajax tapped his comms button immediately.

"General, we have something down here. I suggest you check our feeds."

He then signaled for the rest of his squad to step back. Jack and Wictred did the same without question.

"Sergeant, good work. Stay where you are. I'll send a team down to..."

"General?" he called out, but the communication

outside the cavern had been completely blocked out. He beckoned Jack to come to his side.

"Something's blocking our signal! We need to get out of here, and fast!"

He turned around and took a step forward but stopped as if he'd hit a wall. Jack looked down to see a large metal spike jammed through his armored chest and sticking out of his back. From the ground, the smashed machine started to move, each of its appendages shaking and grinding from the dust and damage. Wictred, Jack and the three remaining marines took a number of steps away from the machine that had so brutally killed Sergeant Ajax. Across the floor, at least half a dozen of the machines were starting to move. It was a fraction of what littered the cavernous space, but it was enough to change their mission from discovery to combat.

"Okay, stay calm and get ready," said Jack in a slow, firm voice.

Though he wasn't military, none of the marines argued. They each lifted their rifles and aimed at the moving shapes.

"Looks like we're in trouble again!" chortled Wictred to himself.

Then the first of the machines pulled its blade from the still corpse of Sergeant Ajax and lifted itself up onto its creaking legs. Although smashed and damaged, it still managed to reach nearly two meters in height before moving menacingly towards them. Jack pointed his weapon at its centre.

"Kill them all!"

CHAPTER ELEVEN

In the shifting political upheaval of the creation of the Alliance, some colonies prospered while others withered in importance. Proxima Prime was one of the few that managed to maintain its position. Though the disparate colonies on its surface still harbored grudges from the violence of the Uprising, they prospered through the new trade opportunities offered via the Interstellar Network. Both Prime and Terra Nova became the most populous and significant planets in the Alliance...until the acquisition of New Charon in the Orion Nebula.

Proxima Prime

The surface of the moon showed numerous sights of impact damage, much like the early photographs of Earth's only moon had shown hundreds of years before; craters from the size of a man's hand through to those as large as a starship covered the surface. But unlike the lunar surface, both a viable atmosphere and the magnetosphere of the planet it orbited protected this moon. By all accounts, this should have reduced the vulnerability to orbital damage. General Rivers looked at one of the holes in the rocks nearby and wondered if there was a possibility the damage was man-made. He was in no doubt that he was seeing damage, but he still had no idea what had caused it.

Those engineers had better get a move on!

A series of flashing indicators lit up on his tactical display. It was a simple, but instant indication, that he had just lost both communication and IFF contact with Sergeant Ajax's unit underground.

"Sergeant, respond!" he repeated for the fifth time, but there was no change.

One of the lieutenants had already redirected their last drone to the area, and it was bringing back surface shots of the location where the squad had entered. It showed nothing of use, unfortunately.

"Wait, the drone is picking up vibrations through the rock walls. Yeah, it's weapons fire."

General Rivers rested his chin in his left hand; this wasn't the news he wanted. Indecision was a killer; however, and he knew from experience that action needed to be taken and fast. He tapped the squad leaders from half of the teams still out searching, as well as Spartan's APS team.

"This is a Code Red priority order. I've lost contact

with 4th Squad, and we're detecting underground weapons fire. These are the exact positions. Get there fast, and get them out of there!"

A stream of acknowledgements came in, and he could see the icons for the squads already making their way to the last known position of Jack and his people. As expected, the fastest of the squads was that of Spartan's. In less than a minute, they'd already covered double the ground of the marine squads.

"General, what did they find?" asked Spartan over the comms channel.

General Rivers tapped a button and sent the last video feeds from Sergeant Ajax directly to Spartan's suit.

"See for yourself. It looks like they found an underground cavern full of something. Possibly ruins, but there were signs of metal."

"Metal...wait...I've seen this place."

"What do you mean?" asked the General.

His next words were slightly muffled as the squad bounced and jumped their way closer to the target.

"Yeah, it looks just like the Biomech assembly area I saw seventeen years ago."

General Rivers looked back at his tactical display in confusion.

"I don't understand it Spartan, that was on Hyperion? I thought we'd already established that the site had been destroyed."

"Well, it sure looks like it. Don't forget it was on the other side of the planetary Rift. Maybe this is where it's connected to?"

This last comment made the General nearly take a step back.

A ground based Rift between galaxies? Is that even possible? He wondered.

"Just get down there, Spartan. Find the squad and get them out of there. Leave the science to the specialists. They'll be here within the hour, and we need this area made safe."

"Understood. Out."

Three marines moved passed, carrying a metal object between them. He recognized the shape as one of the new autonomous supply mules. They placed it on the ground and activated the device. Four legs shook, and it then stood up, waiting patiently. The legs faced inwards like people holding a stretcher, and the middle section looked like an open basket with gaps and spaces for ammunition and gear. He'd seen them many times before but never this small or light. One of the marines turned to him.

"General, we've programmed her for search and rescue."

"Good, get her down to the site and underground. I want our people out!"

The marine saluted and turned back to the machine. As he fiddled with the control system, the General connected directly to the orbiting ships with the communications relay. The face of the Commodore appeared.

"General, what's happening down there?" asked Commodore Lewis.

"We've located man-made structures, bodies and artifacts. It's exactly as we suspected. Somebody has been here before, and by the look of things, a long time ago. We've got trouble, though. One of my squads has lost contact, and I'm detecting gunfire."

There was a moment's pause.

"I see. What can I do to assist?"

"I need engineers to establish a permanent landing site. Also, my reserves need to be ready in case of trouble. We may need their help soon."

"Understood, General. I appreciate you have your hands full, but you might like to know that the recon drones have picked up abandoned settlements on two other moons. Science teams have already landed on one, and more are coming through."

"I see, well make sure they are protected."

"Good hunting, General."

* * *

Jack and Wictred took careful aim at the first machine; unleashing short bursts from their firearms. The L52 Mark II Assault Carbine was a triple-barreled coil weapon that used magnetized projectiles rather than chemicals. They used the high-power mode that expended the capacitor to propel all three projectiles at once. It reduced the rate of fire considerably but did maximum damage. Holes the size of fists appeared in the machine, but it was only when Jack hit it directly in the centre mass, did it drop to the ground.

"What the hell!" shouted the Corporal as he blasted indiscriminately at the other approaching machines. They looked like large mechanical spiders with raised blades and armored shells. Their gunfire caused damage, but failed to drop a single enemy.

"Fall back, slowly!" Jack called out.

Inch by inch, they stepped further from the machines and towards the remains of the arched and heavily damaged structure they had spotted from the ledge above. Seven machines were now moving towards them, but luckily they also appeared badly damaged and took their time to reach them.

"Something happened down here. They have already seen battle," said Wictred with interest as he continued shooting at them.

"Look out!" cried the Corporal, and a dark shape emerged from their flank. It was another of the machines, but this one must have stayed low and in the shadows. It brought down two of its arms, instantly crushing one of the privates, before lurching toward the Corporal. In a fluid motion, Wictred removed a crude looking blade from his flank and hacked down at the machine. It was shaped much like a Kopis blade from old Earth. It was slightly crooked and front heavy, making it ideal for hacking. Like the glaives used by his more senior brethren, this was built from the latest alloys and was able to smash and damage the limbs of the machine as it struggled to reach the Corporal.

"Out of the way!" shouted Jack. He jumped sideways and blasted the machine in the centre with a single high-power shot from his carbine. It destroyed the machine but also sent shards of metal in multiple directions. One piece embedded into the collar of Wictred, and a second struck Jack in the thigh, instantly causing a pressure leak.

"Alert! Alert!" called the suit's internal alarm system. "Pressure Malfunction!"

The interior quickly filled with a haze as the internal repair system attempted to perform a temporary seal. It took just a few seconds to perform before clearing. The surviving four stepped back until their backs were against the smashed arch structure. They all kept shooting, but the machines were now staying low to the ground and using the debris and their broken brethren to stay out of sight as they covered the open ground.

"Suppression fire, slow them down!" Jack ordered, and with a quick flick changed his weapon to the lower powered mode that fired each chamber in succession. The rate of fire went up considerably so that it made a buzzing sound more like a power saw. Streaks of superheated energy rippled through the space, as the projectiles picked at the targets whenever they could be seen.

"It's working," said the Corporal optimistically.

"Yeah, for now. It won't last forever," said Wictred, but with less humor this time.

* * *

Spartan reached the entrance to the ruined site first, closely followed by Khan and the other Jötnar. He didn't even hesitate, throwing himself through the damaged entrance, ripped open just minutes before by Wictred. Khan followed, hot on his heels, but with his glaive hung low and ready for trouble. The Jötnar had learnt very early on that in underground combat, it was just as important to carry heavy edged weapons, as it was to carry firearms. It was a lesson they had picked up on during the many hunts in the jungle of Hyperion, and especially when searching the ruins.

"General, we're inside. My suit is picking up an increasing power source. I'd say that is the source of the comms blocking. We need to shut it down fast."

"Very well. More squads are on the way. Get it done, Spartan. I will meet you down there."

Spartan moved on and continued to follow the footprints in the dusty ground that clearly marked the passage of the previous marine party. Intermixed with the prints of the marines were the even larger footprints, indicating the presence of Wictred. He turned to Khan.

"This is definitely the way they went."

As if to answer his comment, a stream of heavy gunfire reverberated through the chamber. Instinctively, each of the APS team ducked down to avoid what could have been devastating gunfire. Nothing came their way, just the sound of bursts of fire that Spartan quickly recognized.

"That's coilgun fire. They need help, let's go!"

He rushed off, without even checking on the rest of his group and headed deeper inside the tunnel. Every extra meter they travelled, the louder the gunfire became.

Why only coilguns, though? He wondered.

The weapons had only entered full service through the Alliance in the last decade, and very few had made it to the black market. The chances of somebody, other than those officially supplied by the Alliance arsenals actually using them, was almost nil.

"Spartan...drones...be" came a crackled and badly damaged message from General Rivers. It finally succumbed to whatever was causing the signal interference inside. Luckily, the suits were designed with a separate short-range system that utilized both radio waves and line of sight microwaves to avoid jamming.

"Stay close, we're not far from them now," he said calmly, rounding the final corner to reach the ledge that

Jack and the others had recently vacated. The sight of the great cavern sent a shudder through Spartan's spine. Khan moved alongside him and scanned the area with his equipment. They easily spotted the heat signatures of the marines at the far end, but all around them moved the metallic machines.

"Jack, can you hear me?" he pleaded over his comms system.

A high-pitched whine tore though his speaker, intermixed with the sounds of Jack speaking.

"Jack, watch your fire. We're coming in," he said and then leapt from the ledge.

The rest of the Jötnar followed behind, and they all hit the ground within two seconds of each other. From their landing spot, to the shattered structure where Jack and his comrades were, was no more than fifty meters.

"Stop them!" roared Khan, as the entire team surged forward.

The low gravity made it hard to run. Instead, they made use of the short leaps they had all practiced in multiple low gravity training scenarios. It took a great deal of practice to cover ground quickly and safely. Most made the mistake of making large leaps, but this could easily result in the person wasting more time on the bounce and recovery than actually moving forward. Khan reached the back of the first attacker. Without hesitating, he brought down his glaive in a mighty arc onto its body. A flash of sparks and metal indicated its quick death. He jumped over the body and landed directly opposite Wictred, who almost took his head off with a slash from his Kopis.

"Duck!" shouted his son.

Not giving it a moment's thought, he rolled down and to the right, just as one of the heavy metal arms crashed down. Spartan and the others were now in the middle of the group, and blades and gunfire tore apart the machines until just one remained. It stood in front of Jack who knelt on the ground with three holes punched through his body armor. Its front legs were lifted like blades and only a meter away from Jack's face.

"Wait!" called out Spartan, a flicker of fear and doubt appearing on his face. The group of Jötnar lowered their glaives but only slightly. Each was alert, with their bloodlust making it almost impossible for them to not continue their rampage. Spartan glanced about and noted the shredded remains of two marines. Then he spotted a series of gears start to move inside the body of the machine.

It's going to kill him!

He lifted his carbine, but it was too late. A bright flash almost blinded him, and the machine tipped backwards, collapsing to the side. There was a hole the size of his fist through its central torso. As the dust cleared, the shape of a young female marine stood with her L52 Mark II Assault Carbine still pointed at the machine. The triple muzzles glowed red with the heat of the last discharge.

Spartan nodded at her in thanks and bent down to check on his son.

"Jack, how bad is it?"

The young man did his best to smile, but he was clearly badly hurt. Spartan tried to connect to the General, but the signal was still being jammed. He glanced over his shoulder to the Jötnar.

"Track the source of the jamming and take it out. We need help down here."

They quickly dispersed, and Spartan could see movement from the ledge above them. The shape of General Rivers and another marine squad appeared.

"Spartan, stay where you are. We have a medical team on the way!"

He nodded in acknowledgement, looking back to Jack.

"Looks like you found trouble after all," he said grimly.

Jack coughed, and his legs gave way. Spartan caught him and lowered him to the ground. The reinforcements were now inside the cavern and working their way towards him.

"Keep still, son. Help is coming."

* * *

Commodore Lewis watched the incoming reports from the multiple teams on the moon below. He'd also seen the information on one of the smaller moons, and it was becoming clear to him and most other commanders that this entire area had once been occupied by an advanced society. The information from General Rivers and his landing party concerned him the most, though. Since his last contact, his signal to the surface had been jammed intermittently. Only in the last minute had contact been resumed.

"General, I don't understand. You say one of your teams came under attack in one of the ruined sites?"

"That is correct. Which part don't you understand, Commodore?" replied an exasperated General Rivers.

Commodore Lewis looked over to Commander Garret Blackford, his senior science officer. The man looked just as surprised as he did at the news. They had no intel, other than the signal beacon, to suggest any kind of existing life out there.

"I don't understand. This place is supposed to be deserted, or at the very least inert. What is down there?"

The man shrugged.

"Without a full engineering and science team down there, I can't tell you anything more."

The Commodore appeared distinctly unimpressed with this information.

"Okay General, what is your current status?"

"My forces have established a secure LZ, and all of the perimeter buildings, ruins and high ground have been searched. We have numerous unusual artifacts and hundreds of the destroyed and non-functioning machines.

Spartan, Khan and I can confirm they match some of the specifications of the machines we've seen before."

Commander Garret Blackford leaned in to the Commodore.

"That will be from the shutting down of the Rift on Hyperion seventeen years ago."

"I see," replied the Commodore to General Rivers. "I have science teams on their way from ANS Endeavour, as well as two engineering ships. My orders from Admiral Anderson are to provide space superiority and support for operations on the moons around this planet. He has requested you make contact in the next thirty minutes via video link. It looks like this part of the sector is going to be the heart of Alliance operations for the next few months."

"Very well, I have a shuttle returning with wounded. Have your medical bays ready to receive them."

The Commodore nodded in acknowledgement and then did his best to soften his expression.

"I heard about Spartan's son. How are his injuries?"

General Rivers sighed.

"They are serious, he took triple stab wounds to the thigh and torso. The armor kept him alive, and our medics have stabilized him. We have two dead, and two wounded Jötnar coming back as well."

"What about the rest of the APS team?"

"They are fine. Spartan is overseeing the security of

the proposed research facility and has already called in more APS teams for the work. It's just as well. My forces are spread thin down here, and we have more moons to investigate and clear."

"That's true. When will you be returning Devastation?"

"As soon as I am satisfied the engineering teams are safe and have started their work, I'll withdraw our forces, and we can move on to the next site."

"There is one more thing, General, and I think it might keep you down there a little longer."

"Oh?"

"One of our Lighting reconnaissance fighters did a high-speed sweep over Colonel Daniels' landing zone. We picked up imagery of a metallic structure below the ground. Only a small part of it is sticking out of the ground, and recent craters surround it. Based on his reports, it looks like the force that attacked him was trying to bombard this place."

"How far away is it?"

"Seventy kilometers, and the trails on the imagery show definite connections between both landing zones."

"This needs to be investigated immediately. I'll discuss it with the Admiral and get back to you. Please send the data down to me. I'll get my people to run over it."

* * *

The communications hall was a new construction at Terra Nova, and something that would have been impossible without the Interstellar Network to provide the infrastructure needed for interplanetary communications. In the past, messages were sent that could take hours, days or even months to reach their destinations. With repeaters stationed at both sides of all the Rift points in the Network, it was now possible to send and receive video communications in a matter of minutes to anywhere connected in the system. There were only two people physically present in the room, and the rest consisted of the latest virtual presence devices.

President Hobbs, the frail but commanding leader of the Alliance, took primary position around the small oval projection table. At her right hand side was Defense Secretary Churchill, the aged but only recently retired Admiral of the fleet; his presence only improved by his scarred face and missing left arm that had been replaced by a prosthetic mechanical arm. Rather than cover it, he left it open and it gave a mechanical, almost brutal look. The others in the rest of the room included the senior representatives from each of the colonies in the Alliance, as well as Admiral Anderson from Prometheus and General Rivers, who was still stationed in Orion. All were standing and waiting patiently until the President spoke. Each of the virtual presence devices for the others present carried a countdown and progress indicator underneath them to show the time delay for the communication.

"Colony representatives and our military commanders, thank you for this meeting. As you know, in this last week, we have seen a number of firsts for our new Alliance. We built and operated an inter-galactic Spacebridge, discovered new worlds, and as of three days ago, we can confirm the discovery of extinct intelligent life."

The was little excitement in the room, partially down to most of the information having already been leaked by the media, but also by the more troubling rumors that overshadowed the discovery.

"We are here because an urgent strategic decision must be made. This decision will affect every single citizen, from farms on Kerberos to miners in Epsilon Eridani. We have been presented with a great opportunity but also with great risks."

She turned to face the shimmering image of General Rivers and nodded. Underneath his name it said there was a seventeen second delay, yet she continued to speak as the counter ran down.

"General Rivers was the first of our people to come across these incredible places, but there has already been a cost in lives. He will now brief us on what his people have been able to discover."

There was a very short delay as the feed from the General finally caught up.

"Thank you, Ms President."

He then looked around the room at each of the figures, pausing for a moment when he spotted a Jötnar warrior standing for Hyperion. The sight amused him, but none of the others could understand why.

"Three days ago, my marines landed on this moon, currently dedicated as NC231. That is the thirty-first moon of the second planet of New Charon. This moon has a viable atmosphere and is partially protected by the planet's magnetosphere that it orbits. Colonel Daniels led a scouting party here prior to my arrival and was attack by unknown forces. His platoon has been recovered, and we have expanded our search in a number of specific sites. We have found human remains at the site, remains that have been here for a long time. A team led by Jack Morato also discovered a heavily damaged Rift generator, as well as a large number of destroyed biomechanical machines. I have platoons at key points on NC231, and engineer parties are already establishing a site here for further work."

He then nodded that he was finished and waited. President Hobbs looked at the people in the room, waiting until the message from the General had reached each of them. It didn't take long, yet the delay seemed to increase the tension significantly. It was one of the most spartan of the official rooms on Terra Nova, with nothing but three simple paintings of the colonization of the planet to adorn the walls.

"Hades, now our official name for NC231, has

complicated our expansion into New Charon. As you can see, the discoveries are impressive but also confusing. We now face great possibilities, but it would appear we have managed to find signs of our enemy once more, an enemy that almost destroyed us, and our way of life. For a long time, many have wondered how the Zealots and their masters were able to fight such a protracted technological war with such limited resources. This information might be the first part in the puzzle. Did this Rift on Hades once connect to our own worlds? Who built these machines, and why did the humans on this moon die? Our decision here today will be ratified in a full session of the Senate, but not for another six months. The question I must ask you all, is whether you will support our strategy?"

With that, she nodded to the Defense Secretary. He tapped a button and brought up a display of the Alliance colonies, along with colored lines that indicated the paths of the Interstellar Network.

"We are self-contained and have access to almost unlimited resources. Yet the Uprising showed us that we have enemies both outside and within. The Zealots have faded, but they are not completely destroyed. Something gave them purpose and provided them with knowledge and technology that even our scientists still do not fully understand. We have two options. We can shut down the Spacebridge and hope the enemy never again tries to tear our Alliance apart. It is a valid strategy and would allow us time to rebuild and strengthen. There is however another choice, and one that will require us to explore, exploit and defend this newly discovered system."

The model changed to show the planets in New Charon.

"There is a reason we were able to build this Spacebridge and at such a long distance. It is to do with the composition of the New Charon star system, and this has thrown up some interesting anomalies that are already being analyzed by Admiral Anderson and his people."

The commander of the research site at Prometheus nodded firmly before taking over.

"That is true. It seems that a small number of star systems contain certain conditions that make long-distance Spacebridges viable. New Charon is one, and Proxima Centauri is another. This would explain why we have been unable to create stable Spacebridges outside of just over four light-years. My scientists hypothesize that only one in a thousand star systems can support a stable bridge over a long distance, perhaps much less. A simple calculation shows that a network, similar to that of a spider's web, can be formed around each of these major hubs that would allow each of them to be connected to another, much like a major spaceport on a colony that is linked to cities and towns, via ground trains and smaller stations."

The image changed to show dozens of interstellar network bridges, appearing to join up hundreds of stars. They formed in tight clusters, like small webs with the occasional long line connecting each of the clusters. One hub clustered around Alpha Centauri with the next nearest being around Barnard's Star.

"By using this information, we could potentially build more of these long-range Spacebridges to places such as Barnard's Star, a system that is over six light-years away. What really stands out though is what you find at New Charon."

The display shifted to the newly discovered star system, but this time a great number of other stars appeared, many of them linked by potential Spacebridges.

"As you can see, New Charon is in range of hundreds of stars that fall within the four light-year limit. Even more importantly, the orbital telescope now deployed by ANS Beagle has confirmed that another twelve star systems within two hundred light-years have the same characteristics as New Charon."

He lifted his hands to emphasize his next point.

"This, ladies and gentlemen, is more than just another star system. It is a hub. A Nexus, if you will, between many more places like this. Whoever controls New Charon, will control access to all of the connected star systems. It is the Nexus of a large part of this Orion Nebula."

The display changed once more and lit up to show how each of the proposed Spacebridges would link to the myriad of nodes around it. The shapes around New Charon appeared to take up the lower corner of the

Nebula.

President Hobbs continued.

"The question is...what are we going to do? Somebody or something has been here before, and there is a chance they could come back. Do we cede this territory and the risk of provocation, or do we expand aggressively and stake a claim to it? I have three options that I want you to consider. Option one, we leave the Spacebridge open and continue to allow military and civilian ships to exploit the area as quickly as possible. Two, we establish a lookout station to monitor the system and withdraw back through the Spacebridge. Three, we withdraw and collapse the Spacebridge."

She looked at each of them, and it was clear there was as much surprise as there was confusion. She turned to Defense Secretary Churchill who spoke quietly.

"Ms President. Haven't we already decided on this matter?"

She shook her head discretely.

"No, not any more. We declared the system Alliance territory to ensure law and order was maintained during exploration and exploitation. With these discoveries, things have become more complicated. By staying, we could be inviting trouble."

He shrugged in response and looked back to the others. A light flashed near the representative of Orthrus.

"Ms President. Over seven thousand workers from my

colony are already at New Charon. If we withdraw, it will result in the collapse of three of our largest employers. I thought the military assessment was that the system was secure and safe for expansion. What are you suggesting?"

President Hobbs smiled inwardly, secretly happy at the question.

"Thank you for your question. Yes, until this discovery, we had assumed it was safe. It would appear otherwise. Even so, the area offers strategic benefits that could result in a golden age for our citizens. In my opinion, we should seize New Charon with open arms, garrison the planets and moons, and establish outposts as soon as possible. Within a decade, this place could be the Nexus of a mighty Alliance of hundreds of new worlds. Think of the opportunities!"

In an instant, the worries of the Zealots, the Biomechs and any other dangers vanished at the simple prospect of missing a great opportunity. She watched them carefully, looking for those who might decide against the plan.

"You have all been provided with full briefings from the military, astrophysics and science divisions. We will reconvene in seventy-two hours for your combined decision. Remember, you are considering not just our future for the next few months, but for the next thousand years."

CHAPTER TWELVE

The Great Exodus that followed the birth of the Confederacy also sowed the seeds for the Great Uprising. Large numbers of men and women brought up children with a distrust of the new system and those that had emerged victorious. The technology, ships and resources they managed to gain access to, were never explained; that was until the Orion expedition. Only then would the true extent of the Zealots' benefactors be fully revealed and the path laid down for the fledgling Alliance.

The Unforeseen Consequences

The events of the struggle to secure Hades had occurred almost a month earlier, and still the news of the battle continued to gather interest. Images of the ruined buildings and hints of a long extinct civilization had awakened every entrepreneurial and adventurous spirit through the Alliance. A decision had been made by the

Defense Committee, a group of colony leaders and the senior members of the Alliance government to expand the settlement and exploration of New Charon. Just weeks after the fighting, and there were science teams on a dozen moons and teams on the way to the many planets. But for Spartan and his friends, it was time to relax for a moment and to reflect on the many decisions that would now have to be made.

Over thirty prefabricated units had been brought to the surface by Alliance engineers to house the hundreds of scientists, engineers and researchers who were busy working on the site. One of these had been handed over to Spartan and the APS Corporation to operate as their command centre for moon security operations. It consisted of a central hub section that contained several rooms, a meeting hall and evacuation station. Around it, like the spokes of a wheel, were another six long sections, each containing a series of small rooms. This was where the power, sleeping and wash facilities were all based. One also contained a full set of weapons, ammunition and equipment for two APS Teams.

Spartan sat at the circular table, along with Khan. The others were busy providing site security for the big excavation work on the largest machine found so far. Spartan had done his best to discourage them from disturbing the great structure, but orders were orders, and the Senate wanted answers, fast.

"How is Jack?" asked Khan in an unusual show of interest.

Spartan smiled grimly.

"He's alright. The injuries to his upper body were severe, and he's still undergoing medical treatment on the Royal Sovereign, the medical frigate that came with the last batch of engineers. She's docked with ANS Beagle, right now."

Khan nodded slowly at the news.

"Good, the boy put up a good fight, so Wictred tells me."

He leaned over the table.

"He won't leave the boy's side," he whispered with a bemused expression.

Spartan raised an eyebrow at his comment.

"And you will leave mine?" he suggested.

Khan appeared nonplussed at the point he was making. In any case, it didn't matter because the door hissed open, and in walked an angry looking Teresa, flanked by two armored Jötnar. Gun, the leader of the Jötnar, and an old friend of theirs, stood to her right while a younger, unfamiliar Jötnar stood to her left.

"Spartan, have you seen what they're doing?" asked Teresa.

She moved closer and stopped directly in front of him. Gun spoke before Spartan could even answer Teresa's question.

"We've just been down there, and they're reopening the dig. I told them what you told me. But would they listen?" he said with a shrug.

Spartan nodded.

"Yeah, I heard. I told them and so did the General, but High Command have made this excavation a high priority. They want whatever is underground to be dug out for study by the Alliance Engineers Corps. Our job is to provide close protection, escort and security services to all Alliance personnel on this moon."

Gun grinned at the last part.

"Yeah, looks like your company expanded at the right time, Spartan."

Spartan glanced at Teresa, who was still angry.

"Look, we can't stop them and..." she glared at him as though she wanted him to do just that.

"If we interfere with Alliance business, we will just be replaced by another corporation. At least this way, we can provide input and be there when they screw things up."

Gun moved over to Khan who approached his leader, grasping his arm in a firm handshake. It was a curious mimicry of what they had seen others do.

"Commander Gun, how is the colonization of the second planet proceeding?"

"Good, very good. Our first ships landed, and we've traded resources on Hyperion for three habitation modules for the surface."

He looked to Spartan.

"Nine hundred of my people are already on the world, and more are following."

Spartan raised an eyebrow at the number; it was larger than he had expected.

"What about others?"

Gun grinned in that classic expression he normally gave before doing something dangerous. In the past, Spartan would have been ducking at this point, in case they were about to be hit by heavy weapons.

"This is the Alliance. We are one happy family. Anybody can settle there."

He looked to Khan who laughed before doing his best to keep silent. Teresa looked at them both and shook her head.

"The heavy gravity and thin atmosphere wouldn't have anything to do with your decision to settle there, now would it?"

Gun said nothing, but his amused expression answered her question. The Jötnar, though human, had been artificially created by the Zealots and their allies, using advanced technology; the end result had been humans with genetic memory that were adept at socializing and combat skills. One thing that had caught many by surprise was how adaptable they were in different environments. The air on Hyperion was a classic example. Though breathable to humans, it wasn't easy and took weeks, sometimes months for a person to fully acclimatize. For some it simply never happened, and they were forced to wear respirators at all times. It was a different story for the Jötnar. Their oversized organs, lungs and modified genetic structure, allowed them to thrive in such conditions. The second planet of the New Charon star system was another such world. It was rocky with no more than a trace atmosphere, mineral rich and very heavy gravity that was almost seventy percent heavier than Earth's gravity.

"What the hell are you planning on doing there, Gun?" asked Spartan with genuine interest.

Khan and Gun looked to each other. Gun moved to the table and sat down. The chair creaked at his great bulk but managed to stay intact.

"We can mine the planet and use it as a source of revenue. But I have other ideas. The high gravity will help keep my people tough and strong. It is our one advantage over humans. I plan on using the planet to guarantee our future."

Spartan listened with interest. The idea was, of course, reasonable, but it also provided a germ of an idea for him as well. Khan saw his expression and became equally curious.

"What is it, Spartan?"

Spartan leaned back in his chair.

"Well, I have an idea that could bring you more money and also keep your reputation as warriors."

Gun looked interested. "Go on."

"Let us establish a training compound on the planet. You will run it, and we will supply specialists and equipment. I can guarantee that APS and the Alliance Marine Corps will definitely want to take advantage of a high gravity training centre."

Khan spoke quietly into Gun's ear and looked back to Spartan.

"Interesting," replied Gun. "You'd have to cycle your people. They won't last long down there with the added weight. It could work, though. It could work very well."

Gun pulled out a secpad and placed it on the table. It displayed a sequence of images from the dig site. Spartan looked at them carefully, noting how a single shallow ramp had been built to work down and around the buried object. He tried to imagine what it might be, but from the rusted shape and broken sections, it was almost impossible. He looked up to Gun.

"Any ideas?"

Gun looked surprised.

"Me?" he answered, pointing to his own chest. "I asked you because we have no idea!"

Spartan looked back at the device. Something caught his attention, and he tapped the unit to enlarge one of the images. It expanded with only a low degree of digital noise to obscure some of the shapes.

"Have you seen this part? It looks burnt."

Gun shrugged.

"I need to speak with the General. One moment."

From his belt, he pulled out his own device and tapped the option to request a conversation with General Rivers. A box appeared with a waiting message. He then looked again at Gun's device.

"Gun, we need to stop this work. Look at the damage to this thing. One way or another, this thing was in some kind of action. Based on what we've seen down here, I think it's clear it wasn't good. So far we..."

He was cut short by the appearance of General Rivers on his own secpad.

"Spartan?"

"General. I have imagery from the dig site here on Hades."

"I don't have long, Spartan. I'm in the middle of landing scouting parties on three other moons around this planet. What do you have?"

Spartan tapped the device and sent the data directly to the General.

"Sir, it looks like these remains saw some serious action at some point in the past. I recommend a halt to the dig until we can learn more."

There was no hesitation from the marine commander, however.

"Negative, Spartan. My orders are clear. Our science teams need complete access to this site and its objects.

The longer we leave it, the greater the chance we might have of hitting a problem once we are overcommitted. I am monitoring the situation from here on ANS Dragon. Keep an eye on things down there and keep me appraised. Understood?"

Spartan sighed but knew it was no good pushing any further.

"Understood, General."

The signal cut, and Spartan looked back to see the inquisitive Jötnar staring right back at him.

"Who is your friend?" he asked.

Gun looked over to the younger Jötnar and laughed.

"This is Hunn, the Champion of Hyperion!"

Spartan turned to Teresa, who said nothing.

"Hunn?" he asked.

"Yes. I have started a fighting program like the one you told me about. Any Jötnar can challenge another. Hunn is the champion of ten fights. He even matched a First."

Spartan felt he'd been separated from the Jötnar for much longer than he realized. Things were happening on Hyperion that he neither knew about nor even fully understood any more. Khan laughed at his confusion.

"The first Jötnar created in the war are now called the First. The survivors are our best and most experienced warriors."

Spartan's secpad lit up with an urgent video feed. He tapped it, and it quickly changed to the face of his Team

Leader operating site security at the dig site. The look on his face sent a shudder of dread through Spartan's body.

"What is it?"

"Sir, the team accessed some kind of damaged computer system down here. It sent out a pulse and then burnt out."

Spartan stood up in a rage.

"What? The mission parameters were simple. Excavation only. No interference with the object until it has been fully examined."

The man shook his head, desperate to say something else. Now Spartan became truly concerned.

"There's more?"

"Yes, Sir. Instruments are picking up movement below the ground, approximately two hundred meters below the surface, but getting nearer. I've ordered a full evacuation back to the base, but there..."

He stopped and spun around. The top right corner of his feed showed a forward view from his helmet as he looked at the scaffolding, ramp and equipment that lay about the great artifact. Dozens of people in suits were moving slowly away from the site. That wasn't what he was looking at, though. It was the shape of a sleek craft about the size of a Cobra shuttle, and it had risen from the ridge just a few hundred meters away.

"What the hell!" he shouted.

Spartan tried to intercede, but a stream of lines flicked around the craft, and simultaneously two of the groundcars at the site exploded. The vehicle rushed out of sight, but another two appeared and continued to strafe the ground around the artifact. Some of the projectiles hit scientific equipment, and some of the rounds even hit the ruined object itself. Then the signal cut completely. Spartan turned to his comrades with a grim expression.

"Teresa, get in touch with the General. Tell him what has happened and fast."

"What are you doing?" she asked nervously, but she already knew the answer.

Gun nodded in silent agreement. Spartan grabbed her about the waist and pulled her close.

"We have to bring them back, all of them. Let the others know."

He walked for the door seal and towards where all the weapons, armor and equipment were stowed. As he moved inside, he threw her a quick look.

"We're not alone after all."

* * *

Jack looked through the window of his ward and out into space. The medical frigate was unlike most other vessels he'd been on before and utilized plate-reinforced glass protected by emergency shutters. It was an old design and one abandoned for over fifty years. As he lay there, he thought of what kind of life the ship must have had in its long career. It lacked rotational sections for artificial gravity, and all but its point defense turrets had been removed to make space for beds and supplies. It was almost sad to see a ship of her age relegated to a non-combat function.

Still, it's better than being scrapped, he thought.

He was positioned so that his upper body was slightly raised, but not too high that he was sitting. The bed was one of eight in the ward; half occupied by marines and engineers that had suffered accidents or injury in the last week. He was young, and his recovery was quicker than some might have expected. The mental scars were more than evident, however, even to him. As he lay there gazing through the window, his mind returned to the short but vicious battle underground on Hades.

Hades, how right they were with that name!

The injuries he'd sustained on that moon were unlike anything his young body had experienced so far. The puncture wounds had penetrated deeply, but according to the doctors, they had managed to avoid all the major arteries and organs. He tried to not think about the blood and wounds; the mere thought of blood sent a dizzy, almost sickening feeling through him. From the window, he watched a group of Navy frigates form up into a neat formation. New Charon appeared even busier than he'd seen Terra Nova or Prime, with military and civilian ships spreading like locusts through the system. He could no longer see the distant shape of ANS Beagle even though the ship had been expanded until it was now almost unrecognizable. They'd left the Beagle Station half a day earlier and were on an elliptical course that would take them past a number of moons but at a leisurely pace. They were in no hurry. Only the faint color of the Rift could just be made out in the distance. He pulled one of the public access secpads from the unit next to his bed and held it in front of his face. It was far less useful than his personal device, but it was tied into the public network feeds. With a few taps, he was able to bring up the headline news stories for the Alliance.

Let's see what's happening out there.

The most common stories were the usual problems; food shortages on Kerberos, public sector protests on Carthago and an armor scandal in the Marine Corps. Even the President seemed to be in some sort of expenses story that seemed to be going nowhere. But the one story that caught his eye was the one given most of the coverage, and it simply stated, 'We are not alone!'

No shit! He laughed to himself.

Reading further into the story, it outlined the most recent developments in New Charon. Preserved skeletal remains, destroyed technology and signs of habitation were now appearing on a large number of moons and on the three planets explored so far. The news story from the Alliance News Network implied the remains were almost certainly early colonists from Earth. The next most important story concerned the usual scapegoats, the Jötnar. Apparently, Commander Gun, leader of the Jötnar, had infiltrated New Charon and was in the process of establishing an independent outpost on one of the high gravity worlds. Jack raised his eyebrows at the story, more in annoyance than surprise.

Why the hell not? If it were anybody else, it wouldn't be a problem.

A shadow appeared at the end of the room, and Jack instinctively went for his sidearm, but he was unarmed. He'd been caught by surprise due simply to the fact that with no gravity the medical personnel moved effortlessly, and often in total silence.

Damn it! He thought for a second.

A flicker of fear rushed through his weakened body before the shape of a young woman appeared. She was barely over 1.6m tall, and her light blonde hair was tied back neatly behind her head. Her face was soft, almost gentle and instantly put him at ease. She floated towards him like a spirit and it made him shiver.

"Jack Morato, how are you feeling today?" she asked.

The nurse approached his bed from the right, using her arms to move about. It was odd to watch her move as she pulled herself through the room. The grab handles were placed at frequent intervals so that she could maintain control, without crashing into fragile equipment. She seemed to float towards his bed, and that was something

Jack was quite enjoying. All thoughts of the Jötnar, New Charon or even the creatures on Hades vanished as he gazed at the young woman. Her face was lightly freckled and her skin almost lilywhite, a common side effect of spending large amounts of time in space. His eyes moved from her waist and lingered on her chest, perhaps a little too long before she coughed politely.

"Ahem, Jack? Can you hear me?"

Jack looked at her jade colored eyes and tried to speak, but his mouth had turned dry. He coughed to clear his throat and answered as quickly as he could.

"Better...Yes, feeling good now...Thank you."

He almost kicked himself for sounding so simple.

You idiot, you sound like a Jötnar juvenile!

She pulled herself down closer and lifted the sheets a little to examine the tubes running into his arm. It was a critical mixture that would provide him with nutrients, as well as the extremely expensive repair agents developed for use in the Alliance military. At least that was what his father had told him. As she bent down, he couldn't avoid her and glanced at her cleavage without even thinking. He could smell her hair and skin at this distance, and it almost overloaded his senses; that was until he heard the sound of breathing that announced the arrival of a second person.

"Jack, I see you've found something soft to look at," came the booming voice.

"Wictred?" he said in surprise and lifted up slightly in

the bed, bumping the young nurse's head with his own. She tipped backwards and drifted away before Wictred grabbed her and held her steady. Jack lifted his hand to his head.

"Oh...What the hell? I'm so sorry!" he said as sensitively as he could but also trying to hide the look of amusement on his face. The nurse shook her head and stepped away from Wictred and back to Jack.

"It's okay." She turned and glared at Wictred. "I've had worse." And then returned to Jack's side to check the seals on the tubes. Wictred raised his shoulder, surprised at her comments, and Jack did his best not to laugh.

"Nurse, uh?" he asked.

"Anne," she answered quickly, lifting a finger to her lips to quiet him.

"The other nurses told me about you yesterday, so don't try any of your moves on me, okay? I've had quite enough of you people hitting on me."

Wictred erupted into a roar of laughter that boomed through the ward. One of the sleeping Alliance engineers in the most distant bed lifted his head, waking instantly from a deep sleep and looked about as if he expected to be assaulted at any moment.

"Please, will you keep your voices down," said the nurse, and then she turned and pushed away from them, shaking her head as she moved effortlessly away.

Jack looked back to his friend and grimaced slightly in

pain as he pulled on one of the deeper wounds. Wictred moved closer to him, pulling himself alongside his friend. With no gravity in the ship, he looked strange as he floated there with nothing but his hand to pin him into place in the ward. The Jötnar, like all of his people, looked completely out of place in a sterile area such as this. He still carried a blade on his side, but even Wictred had been forced to leave his armor behind before he could enter. It seemed like over a year since Jack had seen him like this. He was heavily muscled, in some places in a most grotesque fashion. Like all the Biomechs, they had been created as strong and resilient warriors to be used as food soldiers on the frontline. Jack took a sip of fluid from the pipe that hung nearby and turned his head to Wictred.

"So, you managed to get some time away from Hades, then?"

Wictred nodded.

"Khan and the others are helping with security. He sent me back to the Beagle to arrange for more weapons to come through."

"Weapons?"

Wictred grinned.

"Yeah, Spartan arranged for them to come through as APS equipment. Your father is proving to be quite helpful. I can see why my father treats him like one of us."

Jack looked to the window at the mention of his father. It wasn't that he hated his father. It was just that he'd spent so much time with others that he'd started to view him as more of a distant relative. His military and commercial reputation didn't help either, as everybody knew who he was. Jack wanted to do his own thing, and that meant trying to keep his head down and avoid being connected with one of the most famous Marine Corps Officers since the Great War.

"Look," said Wictred with one hand pointing out of the window. Jack followed the line of his arm and towards the pale, almost colorless Rift in space. He could see nothing of note until he realized it was much larger than it should be.

"What's going on?" he asked.

Wictred then looked off to the right and nodded. Jack followed his line of sight until he could see the Rift back to Prometheus, and it was now a tiny dot in the distance.

Another Rift!

"What the hell is going on?"

They both watched in surprise as the Rift shuddered, and a dark shape almost the size of the Rift itself appeared. Much like when the Alliance ships appeared in a flash, this new ship did exactly the same. Jack watched completely speechless, as the massive vessel seemed to halt just a short distance in front of the tear in space. The lights inside the ward dimmed, and the metal shutters slid down with alarming speed.

"This is the Captain, all crew are to secure wards. We

are setting an escape course to the first planet. This is not a drill. We will engage main thrusters in sixty seconds for emergency burn. To your stations!"

The nurse reappeared along with another. They pulled themselves inside and proceeded to pull down the magnetic seals around the beds that would lock the patients into position, prior to igniting the engines. Jack saw her approaching and leaned back and into the correct position. He reached up and struck the lock button. A semi-circle seal came down, and he felt as if he was being strapped to the bed. She checked the seal.

"I knew you wanted to strap me down," he said, followed by a wink. The nurse smiled and moved on to the next patient.

"Nice moves!" laughed Wictred, who then moved to one of six transit points to pull a series of thick belts and seals around his great torso. The second nurse pulled herself down to him so that she could assist.

"Thirty seconds till burn!" came another slightly muffled message over the speakers. This time the Captain's voice seemed less confident. Jack could feel a vibration coming through the metal of the ship and then as though he was becoming heavier.

"We're under fire, engines activating now!"

The two nurses flew from the middle of the ward to the ceiling with a sickening crack. The nurse from before, Anne, managed to lift her hands in time, but the second slammed headfirst into the metal surface. Jack was certain the impact had broken her neck. After twenty seconds, the engines were still burning, and the ship continued to accelerate.

Whatever is going on out there, it means trouble!

Then the lights cut, and a series of sparks rippled through the ward. They were mainly from the destruction of electronic components, but he also noticed a strange vibration working up through the structure of the ship. He felt weightless again but not a single piece of equipment seemed to work. For a second, he worried that he had been blasted out into the void of space. That couldn't be true because he could breathe, and the temperature of the ward was exactly the same as before. There was a hissing noise, followed by a clump sound. At the same time, the emergency lights partially activated. He reached out to find Wictred's arm pulling him from his bed. His face appeared massive in the low light, and only his crooked teeth showed up.

"Power's gone. We need to find a lifeboat. This is an attack!"

Jack looked at his in shock.

"An attack, by whom?"

Wictred turned, pulling himself along the wall with Jack right behind him.

"Who cares? We need to get off this ship, fast!"

The tube in his arm ripped out, and blobs of fluid drifted

aimlessly inside the gravity-free confines of the ward. Jack could see the shapes of the other patients, struggling as they floated about near their beds. The young nurse was trying to help one of them. Jack grabbed a handrail and stopped his movement for just a second.

"Hey, Anne. We need to get out of here."

She turned around, trying to find the source of the sound, and then she saw the two of them.

"No, my duty is to all of our patients."

She then looked back at the man she was helping and continued to work on his torn bandages that must have come free during the burst of acceleration. The main lights flashed as if they were about to come back online. One managed to stay active, but the others flickered and stayed off. Jack pulled himself towards her and instantly felt a surge of pain, like a knife being stabbed into his ribs. He groaned, but with all the noise, it wasn't noticed. Wictred stopped and look back.

"Leave her, Jack. We have to go!" he snapped at him.

"No, I'm not leaving her!"

"Anne, there isn't..."

He was cut short as part of the ward started to glow red. They could instantly feel the increase in temperature. Jack grabbed Anne and yanked her from the patient and towards the door. She spun out of control, shouting wildly at him until Wictred caught her foot and pulled her out of the main doorway. Jack followed close behind and made it through the doorway in time to see parts of the interior furnishings begin to melt. Wictred grabbed the metal rod that was the emergency door override, a standard design fitted to all compartments in the ship. He didn't even hesitate and forced it down, even as a patient tried to make it to the frame. Anne pulled at him, trying to keep the door open.

"Bastards!" she screamed. "Open it, now!"

The tiny porthole in the door flashed blue, and a flood of energy washed about inside the compartment, instantly vaporizing anything other than the bulkheads and heavy equipment. The patients caught fire before being sucked out of the gaping hole in the side of the ship. Jack pulled her close so that her bruised face was only inches from his.

"Anne...Anne!" he repeated, trying to calm her down. "We had no choice. They are attacking us. If you stayed, you'd be dead as well."

Wictred reached out to her.

"If you want to live, follow us."

Wictred pulled himself through the main shaft and Jack followed. They travelled almost ten meters before he looked back to see what the nurse was doing. To his surprise, the young woman was directly behind him, pulling herself along with surprising speed and efficiency. The speakers crackled, and a high-pitched whine screamed down the system.

"Large formation...abandon ship, boarding on the..."

then it continued as nothing but noise. Wictred reached the first junction and checked his friend was still there.

"We're under attack. If they board us, we're finished. We need to get off this frigate and join the fight!" he said sternly. Jack looked to Anne, expecting her to argue yet again. Instead, he saw nothing but resolve on her face.

"Don't wait for me, come on!"

CHAPTER THIRTEEN

The religious artifacts that appeared after the Hyperion Incident quickly turned from the mythical and into the biomechanical. Just seven months after the end of the fighting, a suicide cell was captured and interrogated. Amongst their weapons and explosives were a dozen small metal objects, each one the epitome of the half woman and half snake Echidna. This time, however, the snake was fully mechanical and the resulting creature was some foul mixture of the two. Over time, the last Zealot cells disappeared with most returning to their families and societies as before. With the link to Hyperion gone, so went their strategy and support. It should have been obvious; with hindsight, it couldn't have been more straightforward.

Holy Icons

Spartan drove as quickly as he could from their encampment without tipping the Bulldog armored transporter over. It was a large six-wheeled vehicle with four exit doors and a single top-mounted turret position. Although it was mainly designed for the military market, this version of the Bulldog was the civilian issued version, and therefore not equipped with weapons or countermeasures. At least, that was how it had been before the APS Corporation had got their hand on a dozen of them in the military surplus market. Now the vehicle was fitted with what looked like a cage around its hull to trigger explosive charges before they penetrated the hull, as well as a modified 'v' shaped hull and reactive armor. They struck a ridge, and the vehicle left the ground for a short time before crashing back down.

"Hey, nice driving Spartan!" snapped Gun.

In the back of the vehicle sat the small group of Jötnar, as well as Teresa and two APS operatives. Everybody was armored, and with just a few minor changes, they could easily have been a Marine Corps unit from twenty years earlier. The vehicle was specifically designed so that it could be driven and operated by personnel in full PDS tactical armor without compromises. Teresa sat directly behind Spartan in his driving position and tapped the side of his helmet. Both of their visors were open, and it was surprisingly quiet inside the armored hull.

"How much further?" she asked nervously.

They hit another bump, and only the gas suspension and magnetic seal for each of the passengers stopped them from coming to harm. The Bulldog settled back down, and Spartan was able to turn back for just a second.

"Over the next ridge, then we circle down three hundred meters to the excavation site."

One of the APS operatives, a middle-aged man called Issac Ocano, sat at the bank of computer displays and controls. He was a senior Team Leader in the Corporation and the controller for some of the most violent APS teams in the Alliance. Today, however, Spartan had given him tactical command. There had been protests, but Spartan needed his skills and experience to control what could become a very messy operation. From inside, he had access to all the remaining data feeds. The most prominent was from the high-level security drone that was monitoring the site from above. There were also two active data streams coming back from the two APS teams near the area who were also moving in to assist. Issac was one of APS Corporation's most successful commanders, and with a violent reputation. He had already redirected seven reconnaissance assets as well as all available APS units to the area.

"Spartan, I've managed to get a signal out to ANS Dragon. Their real-time streams are being hacked, but it looks like something is going on up there. The data indicates something has entered the system and is blockading the Spacebridge."

"Something?" growled Gun.

He was well known for being short of temper, and one thing he disliked more than anything else was ambiguity. Instead of saying more, he checked the hilt of his weapon. It was an odd device, similar to the glaives of the Jötnar, but with a shorter shaft that could be wielded in one hand. Spartan was busy controlling the vehicle, and it was taking a supreme effort to keep the thing on the roughly cut track. The only times in the last few weeks he'd done this same trip had been at no more than a quarter of his current speed. Even so, none of the passengers complained, other than the occasional sarcastic comment from Gun.

"Nearly there!" he called out, and with a sliding turn, they finally reached the peak. The vehicle lurched slightly as it changed its orientation and started the winding descent down to the dig site. With the worst of the drive out of the way, he spoke through the Team Network that connected them all, both visually and orally.

"Whatever is happening in orbit and beyond is out of our control. Our job is to protect our people. We will assess the situation when we get there. Our priority is to keep the workers, engineers and security teams safe."

"What about the site?" asked Hunn, the young Jötnar warrior.

Spartan threw him a quick look and turned back, shaking his head.

"To hell with the site, the people come first. I warned them to not touch anything. Have we learnt nothing from these places? Didn't they see what happened when Jack and Wictred activated the machines down there?"

Gun and Khan both looked at the young Jötnar with amusement. Khan leaned in slightly and thumped him playfully in the chest. To a Jötnar it was nothing, but for anyone else it would have broken bones.

"Like I told you, Spartan is his own man. There's only one human who hates the feral Biomechs more than us."

Khan nodded towards Spartan.

"It's him. If you want the taste of battle, then listen to Spartan."

Gun nodded in agreement.

"True. Spartan always finds the best fights."

Teresa watched and listened to them all, but she was more interested in the aerial video streams than their macho posturing. The low level drones kept being disabled, but the high level drone was still transmitting. It showed a number of fast moving machines that seemed to be hovering about two hundred meters from the surface. The dark shapes surrounding it by a myriad of paths and tracks, easily identified the dig site. Then she spotted movement in the lower left.

"Look!" she cried.

Issac Ocano had already seen it and enlarged that segment to show a group of five people sheltering behind what appeared to be rubble, or perhaps a broken wall. They were firing their weapons at something near the artifact. Then a blue pulse tore at the ground around them, knocking them back. Incredibly, all of them returned to their feet and continued to move away from the object. Teresa sat up straight and stared at Issac.

"Is it me, or does it look like something is trying to get them away from the dig site?"

* * *

Jack and Wictred had reached three evacuation points on the stricken frigate, and still there were no available lifeboats. In their journey through the ship's hull, they'd come across multiple bodies but no survivors.

"Where is everybody?" asked Anne.

Wictred ripped open the entrance to another compartment to find it was empty, like most of the others. He snorted and pulled himself further inside. Jack followed close behind and threw just a brief look back to Anne.

"They're gone. Looks like the crew just went for the lifeboats and jumped ship."

She shook her head in horror.

"No...They would never abandon the wounded and our staff like that."

She tried to sound sure of herself, but it was clear that the poor woman was already doubting the integrity of the ship's crew. They continued on through section after section, each time doing their best to avoid the debris, broken pieces of plastic and the drifting bodies of those killed. Nothing compared to when they reached the medical laboratory though, where seven of the crew spun aimlessly about the place. All of them suffered multiple puncture wounds. Jack and Wictred moved about, looking for signs of what might have happened to them. Anne, meanwhile, examined the bodies. After checking the first, she started to wretch and had to wait for a few seconds to calm down.

"Who did this to them?" she said bitterly.

Jack was already at one of the computer units, but nothing he did seemed to help. The screen was black, and even the battery backups did nothing, other than light a few status indicators.

"Everything is out," he announced, pulling himself around the unit to check the cables.

Anne stayed where she was but glanced about the place. There was no sign of power or life, other than their small group and the low level battery powered lights fitted at fixed intervals through the ship. She looked down at a device on her arm. It was a medical secpad with built-in atmosphere and biological monitoring sensors.

"We need to get out of here before the air runs out," she shouted in a hurry. "My secpad says the oxygen levels are already dropping."

Jack looked back to her.

"Life support is out then. This ship is toast. If we stay, they'll find us."

Something major shook the ship, and they were all forced to grab anything nearby to stop drifting about inside the room. Wictred spotted something and pulled himself across the width of the room to a series of wheels near the wall. He braced himself and started to twist the largest of the wheels. With each turn, the metal safety shutters started to lift. Four full evolutions, and he had opened it almost a meter. The three of them watched in awe at what was happening outside of the frigate. A large, but crudely constructed vessel, lay alongside it. It bristled with plating and what seemed to be weapon turrets. The shape was impossible to determine at that distance, as the great bulk blotted out much of the view.

"Whose ship is that?" asked Anne.

Jack shook his head.

"Uh, that isn't an Alliance ship."

As if to emphasize the point, a flight of Lightning fighters moved past on the left. As they came closer to the ship, a number of projectiles streaked towards them from one of the dozens of turrets and picked them apart. All four were totally destroyed in seconds.

"They aren't friendly. Let's go! I've got an idea!" said Wictred. The Jötnar pulled himself out of the room and into one of the many identical looking service corridors. These were smaller than the main corridors of the ship but did lead to a greater number of places. Jack pulled as hard as he could to catch up with his friend.

"Mind sharing your plan?" he asked.

Anne followed quickly behind them with speed that surprised them both. Wictred didn't stop, and Jack was forced to chase him, just to hear what he had to say.

"The loading bay up there. It faces that ship."

"So?" asked Jack.

Wictred finally stopped, facing his friend with a wry smile.

"I say we board her!"

Jack looked in Wictred's face and saw a mixture of excitement of nerves.

Board her, you crazy bastard!

He looked at Anne, who was waiting patiently, and then into the corridor. He shook his head as he returned his gaze to the Jötnar.

"There has to be another way?"

Wictred pulled himself a few more meters before replying.

"Life support is gone and so are the lifeboats. There are suits and weapons in the loading bay. We get there, suit up and leave. Either we wait in space to be found, or we attack them. Let's go, now!"

With that, he was gone, leaving Jack to wonder how they would board and attack a ship the size of which even he didn't yet know. Anne grabbed his shoulder.

"Is he mad? That ship has crippled an Alliance frigate. We can't board it!"

Jack guffawed.

"Really? You've never met Jötnar before, I assume?"

A terrifying howl echoed through the innards of the ship, and Jack knew immediately it was the sound of sheer terror. He'd only heard it a few times in his life, and each time he'd wanted to move away from it, not closer. He grabbed a handrail and pushed out through the hallway and into the corridor. The screaming instantly increased in volume, and he almost ran into the bloodied nurse before coming to a stop. A marine pulled at a hastily applied bandage on his shoulder and blazed away down the corridor with his carbine at some dark shape. Jack reached him and moved to the woman to check her injuries. She was breathing quickly and lost consciousness. Anne followed close behind, pushing him out of the way to see what she could do.

"Who the hell are you?" snapped the marine.

"Jack, Anne, Wictred," he answered quickly, pointing to each of his tiny band.

"Can you shoot?" he asked, completely disinterested in what Jack had to say.

Jack reached down to the spare carbine on the ground, lifted it and removed the safety.

"Yeah, I've fired a few shots. What happened here?"

The marine checked his carbine, adjusted the power

setting and continued.

"We were hit in three places on the starboard side. It was a boarding craft of some type. They smashed through the armor, and then these soldiers came aboard. They took out the power, engines and weapons in less than two minutes."

Wictred seemed especially interested in the last bit.

"Soldiers? Whose soldiers?"

The marine looked at the oversized Jötnar with disdain before answering.

"I don't know. They were heavily armored, like marines but bulkier and stronger. Their weapons cut through our armor like tissue paper."

Anne sighed and moved away from the bloodied and now motionless nurse.

"She's gone, her injuries, they were..."

Jack placed a hand on her shoulder.

"It's okay, there's nothing you could do. We need to save whoever is left. Right now, that looks like just the four of us."

The marine grabbed Jack's arm and pulled him down to his face.

"It wasn't just them, though. They had a machine with them as well. It was like a mechanical spider or crab, or something. It was bigger than a man and thickly armored. I've never seen anything like it. It was horrible, and its legs had blades. I saw three of my men butchered by them before we got to this point."

Jack looked to Wictred who nodded slowly. The description matched some of the details of the machines that had appeared briefly on Hyperion before the Rift had been destroyed.

"There's something else," the marine said seriously.

"What?" Anne asked.

"The machine, it...well, it looked like it was giving the orders."

Jack, Anne and Wictred looked at each other. It didn't take Wictred long for him to pull his heavy looking blade from his belt and start moving along the corridor.

"Hey, where are you going?" shouted the marine.

Wictred ignored him, so it fell to Jack to explain.

"We're heading to the loading deck. Going to grab gear and leave the ship."

The marine almost choked in amusement at the idea. It wasn't easy to make out his expression, but his tone was clear enough.

"Forget it, the landing bay is gone," he said grimly. "I would probably have done the same, but one of their craft took it out. Where do you think they attacked from?"

Jack sighed, and even Wictred appeared to have noticed because he slowed down and finally stopped.

"If you're serious, there's only one way of this ship now. The port side weapons array is undamaged. Since this ship was converted to medical use, the weapons were taken out and replaced with stores and all kinds of medical junk. Behind that section are two lifeboats. They were for the gun crews and engineers, and that's why nobody went for them, simply because this old bird doesn't have any gunners anymore. My squad was heading that way when we ran into their soldiers."

Jack didn't need much more encouragement and called out to Wictred.

"Get back here. We're going for the port side weapons array."

Wictred looked at him but didn't move.

"Where is it?" he asked suspiciously.

Anne pulled at the marine's arm and helped drag him out of the room.

"I know the way!" she called out and disappeared out of the door.

* * *

Spartan pulled on the control column as hard as he could, but it was too late. The broken gravel and rock had loosened to such an extent that he finally lost control, and the Bulldog started to slip down the steep embankment. As they slid down, they could make out a rough ridge, and beyond that a steep incline that ran down to the artifact and the dig site. Swirls of smoke drifted up into the sky from the already burning vehicles.

"Crap! Hold on!" he shouted.

They increased speed, and only Spartan's steady hand stopped them from tumbling over. The reduced gravity made it harder to control, and each time they left the ground, it seemed they might never come back down. It seemed like an age, but was in reality less than ten seconds until they reached the bottom. The chin of the vehicle crunched into the rock with a screeching sound. It would have knocked the passengers unconscious if they hadn't been strapped in with the magnetic couplings. The bumping and shaking stopped as quickly as it had started, and they all stared at the multitude of video displays fitted inside. They were surrounded by dust, but the scanners had already identified where they were, using the IFF gear fitted to every APS operative. Khan thumped Spartan in the back.

"Good driving, Spartan. We're in the right place."

Teresa unlocked her harness first and moved to the nearest doorway. Her close fitting armor looked almost identical to the gear she'd worn back in the Marine Corps, and Spartan noted that she moved just the same as well.

So the working out wasn't a total waste of time, then! He thought to himself.

Gun hit the release button on his magnetic coupling and leapt from his seat and towards the left-hand door. Without checking with Spartan, he struck the button, and the door ripped open with a hissing sound. Gun was out first with his weapon in his hand, and closely followed by Khan and the rest of the team. Spartan and Teresa looked at each other and then chased after them. Once on the exit ramp, Spartan looked back at Issac Ocano who was still managing the disparate units about the dig site.

"I've got this, Spartan. I'm bringing in two support drones to assist you. Get the rest to fall back here. I'll establish a defensive perimeter while you secure the dig site. We've got more help on the way."

Spartan nodded, impressed with his cool handling of the situation. Technically, Spartan should have stayed back, but his skills had always been in the execution of operations, not the management of them. Issac Ocano might be a ruthless fighter, but he was also a quick-thinking commander and extremely cool under pressure, exactly what was needed in a tricky situation like this one. Two APS operatives moved from the right-hand side of the vehicle and carried an automated sentry turret between them. As soon as they placed it on the ground, a set of six legs extended out and embedded in the ground. A gyroscopic head lifted out from the middle and then waited. It was one of the newer pieces of equipment the APS Corporation was trialing, and for just a moment, Spartan's professional interest almost took his attention from the mission. But his focus was strong enough that he turned back to his team.

"Spread out!" he called, and the group increased their

spacing. They were only a few hundred meters from the target; a large crater-shaped dig site that lay before them. Multiple vehicles were burning, and Spartan could see at least three bodies near the crater itself. A number of personnel were climbing up one of the further ridges to escape, but most were following the commands of Issac Ocano and working up to the craggy ridge where the Bulldog waited patiently. A motorized turret on the top of the vehicle moved silently with its dual L52 Mark II Assault carbines tracking the horizon; only its movement catching Spartan's attention. A blast struck near a small group, and dark sharps darted about.

There they are!

"Team, follow me!" he cried and leapt over the ridge and down the slope. The Jötnar were close behind him, each keen to embed their blades into the nearest enemy. Most carried modified firearms to suit their size, but Gun and one other still carried their ranged weapons strapped onto their arms. Though less accurate, it left both hands free to wield close quarter weapons. Spartan reached the first two engineers who were running for all they were worth. Only one stopped; the other streamed past.

"What's happening?" asked Spartan.

The man pointed behind him and started muttering.

"They...they came from under the ground. There was no warning!"

He stumbled over and dropped to his knee but then

lifted himself up and continued moving up to the ridge. More of the civilians appeared from the dust, and then he saw them. At first it looked like a heavily armored marine, but then he spotted the closely fitted armor, the smooth metallic plates and the oddly shaped helmets.

These aren't ours!

There were three of these warriors, and they must have seen him because one looked directly at him. Spartan had been in combat enough to tell when somebody was about to shoot. He instinctively rolled to the right and narrowly avoided being struck by a pulse of energy. The impact sent debris and rock in the air, but luckily none of it hit him. The gun turret on the Bulldog opened fire, sending its load of magnetized projectiles over their heads and into the soldiers' position. As soon as he recovered, he lifted his own weapon and aimed directly at their position. There was nobody there though, just a trail of vapor that disappeared off into the air, and the marks of where the rounds had struck home.

Damn, these guys are good.

"Spartan, I'm picking an airborne unit near you. It's not ours," said Issac Ocano on the comms link.

You don't say!

Spartan looked up at the sky and saw three shapes moving at speed back towards the artifact. Two streaks of energy appeared from them and struck the higher ridges around it. That was when Spartan noticed they were sending down rocks that were helping to bury the thing.

"Incoming!" shouted Khan as he waved his blade in the air.

A small vessel flashed past them overhead, and an object fell towards the dig site. It was round and about the size of a man. Just before it struck the ground the object vaporized and sent a shockwave in all directions. The blast was substantial, and all the APS operatives were thrown to their backs. Spartan landed hard, and the internal sensors showed minor breaches in the suit's joints. It wasn't serious, and already the suit's control unit was sending small clouds of vapor to the breaches to assist in the temporary repairs. Spartan lifted himself up to find nothing but dust around him. He shook his head only to see one of the unidentified enemy soldiers stood just two meters away. They stared at each other through their armor but neither moved. Khan appeared to his left, and upon spotting the soldier, started to lift his blade. Their enemy raised his odd looking firearm but did not fire.

"Who are you?" asked Spartan.

The soldier said nothing.

"Spartan, I've got the engineers, what the hell is going on down there? The aerial drones are all down. Bravo team has just arrived, and I've set them to deploy fire-support teams to look down on the artifact. Spartan?"

Spartan continued staring at the enemy soldier and slowly lifted his left arm up with the palm facing towards the armored shape.

"Spartan here. Good work. Get them out of here and back to base. Send a Bulldog to the secondary coordinates when you're done."

"What?" came back a surprised reply from Issac Ocano.

"We have guests, and they are heavily armed. Get the civvies out of here, now!"

A little more of the dust cleared to give him a better view of the artifact and the level of destruction caused by the soldiers. The bomb that had been dropped had completely covered the dig site with rubble so that it looked little different to the rest of the area around it. There was no sign of the dead or the destroyed vehicles, as they were all now buried beneath tones of rock. The soldier, on the other hand, looked bizarre. His armor was of a similar color to the rock itself. It stood slightly taller than Spartan, but that could easily have been the suit. The other two were now stood alongside him and dressed in the same gear. Gun rested his blade on his shoulder and turned his head to Spartan.

"So what happens now?" he asked sarcastically.

The soldier started to move forward and then stopped; something appeared to have caught his attention. He looked around, turning his gaze to the sky. The other two soldiers did the same. Spartan considered jumping in and striking them, but there was something about their behavior, apart from not attacking him, that suggested they were not quite as they appeared.

"Spartan!" came back the transmission from Issac Ocano.

"We've got something coming down from orbit. Transmissions from the fleet say a vessel has entered New Charon and is blockading the Spacebridge back to Prometheus. The signal is broken, but it looks like there's a shooting war going on up there."

Spartan shook his head, but for some reason, he didn't feel particularly surprised. He turned to his left to see Teresa stood there, looking right back at him. She looked worried. In fact, her expression was much more serious than that.

"Jack," she said quietly.

Spartan's heart almost skipped at the mention of his son's name.

"Uh, Spartan, look!" said Gun.

Spartan followed his gaze and quickly identified the glowing shape of a superheated object dropping out of orbit. No sooner had it leveled off before three much smaller vessels gave chase. Spartan didn't recognize any of them, but it was clear they weren't friends. The largest of the four seemed to split up into smaller components. Each of them moved apart and turned in the direction of the valley leading to the artifact. The pursuing craft fired a variety of weapons at the targets, but in just seconds two had vaporized, leaving the third to turn and desperately try to escape. The pursued turned to the pursuer, chasing it relentlessly until finally striking it with continuous gunfire.

""I don't like this," said Spartan. "We need to fall back. They're coming this way."

With that, he took a few steps back from the soldiers. One of them spotted his movement and watched him move away. The soldier tapped the side of his helmet and the front lifted up and into the back of the armor, revealing a pale white, almost alabaster looking face. A face that was female and definitely human. The soldier spoke, but her language was completely alien to him. He was about to lift his hand in confusion when the rough synthesized sound of the soldier's suit started speaking.

"We...danger, must leave...follow!"

Her visor clamped back shut, hiding her face as before. The soldier extended her right hand, exposing a control unit on her arm. She tapped three buttons, and a gentle rumble started from her left. Spartan glanced in the direction of the sound to see a sliding door expose a tunnel under the ground. The entrance was at least the height of the Jötnar and wide enough for three of them to stand abreast. It was no simple door either. As the three soldiers ran over to the hole in the ground, it was clear the outer layer was almost half a meter thick and plated with multiple sections on the inside. The three disappeared inside, leaving just Spartan and his team to await the arrival of the other vessels. The female soldier moved back and looked towards Spartan.

"They come for us...follow," and with that she was gone.

Spartan connected back to the Bulldog.

"Issac, what's your status?"

The reply was rough, probably from the jostling and jumping about as the Bulldog made its way back to the base.

"We're almost back to the ridge. Team Bravo has already left with two engineer teams, and they're halfway back. My sensors show those craft are coming down to land. They're after you with a purpose, old friend."

Teresa grabbed Spartan's shoulder.

"We have to get back to the camp. If we wait any..." The whistle of missiles from the approaching vessels cut her off. Now that they were closer, they could see the craft were almost the size of Alliance transports and heavily armed. The missiles slammed into the positions around the retreating engineers, and at least one struck Issac Ocano's Bulldog as it continued its final struggle up the ridge. Gun grabbed Spartan and threw him inside the hatch, and the others all rushed to follow. As Teresa reached it, another volley of missiles exploded around them, and she was thrown full force to the ground. She blacked out, but not before she spotted the hatch starting to close. The last thing she saw was movement outside, then blackness.

CHAPTER FOURTEEN

Titan, the old moon of Saturn saw new life with the creation of the Interstellar Network. The moon had been settled for centuries, but its standing as the first among many colonies gave it an almost mythical reputation. As the development of the Old Solar System began, so did the interest and pilgrimages to what was considered by some to be the spiritual home of those who had left Earth for a new life. Titan became to the Alliance what the Holy Lands had been for Western Civilization on Earth.

The Lost World

Jack was the first to reach the port side weapons array on board the stricken frigate. It had taken almost fifteen minutes to get there, but luckily, they'd managed to avoid running into any hostile forces or problems. That was at least, until they approached the large metal blast door that led into the compartment. Not only was it shut, but it was mechanically sealed from the inside.

"We've got a problem," said Jack in a dour tone.

Wictred pulled himself into position around the door, jamming his body to the wall so that he could exert as much effort as possible onto the lever. He groaned as he used every ounce of strength to try and force it, but to no avail. He loosened his hold and looked back to Jack.

"It's locked."

Jack shook his head at his old friend.

"You don't say."

Anne tapped her hand on the thick metal three times and then called out.

"Is there anybody there? This is Nurse Anne Fitzgerald. We need to come in."

A dull clanging sound issued from the other side, and in one slow movement, the door slid open. Wictred moved to the opening, only to stop himself at the sight of three rifle barrels. Jack lifted his hands and placed them in front of his friend.

"He's with us. We're from APS Corporation."

"Get in here, fast!" said a gruff voice from in the shadows.

Jack moved in first, and the other three followed right behind him. As soon as they made it inside, the great metal door slammed shut behind them. A gentle glow from the far corner showed up the shapes of the marines hiding behind what cover they could find.

"Who's in charge here?" demanded Jack.

A shape moved closer, until a squat looking man wearing half of his PDS armor stood just half a meter to his front.

"Lieutenant Veeranki, ship's security. What the hell are you doing on my ship? The order to evacuate has already been given."

"No shit!" said the marine that had come with them. "We are all that's left. What are you doing holed up in here?"

The Lieutenant seemed to soften at the sight of one of his own.

"The lifeboat isn't functioning properly. We've got a Navy tech guy working on it, but he reckons it will be another thirty minutes before the system is in place. You know what's going on here?"

Jack looked to Wictred, who seemed to have little interest in contributing to the conversation. It was one of those peculiarities of the Jötnar. Although they were interested in battle and adventure, they rarely said anything unless they had something genuinely to contribute. It was both a benefit and a curse, and right now, Jack would have liked to hear something from his friend. His attention was drawn to Anne. She was moving about, speaking quietly to the other marines. Even in this situation, she seemed more interested in doing her job. At least one of them was badly in need of some help, with two arm wounds.

Maybe it's just keeping her busy.

He looked back to the marine.

"There's a fleet of ships out there, and they are attacking Alliance vessels. I don't know what they want, but negotiation doesn't seem to be at the top of the list."

He pointed back to the door.

"They have a ship running abeam and had troops move inside to disable us."

A head appeared from the entrance to the lifeboat. It was a much older looking man in grubby overalls, and the interior lighting of the lifeboat backlit him neatly.

"Did you say one of them is alongside us? I thought they would have left some time ago."

Jack nodded. "Yeah, why?"

"Well, as the Chief Engineer, I'm the only one of us here with access codes for the primary server. With my information, you can trigger the auto destruct. It might be the only way to stop this ship getting any closer to the Spacebridge."

"So?" asked one of the marines.

Wictred looked at the man and then slammed his oversized fist into the bulkhead.

"He means we can destroy the ship, and maybe take theirs with us, before they can cause any more trouble."

At that one comment, the small storage area seemed to fill with agreeable faces.

"Alright, sounds like a plan, but you're forgetting one

small detail. We are still stuck here. I don't know about you, but I have no interest in burning here. What did you have in mind?"

"I'll show you the route. It will take you about fifteen minutes to get there, and then sixty seconds to start the sequence. It's only a three minute countdown, so you won't have time to get back."

"Great, I assume you have a plan for that as well?" asked Wictred.

"Yeah," answered the Chief smugly. "I'll meet you at the Six Alpha docking point. It's three sections from where you'll be anyway. It's normally only used for cargo and the like, but there's no reason why a pod or lifeboat can't dock there, force a magnetic seal, and trigger the airlock. It will need some pretty good flying. Lucky I'm good at that, as well!"

"Isn't that cutting it a bit fine? What if you can't get the lifeboat working?"

He looked inside the craft and back to Jack.

"Oh, she'll fly, don't worry about that. What you need to worry about is the guns on that thing outside. The last lifeboat we launched was vaporized once it hit the ten thousand meters marker. This might be our only way out of here. We need to be outside of the five thousand meters mark when the auto-destruct activates."

"What about the shock wave?" Wictred asked.

The Chief shook his head in an irritated fashion.

"Don't you kids learn anything in school now? There won't be a shockwave in space. There will be a very short-lived heat bloom though that will vaporize anything within a kilometer of the frigate, probably more with the enemy ship combined. Depends what's on board and how they built her."

Jack nodded slowly. "Okay, what do we need to know?"

* * *

Spartan activated his thermal and infrared overlay as they continued deeper underground and through the tunnel system. Teresa stood at his side, and the rest of the APS team followed directly behind, with their blades drawn and at the ready. They'd been inside now for almost five minutes and continued on the gentle gradient deeper into the site. The three soldiers had vanished long ago, as they moved with greater speed. Spartan was not happy, and it was just as well he was at the front, so none of the others could see his expression.

We have a lot of good people on the surface. Are any of them still there?

He checked his IFF system, but even this short distance underground had completely blocked his medium to long range communications. The only good news that he could see was that a small number of his people had made it to the vicinity of the encampment. That was all he had, but he did know the site was well protected with automated turrets and contained enough weapons and supplies for multiple APS teams if needed.

I just hope they keep their heads down. Last thing we need is a massacre on Hades.

Teresa nursed her head as she did her best to maintain Spartan's fast pace. The blast as they'd entered the tunnel had knocked her out cold, and the pain in her skull was ever present. Even so, not one of them wanted to lurk near the surface to face whatever was going about its business.

"Where are they taking us?" she asked suspiciously.

Spartan trudged onwards and shrugged at her.

"Who knows? It's pretty clear they live here though, and they were trying to keep us away from the artifact at the dig site. We must have disturbed something down there."

Teresa nodded as ideas gelled together in her mind.

"Like Jack and Wictred did when they found those machines?"

"Maybe," he replied.

The idea made sense. There had been no violence until particular sites on the moon had been interfered with. First was the marine unit under Colonel Daniels. Then had came Jack, and now this catastrophe at the dig site.

His attention was drawn ahead as a bright light appeared directly in front of them. It took a moment for the suit to adjust to the brightness, but Spartan kept moving forwards. After few more steps, they reached the end of the corridor and stood on the perimeter of a vast cavern that had been cut into a beautifully intricate structure. It immediately reminded him of the exquisite architecture of Terran Nova with its detailed arches and columns. The designs here were not identical, but the artistic design and quality of work were evident. Most of the area was open, but the walls were filled with columns and small buildings that although very narrow, seemed to reach up and merge with the very rock itself.

Waiting almost fifty meters away were two-dozen of the warriors. They stood in what looked like an open plan temple. Columns ran in a circle around them, and in the centre was a hexagonal stone object covered in tubes and wiring. Above it floated a holographic model of a dozen spheres.

Planets? Spartan wondered.

All were armored in the same fashion, apart from the woman they'd met previously. She took one step away from them and waved her right arm in some odd and flamboyant fashion before stepping back. A different soldier stepped forward and deactivated the complex helmet arrangement; to Spartan's surprise it was another female face. She then spoke in much the same fashion as the first; her alien sounding tongue quickly masked by the synthetic tones of her suit.

"Greetings, Spartan, Commander of the Alliance.

Welcome to our home."

Spartan looked over to Teresa and then to Gun, but neither said anything. Every one of them seemed as surprised as him. He returned his look to the pale, pallid face of the soldier.

"Greetings to you. What is your name? Who are you?"

The pale-faced soldier moved her head and looked around at the underground facility, returning her gaze to Spartan.

"I am Ayndir," she said slowly, lifting her hands to indicate those behind her, "and we are the T'Kari. The last of our race."

Spartan's mind rushed as a hundred questions entered his thoughts.

"How can you understand us?" It was the first question he really wanted answered.

The woman nodded and continued speaking.

"We have listened to your data since you came here. Our technology has deciphered your tongue. Our suits can translate for us."

She paused as though wanting to say something uncomfortable.

"Spartan, Commander of the Alliance. Why have you come here? Why have you disturbed our buried dead?"

She then stepped closer and raised her tone.

"Why did you awaken the machine?"

The inside of the structure vibrated violently. Small

chunks of stone broke from the ceiling, dropping down almost a hundred meters and then crashing to the ground. Teresa grabbed him as he lost his footing from the shaking, but then it died back as quickly as it had arrived. Off to the sides of the open space, a number of armored doors opened. Small groups of people, this time unarmored, appeared to look at the new arrivals. One, a tall woman with long white hair approached, looked at them and launched into a long discussion with Ayndir. Half way through their conversation, the woman lifted out an object from her robes. It flashed and displayed a holographic image of the surface of the moon. It showed the Alliance encampment and the arrival of four APS Bulldog vehicles. Dozens of people were rushing about, and Spartan was sure he could see several of his operatives in full armor taking up positions on the perimeter.

"Hey, what's going on?" he demanded.

Ayndir lifted her eyes to him but waited until the unarmored woman finished speaking.

"Your people, up there," she explained, looking to the ceiling. "They have brought the wrath of machines back to our worlds. It will not be long now."

Gun stepped forwards to Spartan.

"What's the plan? We can't leave them alone up there. This is a war!"

The other Jötnar growled in agreement. Khan even turned to head back the way they had arrived, but Ayndir lifted her hand in an obvious gesture.

"Your people will be safe up there...for now," she said calmly.

In the background, another group of a dozen of the soldiers ran past and into a different tunnel entrance. Gun immediately suspected betrayal; his patience now starting to wear thin.

"Explain!" snapped Gun.

"The machines know some of our people still live. They will finish what they started nine hundred solar cycles ago. Our doom approaches. Your people will suffer...after our fall."

"Bullshit!" shouted Khan angrily. He swung his blade, creating a whirring sound that caught the attention of all the soldiers. Spartan noticed their interest and could only assume it was the complete difference between the Jötnar and him and Teresa.

Activity inside the open area continued, as what could only be assumed were civilians lined up near to two large structures. They were being handed weapons, much like those carried by the soldiers. Interestingly, these civilians were a mixture of male and female, but he spotted no children or youths of any age. Spartan knew immediately that something bad was about to happen. He grabbed Teresa by the shoulder.

"You don't arm civilians unless things are bad."

He then turned to the others.

"Get ready."

The soldiers split from the centre of the space and rushed to a variety of doorways along the outer rim. Only four remained, including Ayndir as well as the civilian. The civilian spoke in hushed tones to Ayndir who then repeated them through her suit's translator.

"The machines left this sector seventeen of your solar cycles ago. Their military base was destroyed, and our race was extinct. At least, they thought we were, until now. They have many enemies, but you have reminded them of us, and our resistance. Now it is the end."

A repeating tone appeared from nowhere, and it seemed to galvanize the T'Kari who rushed to cover, preparing for the end. Every structure, column and building seemed built with the dual purpose of being a defensive position. Loud thuds came from multiple directions deep inside the thick stone.

"You are all ready?" asked Spartan to his tiny group. Teresa and Spartan both had their carbines loaded and lifted to the shoulder. The Jötnar lifted their weapons while Gun raised his arm-mounted weapon.

"You should use cover. They are strong!" said Ayndir.

She took up a position behind the nearest column of the centre structure. The shape was perfectly formed with gaps for shooting while staying protected. Spartan was fascinated, but snapped back to attention when a booming sound to his left announced the arrival of the enemy. The great metal blast shield ripped from its mountings. Right away, a number of small objects rolled inside, followed by a bright flash and sonic burst. Luckily, the PDS suit was able to filter it all out, and in they came. To Spartan's astonishment, the figures looked almost identical to the T'Kari, except for their flowing robes, gold colored armor and large ration of edged weapons. Their armor and clothing style were just the same, yet there was a familiarity about them he couldn't shake off.

"Uh, Spartan...do these guys look familiar to you?" asked Gun, at the same time as he opened fire with his Gatling gun. He was the first to fire, and the overwhelming volume of fire from his weapon cut a dozen figures before the rest joined in. It didn't take long before more breaches were made, and the entire underground site turned from calm tranquilly into yet another blood soaked battlefield. As Spartan loaded a new magpack into his carbine, he spotted the faces of the Jötnar. Each of them howled with bloodlust as they blasted away.

Gods help them if any of those things get near Gun and his people. He thought with surprising amusement.

* * *

Jack and Wictred worked their way through the damaged corridors of the long abandoned frigate. The systems were still off, and the temperature had already fallen over ten degrees and was continuing to worsen. They'd left the others under the command of the Chief, who seemed to be the only one with any idea as to how they could get away from the ship. As they continued onwards, Jack wondered what else was happening through the New Charon system. From what he'd seen, it was clear that somebody wanted them gone. The thing he really wanted to know was who they were and what they wanted.

"Jack, it's through here," Wictred said quietly.

The two entered the computer room to find cables and equipment drifting about the place. Jack thought back to his last conversation with the Chief and tried to remember where he said they needed to go.

The control nodes on the primary console.

He looked about and found the unit with the static body of a dead crewman draped over it. Jack kicked at the wall and moved effortlessly to the unit. He traced the control node with his hand, until reaching a flat panel about the size of his head. He pushed it in about a centimeter until it clicked and then slid open to reveal three circles, each with an analogue dial sat on top of it. Between the three circles was a small hexagonal hole. Jack reached for the control-key the Chief had given him. As expected, it matched the hole perfectly.

"Wictred, we need the other one," he called out.

Wictred was already moving from one body to the next, but so far had found nothing of use, other than a half loaded navy issue pistol. He tucked it inside his belt and continued the search. Jack looked below their position, now nervous that they might not find a senior member of the crew in this part of the ship.

"Maybe they got out," suggested Wictred.

"Wait!" said Jack. He could see a shape jammed down behind one of the shattered computer displays. "Look, if I'm not mistaken, that's the body of a sub-lieutenant. Check him out."

It didn't take Wictred long to get to the man, and within a few seconds, he held up the control-key triumphantly. According to the Chief, all senior command staff carried one, as well as the commanding officer of this part of the ship. It needed both keys to activate and would also send an automated message to all other command staff. They could then instantly override the self-destruct system in case of accident or sabotage. Jack just hoped there was nobody left on board that might stop them. The idea that others might still be alive on the ship was a thought he did his best to avoid, but from what he could see, the ship was a barren vessel and one that would kill anybody within the hour, no matter what he did.

At least this way we can take some of those bastards with us!

"Okay, over there and open up the secondary port," he said, pointing to a partially damaged computer system.

Wictred wasted no time and quickly covered the space to the unit. With a quick push, the slat at the front popped open to reveal a smaller but similar entry unit to the one near Jack. Wictred placed the key near the hexagonal hole and looked over to Jack. On his nod, the two pushed in their keys, and both units flashed yellow.

"Yes!" cried out Jack, pleasantly surprised that this part had worked at all. He'd half expected something to fail or interfere with their task. He checked the time displayed on the front of the unit, quickly calculating how long they had.

Two minutes till the lifeboat gets here. Crap! We're behind schedule!

Each of the circular parts lit up, and he thought back to when the Chief had given him the details of what to do. The circles clicked as they were twisted, and he recalled the nine-digit code needed for the trigger. He started with the first wheel, and immediately a color display showed the first character speeding through numbers and letters.

"You sure you remember what the Chief said?" asked Wictred suspiciously.

Jack continued entering the code.

"Thanks for the vote of confidence, but yeah, I've got it."

With each series of twists, the list of numbers and letters increased until finally, the entire nine-letter code was finished. Upon adding the very last one, the system beeped, and its lights turned red. A quiet voice came directly from the unit.

"Auto-destruct sequence activated. Three-minute silent countdown is in progress. Please evacuate the ship immediately."

Jack looked to Wictred, who actually appeared nervous for the first time.

"What the hell are you waiting for? Go, now!" he cried.

With that, the two pushed away from the units and to the far door. It was a short route to the Six Alpha docking point, only three sections, but with the silent countdown ticking away in their ears, the two of them moved as fast as their bodies would let them. Wictred made it to the Six Alpha section and turned, waiting for Jack to arrive. He moved in a few seconds later, and the young Jötnar pushed the door shut behind him and pulled on the seals. The two then turned to face the external airlock, a double layered system that was designed to allow automated supply units to dock with the frigate. Jack hit the first manual control that triggered the opening of the seal. There were three seals in this section, and the final two could only be activated once a unit was connected to the exterior of the ship. It was a simple system, designed to avoid accidental breaches and fatal accidents. Wictred smashed his fist onto the panel, but the final two sections didn't open. Even more serious though, his fist managed to break the panel to leave nothing but exposed circuits boards and wiring.

"Wictred! What have you done?" exclaimed Jack.

He pulled himself over to the panel and reached in, only to find smashed components and a scorch mark running along the metalwork. He turned back to Wictred, shaking his head.

"We've got a big problem."

* * *

Captain Thomas stared with cold, expressionless eyes at the formation of enemy ships on the main display. The six ships appeared to be almost the same size as ANS Devastation, but their design, intentions or even capabilities were a total unknown to him. The shapes were similar to images he had seen of prehistoric fish back on Earth, with the thickly ribbed hulls and chunks of plating fitted at every point. One of them had reached an Alliance frigate, but they were too far away to assist, and by all accounts, the sensors showed the abandoned ship looked no better than a hulk.

"Tactical, what's our status?" he asked for confirmation, even though he could see the icons on his own status board. He just needed to hear it from somebody else. The assault on the medical frigate was a shock, but there were even greater concerns in New Charon, right now. Lights flashed up on the mainscreen, and it quickly altered its focus to show the spot that had been occupied by the medical frigate and the large enemy ship. In their place was a great cloud of metal and debris. Colored flashes ripped through both structures, until a great color ball of energy tore the two vessels into tiny fragments.

"Holy crap!" uttered the Tactical Officer, before realizing what he'd said.

"Uh...the medical frigate is gone. Sensors indicate a strong possibility that she triggered an autodestruct sequence. The enemy ship's gone as well."

The display altered again to show all the changes that were occurring. The large structure of the primary enemy vessel had moved only a short distance from where it had arrived. The Tactical Officer highlighted the vessel on the computer system so that it indicated red on the display.

"The main vessel has taken a stationary position at the mouth of its Spacebridge. We have six other vessels, roughly cruiser class, and they have split up with each on an intercept course with the moons around the gas giant. No...Wait! They are all altering their course."

Captain Thomas scratched his chin as he considered their options. The major Alliance ships in this sector were spread out over a wide distance with none, other than ANS Devastation, anywhere near the Spacebridge.

"Uh...Sir. They are on an intercept course with our Spacebridge and ANS Beagle."

That last part snapped him out of his thoughts.

Beagle? What do they want with the bridge?

He nodded to the helmsman.

"Put us between them. They aren't getting near our station."

"Aye, Sir," answered Lieutenant Glinda Scookins. She was a short, white-haired woman with a clipped accent. She was fast though, and in just a few seconds, the course changes were laid in. Captain Thomas indicated for Commander Parker, his XO to approach.

"Get the crew ready. I think we're going to war."

"Aye, Sir," replied the XO, who then turned to the communications with confidence.

"This is the XO. Action stations! Marines, to your posts! Charge weapons systems! Medical staff to your posts! This is not a drill, I repeat, this is not a drill."

The Tactical Officer did one final check before nodding to the Captain.

"Sir, particle beams capacitors are charging, approximately ninety seconds until ready."

Captain Thomas nodded.

"Good, let's hope they work as well as the tests suggested. Get me Captain Vinson on the horn."

The face of ANS Devastation's CAG appeared in seconds on the smaller screen to the right of where Captain Thomas sat.

"Captain, I need your birds in the air. Put fighters out as escort. We have hostiles on the way."

"Understood, Sir, they'll be out in less than sixty seconds."

* * *

The destruction of the medical frigate and the enemy warship was the first major action in the space-borne struggle for supremacy in the New Charon sector. Even as the wrecked hulks drifted apart, the deployment of every ship in the system altered. All civilian ships and traffic in range of the Spacebridge returned to Prometheus immediately. All other military vessels set their course for ANS Beagle and the entrance to the Spacebridge itself. From the bridge of the ship, now nicknamed Charon Station, Captain Raikes watched the movement of ships around the nearby gas giant and its moons.

"Confirm that, all unidentified ships have changed course to intercept this station?"

The XO nodded.

"Affirmative, Sir, with the destruction of our frigate and the enemy ship, they have redirected their efforts towards us. It looks like their objectives have changed."

"And the only defensive capabilities we have are two frigates?"

The XO nodded but said no more. On the tactical display were the icons for all the major warships in the system. Icons over the heavy gravity world showed the Jötnar transports and one Alliance crusader class vessel. ANS Dragon and her small taskforce were busy establishing monitoring posts and a resupply station in the asteroid belt. He'd already spoken with Admiral Anderson, who was mustering every ship he could find in the vicinity of Prometheus. He'd already sent through the second frigate to assist the station, but it wasn't enough.

That left only ANS Devastation anywhere within range of the Spacebridge for at least two days. The display also showed quite clearly that the six enemy ships would have to move past Devastation. The status markers showed the intentions of her commander, and the hold action he was taking made Captain Raikes nervous. He tapped the communication button and immediately reached the pale face of Captain Thomas.

"Captain Raikes, good to see you. I'm deploying fighters and setting up a perimeter from the Rift."

"I see. You understand that the enemy vessels appear of a similar size and capability of one of our own cruisers? You won't last long out there."

Captain Thomas nodded.

"I understand. Even so, once they get past us, they will hit you. If ANS Beagle is damaged or destroyed, we'll be trapped here and at their mercy. We need reinforcements and fast."

"Anderson is sending a taskforce in two hours. How long until the enemy reaches you?"

The Captain moved away for a moment before returning to the screen.

"They'll be in weapons range in just over ninety minutes."

"Ninety?" replied Captain Raikes with surprise. "Can you hold for thirty minutes with six ships on you?"

Captain Thomas simply smiled back at him.

"Ask me again in two hours."

CHAPTER FIFTEEN

The space battle at the Siege of Titan proved once and for all that the actions of a single ship could change the course of a battle. The heroic stand of the Battlecruiser Crusader against incredible odds made the assault landings on the station possible, and with it the first real victory in the Great Uprising. Though the great warship finally met her end at the fall of Terra Nova, she did provide the inspiration for an entire new class of ship. This class of warship would be proudly named Crusader and be fully battletested in the struggle for supremacy in the Orion Nebula at New Charon.

Naval Cadet's Handbook

The first wave had been easily repulsed with only minimal losses to the T'Kari. Spartan, Teresa and their Jötnar allies were still stood outside the perimeter of the temple location in the centre of the room, much to the apparent dismay of Ayndir who continued to call them over to make use of the cover. Spartan, however, knew full well the strengths and weaknesses of his own people. They were bigger and bulkier than the T'Kari, and the limited cover offered them little protection. The open space gave them room to use their weapons.

"Listen!" barked Gun.

Spartan could hear nothing, but he understood the senses of the Jötnar and had grown to trust them without hesitation.

"Get ready!" called out Teresa, and once more they lifted their weapons for battle.

But this time the sound was different. The sound of hundreds of feet was replaced by dull thuds and grinding sounds. Teresa wasn't sure, but Khan and Spartan knew what was coming.

"Get back, it's machines!"

On cue, the damaged entrance ripped open and in walked one of the eight-legged machines, just like those Jack and Wictred had discovered long dormant. They surged forward in a rush as gunfire licked around them. Five more entrances ripped open, and more of the machines broke through, closely followed by scores of the T'Kari looking enemies. One of the machines managed to reach the temple, cutting down a T'Kari guard before Spartan and Khan jumped at it. Khan embedded his blade into its torso, and Spartan jammed his barrel against the thing's back, blasting it with continuous gunfire. It flailed and struggled before collapsing but still managed to shred Spartan's carbine at the same time.

"Spartan, over here!" shouted Gun as he continued blasting away. With his free arm, he withdrew one of the primitive looking slightly curved blades and tossed it over to him. A Jötnar could swing it with one hand, but it took both for Spartan to swing the three kilogram weapon with speed and precision. Like a tidal wave, the enemy surged over them, and all the defenders could do was shoot, hack and stab for all they were worth.

* * *

Captain Thomas watched the approaching ships with trepidation. He'd given as much ground as he dared to them but any closer to ANS Beagle, and they could simply ignore him and attack the station. Deep down, he worried they would do that anyway. It was not like a ground or even an ocean based battle. Ship ranges were almost irrelevant in space, as were the gaps between ships. His plan was a simple one. He would put on one hell of a show to distract them, and hope he looked more hostile and dangerous than he actually was. Either way, it was a matter of minutes now before he would find out.

"Sir, our weapon arrays are in range. From their current course and velocity, it looks like they are ignoring us and heading directly for the Spacebridge," explained the Tactical Officer.

Damn, he thought. That was the news he had been dreading.

"We cannot let them get past us. Send the word to Captain Vinson. I want his air group in action."

He then turned slightly to Lieutenant Jesse Powalk, the Tactical Officer.

"I want their attention, get it for me!"

"Aye, Sir!"

Unlike her sister ships, ANS Devastation was equipped with the latest particle beam direct-energy weapons. As they opened fire, the crew were surprised to see red streaks of energy as they bounced and reflected off the dust and gas that was prevalent in this sector, especially around the gas giant. The parallel beams struck the first heavily armored ship directly on the bow section, but appeared to show no discernible effect.

"Status?" called out Captain Thomas nervously.

"It's taking time, Sir. The weapons are burning through her hull. I don't know what they make those ships out of, but it is layered and very thick."

The optical scopes had magnified the lead three enemy ships so that they filled the mainscreen. The two red beams seemed to been locked onto the bow of the first ship for an age, before a series of explosions started a quarter the way along her hull from the bow; quickly followed by ripples and flashes. Then the bow tore off with a mighty flash, sending broken metal and debris around the vessel.

"Yes!" cried the XO before quickly calming down. Even so, the cheer of excitement through the bridge quickly spread.

"Good work," announced the Captain. "I think that will get their attention."

He was answered in the simplest of fashion as four of the ships made subtle changes in their course direction. Flashes of light ran along their hulls, followed quickly by the emergency alarms inside the bridge.

"Alert, incoming warheads!" announced the computer.

There was no time for the officers to give orders. The computer had already told them all they needed to know. In just three seconds, the hypersonic projectiles slammed into the port side of the ship with terrible effect. The massive warship shuddered from hundreds of impacts, and alarms blared on multiple screens.

"One powerplant's offline, breaches on six levels. Those are powerful weapons, Sir," said Lieutenant Powalk.

"Take us closer. I want every defensive turret online and firing. I don't care how much damage we cause, just keep as many of them busy as you can."

The great ship shifted a few degrees until the four enemy ships and ANS Devastation became locked in a bloody close-ranged battle of kinetic and particle beam weaponry. The turrets of the Alliance ship were designed for stopping fighters or missiles, but on this occasion they sent thousands of projectiles at the ships. The damage was minimal, but they did cause minor damage on all four ships.

It wasn't just the capital ships that were busy in the battle; at the same time, the squadron of Lightning MK II fighters entered the fray. The group of agile fighters split apart and loosed off their Sea Skua missiles at two of the ships. All missiles impacted, with the enemy ships appearing to make little, or no use of countermeasures of defensive systems. Unfortunately, they struggled to penetrate the thickly layered armor and did little more than blast great hole in their flanks. Even so, one more pass by the Alliance warship put her in position behind the hostile vessels. Another long burst of particle-beam fire, and she was left as a burning hulk from the inside out. The particle beam emitted by the ship had the potential to release over a gigajoule of kinetic energy, at speeds approaching the speed of a light. Tests had shown the weapon should negate any realistic means of defending a target, providing the power and focus could be maintained. The explosive impact of the particle beam had the capacity to literally explode the target upon impact. With one ship down, it was starting to look like ANS Devastation might be more than capable of fighting off the enemy. That was until they were finally able to face their flanks to the gallant ship.

"Captain, they're building up power. Something is coming!" cried Lieutenant Powalk.

The crew did their best to maneuver past the enemy ships, but it was too little too late. Two of the heavily armored warships unleashed a volley of much lower powered direct-energy weapons. The effect was very different to the weapons on ANS Devastation but was equally terrible. Streaks of blue matter blasted from their flanks and slammed into the much thinner hull of the Alliance ship. Each round ripped through the outer skin and proceeded to burn slowly through several meters before coming to a halt.

More alarms triggered inside the ship, but incredibly, none had reached the main crew areas or the powerplants. Even so, the alarms warned of hull breaches and losses of power to a number of minor systems. Captain Thomas paced back and forth as he checked each of the stations and encouraged them on. At this range, he had to rely on their training and reactions, and so far he could find nothing to fault.

"Captain, the port emitter has overheated. We're down to just one," explained Lieutenant Powalk bitterly.

"Just use what you have, Lieutenant, and bring us around to burn a hole in the closest ship."

She opened her mouth to speak, but a great shudder forced most of the crew about and to the floor. The mainscreen split down the middle, and a number of screens stopped working altogether. Emergency alarms activated, and jets of steam and gas burst in at least seven locations. Captain Thomas picked himself up and looked over to the XO.

"What the hell was that?"

"Unknown, Sir, it came from the lead warship. Our main engines show as out of action, and the particle beam capacitors have overloaded. We're dead in the water."

As if to emphasize the point, another three volleys of weapons fire crashed into the hull, sending a flurry of damage reports and warnings about the remaining computers.

"Your orders, Sir?" asked the XO.

Captain Thomas pulled one of the smaller screens closer, so he could get an external view of the battle. One enemy ship was gone, and a second was burning about its centre section. But there were still four remaining, and he knew where they would go next. Right now, though, they were moving into position to protect the damaged ship from the cloud of turret fire still pouring from ANS Devastation's close in weapon systems. All of the remaining ships were now moving on the same linear course to ANS Beagle. It looked almost as if they were in a running race to the finish, but in reality, they were all in the deceleration stages so that they could move into position around the target, rather than fly right past it. That was what gave Captain Thomas an idea.

"Helm, we still have maneuvering thrusters, do we not?"

He was greeted with a quick nod.

"Good. Get me closer to the ship protecting the damaged vessel."

The XO walked over to him and leaned close to his ear.

"Sir, what are you thinking?"

Captain Thomas just smiled back.

"I mean to use our last remaining asset against them."

The XO looked confused. Their fighters were engaged, their main engines and weapons were offline, and their only offensive system was either the small-caliber point defense grid or the bulk of the ship itself. Another volley of gunfire tore into the warship, causing even more breaches.

"Captain, powerplants are fluctuating, and we have containments breaches. I'm evacuating the entire level!" announced the Chief Engineer.

Captain Thomas didn't seem particularly concerned. He was well aware their options were limited and that ANS Devastation was facing her final minutes. Instead, he made direct contact with Lt Colonel Maria Barnett, the commander of his embarked marine unit. Her image appeared but crackled with digital distortion as more gunfire rained down on them.

"Colonel, your marines, are they ready?"

"Aye, Sir, armored and waiting."

"Good, to your boats, Colonel. I want you to board the two nearest ships."

"Sir?" she asked in surprise.

The warship shuddered from yet another powerful blast.

"Colonel, we don't have much time. Split your teams and hit both ships. Do what you can. We'll cover you with as much point-defense fire as we can muster."

The Colonel saluted smartly; painfully aware her mission was almost certainly a suicide run. The video cut, but the status indicators on the computer showed the landing craft and shuttles were already primed and moving into the launch bays at the rear. Captain Thomas watched as the first craft moved away from the ship amid streams of fire and flashes of energy.

"Tactical, protect our people!"

* * *

The view from the boarding shuttle was one of destruction and carnage. The group of ships were still travelling together like a shoal of fish. Lt Colonel Maria Barnett could see the grey hulk of ANS Devastation nestled between the crude but thickly armored enemy warships. Like a battle from Earth's eighteenth century, they continued to blast each other with powerful broadsides. The Alliance ship was taking the worst of it, and she spotted at least seven major fires as the gallant ship burned from the inside. She tore her eyes away from the crippled vessel and to her target. She'd sent one company to the damaged ship, but she was heading for the undamaged one that had moved into position to protect the other from any more fire.

What the hell are we going to find on that thing? She wondered.

"Colonel, where do you want to land?" asked the pilot nervously.

She looked carefully at the design of the ship. There were many gaps on the hull that gave the impression of landing bays or docking areas. She couldn't be certain, but they didn't have the time to perform a more thorough examination.

"There!" she said, pointing at the schematic. "Get us there as fast as you can. Co-ordinate with the others. I want maximum deployment at the landing zone."

"Understood, Sir."

She looked at the other marines waiting patiently in the armored craft. All wore the general purpose PDS armored suits, and in their hands, they cradled their fabled L52 Mark II Assault Carbines. The enemy vessel seemed to approach them quickly but, of course, it was the other way around. At a distance of just fifty meters, she could clearly see a flat landing area with three small vessels clamped into place.

"That's the spot. Put us down."

She then hit the Marine Corps open channel. It was

encrypted but went to every marine in her unit.

"Marines, we don't have much time. Fix yourself to the hull and assist with the entry points. Once we're inside, use your scanners to identify energy blooms and hit them hard. I want power systems, fuel, weapons, and anything of value destroyed. We'll tear them apart from the inside. Good hunting!"

They moved slightly closer, and the doors of the craft opened before they even touched the metal. The Colonel was the first out, and she drifted right up to the hull before her boots performed the final link with the surface. She glanced back to see the small flotilla of craft disgorging the rest of the marines onto the spacious landing area.

Right, what next?

A quick glance showed two circular hatches that looked suspiciously like an airlock seal. She signaled to one of her personal guards who made quick progress towards the hatch. He pulled a tool from his suit and proceeded to start placing a compact thermite charge, designed especially for spacecraft breaches. More marines arrived, and in less than thirty seconds, there were charges set at three separate locations on the platform.

"Now!" she cried.

A brief flicker of white was the only effect until the hatches themselves ripped off and blasted out into space. It depressurized the inner section immediately, and she watched with a mixture of pleasure and sickness as three of the crew were sucked out into the void. There wasn't time to look any more closely at them, but they were clearly human, of a fashion.

This is it then!

She didn't hesitate, and instead, pulled herself through the hatch into the ship, her carbine at her hip and ready for battle. The other marines did the same and very quickly they secured the empty sections of the ship. They appeared to have gained control of almost a complete rear deck of the ship, and nearly forty marines moved inside. The design was more cramped that an Alliance ship, but the level of technology appeared highly advanced. There were no exposed machines of any kind, just glowing tubes and cabling, as well as granite-looking slabs coming up from the floor. Some of them flashed with blue energy, as information in a foreign tongue appeared, much like on a monitor. There was little time to investigate, as two large doorways flipped upwards to reveal small groups of warriors. They were of a similar size to the marines but slighter in build. They blasted away with unknown weapons, but the effect as terrible. Streaks of energy tore through the marines' armor as if it were nothing but thin plastic.

"Stop them!" she screamed over the communications gear.

The deck turned into a savage warzone, with defender and attacker alike falling and being blown apart by terrible weapons. Lt Colonel Barnett reached them first, and she kicked away from the wall, smashing her weapon at the nearest armored soldier. Surprisingly, the enemy troops seemed to instantly fall back when confronted by the ferocity of close quarter battle, even in a zero gravity environment. More marines joined her, and the firefight quickly turned into a close quarter brawl, a situation that perfectly favored her marines.

"Keep pushing forward!" were her last words, as two of the enemy pinned her to the wall and blasted her helmet apart with close-range gunfire.

* * *

The area of space around the entrance to the Spacebridge was surprisingly busy, as over thirty civilian vessels formed up in a widely space cloud around the station. They were operating under automated control or skeleton crews, just to give the enemy something else to shoot at. So far, the only military presence was the two Alliance frigates posted there. Like two small guard dogs, they moved out to form a pathetic skirmish line. It was nothing but a token gesture, as the group of enemy ships could easily hit ANS Beagle with their long-range guns, and there was little they could do about it. Even so, both ships waited with weapons systems active and ready for the inevitable attack.

Captain Raikes watched patiently as ANS Devastation

and the enemy ships continued their violent battle, but minute by minute the group came closer to his position.

She's doing her job, though. Forty minutes now, and they are still fighting. He thought with amazement.

"Sir, close-range sensors have just picked up an approaching ship. Unknown configuration and they are only a kilometer away!" shouted the Tactical Officer in surprise.

Captain Raikes approached the monitor and examined the vessel. It was completely different in size and configuration to the enemy craft or anything else he'd seen. The computer system brought up a comparable image of one of the craft spotted, bombing Hades, prior to the arrival the large enemy ship.

"Uh...Sir, they are hailing us," announced his Communications Officer.

A quick hand gesture was all that was needed to transfer the communications from the vessel to the mainscreen. It showed digital noise until segment by segment it rendered to a high-quality video feed. A group of three armored warriors appeared inside a cramped command deck of some kind. One of them started to speak in an odd tongue, before a synthesized voice spoke in broken English.

"Greetings, Commander. We offer you our assistance."

On the tactical screen, Captain Raikes watched the vessel take up position alongside the two frigates and then wait as if it was no more than another Alliance frigate. He looked to his XO with a look of outright surprise on his face.

"Uh...what is this?" he asked slowly.

ANS Beagle's internal warning system activated, and just as on all Alliance ships, the lights slowly altered to low level red as a warning to all crewmembers.

"Sir, the enemy formation is moving into weapons range. One is badly damaged, and three of the others are making course adjustments. I think they're going to attack."

The Captain nodded. He'd expected this.

"Send the signal through the Rift, and start the shutdown sequence. If anything happens to jeopardize Prometheus, we'll cut the link."

He then looked to his XO.

"Get them ready. It's time."

As if in response to his comments, a great volley of projectiles and missiles appeared on the scanner. At the current range and velocity, the first would hit in a matter of seconds.

"Defensive fire, now!" he shouted.

The area of space around ANS Beagle instantly filled with clouds of metal shards, and scores of multi-barreled turrets opened fire. They were designed to pinpoint and blast tiny, high-speed objects in a fraction of a second. Both the station and the two frigates concentrated every weapon they had into a broad corridor towards the slowing ships. It was an impressive sight, and by all accounts, stopped over ninety percent of all incoming fire. But that was still enough to devastate one of the large cargo ships waiting five hundred meters away from the entrance of the Rift. Explosions rippled around the engine area, but incredibly, the vessel stayed intact.

"Sir, they are moving to present their broadsides to us!" shouted one of the officers, but the Captain barely registered it. His eyes were drawn to the new arrival; the alien ship that had accelerated away and was jinxing around the enemy capital ships, bombarding them with heavy fire. The effect was impressive, but he still doubted it would change an awful lot.

The interior of the bridge flashed light blue as a ship came through the Rift, quickly followed by many more until a force of twelve capital ships, including five of the new Crusader class, poured out of the tear in space. They must have been ready because no sooner had they arrived, and they were already firing. The five Crusader class tore into the exposed flanks of the enemy ships with devastating effect, and two were cut clean in half by the coordinated and concentrated fire. The image of Admiral Anderson appeared on ANS Beagle's main screen.

"Sorry we're late, Captain. Leave this to us. We'll drive them back to the abyss!"

With that one announcement, the battle for the Spacebridge turned around. In minutes, those enemy ships still able to maneuver had turned and accelerated at maximum speed back towards their own Rift and command ship. Three ships remained; ANS Devastation and the two now heavily damaged enemy ships. All three were so close, they now looked like a single vessel, and from what Captain Raikes had heard; they were a warzone.

* * *

The defenders of the underground complex had now held off four attacks, but already their ranks were starting to falter. Khan and two other Jötnar were quite badly wounded and forced to withdraw to the fallen columns around the centre of the room for defense. Over half of the T'Kari were now dead or wounded, and even worse, those that remained seem incapable of fighting at close range. Spartan had never seen anything quite like it. He'd witnessed three of the T'Kari simply kneel down to be killed by edged weapons. It seemed they were either not trained for close quarters combat, or they were unwilling. Either way, it had fallen to the depleted group to fight when the enemy came again.

How many more attacks must we face?

To answer his question, another rumble shook the ground, and he could see flashing lights approaching from the nearest tunnel. Ayndir beckoned towards him and threw one of her rifles at him. He grabbed it, lifting it to his shoulder, ready for battle. Gun and Teresa stepped alongside him, both holding their weapons up and ready.

* * *

The enemy ships needed several hours to reach their Rift, but Admiral Anderson was having none of it. His force of warships continued right behind them, firing their railguns and particle beams as frequently as they could. It was more a chase than a battle, and in less than twenty minutes, only one of the ships was able to keep moving.

Captain Thomas grabbed onto the handrail as his marine bodyguard helped him to the lifeboats. The valiant warship was burning, and he'd already given them his orders. Incredibly, the ship had survived the battle long enough for the reinforcements under Admiral Anderson to arrive. Now that they were being pursued, he had given his last order aboard ANS Devastation. There were no more explosions, but it was clear that the ship was no longer habitable with her powerplants off-line, engines out and hundreds of major hull breaches.

"Sir, Colonel Barnett's deputy reports the remaining enemy vessel has been captured. She has just under a hundred prisoners and says the ship is habitable."

"What happened to Barnett?" he replied suspiciously.

"It looks like she died in the first wave, Sir."

He shook his head.

"Damn it. She was a fine officer. Still, there will be time for mourning later. The enemy warship, we shall claim her as a prize. Move the crew over as quickly as possible. I will transfer my flag to the enemy ship."

Commander Parker saluted and then continued with her work to help evacuate the crew. As she moved away, she even considered the possibility that the ship might be salvageable, assuming they survived. They were not far from the starboard evacuation deck, and the blast doors had been torn off. Luckily, all of the crew were now wearing sealed suits and pulling themselves past the debris to the waiting shuttles and lifeboats. Captain Thomas waited for a moment as he spotted the enemy's Rift, like a second sun in the distance. Though the enemy command ship was far away, he could work out the silhouette against the colors of the space phenomena.

Who are you? He thought bitterly.

* * *

Admiral Anderson had the perfect view from the CIC of ANS Crusader, the lead ship in the new class of Alliance warship. The magnified view on the mainscreen showed the enemy command ship was moving back through its own Rift, presumably withdrawing from battle. Tempted as he was to pursue it further, he had already ordered all of his ships to turn on those few ships still in the system. He was going to make sure New Charon was secure before he let a single vessel head anywhere near the new Rift.

"Admiral, the T'Kari ship is continuing on its course to the Rift."

"What? Why?"

Captain Harris, the commander of the ship shook his head.

"Unknown, Admiral. Wait, they're firing something into the Rift."

They watched as a blue pulse of energy, much like a magnetized railgun round, but it emitted massive amounts of energy. It moved at almost the speed of light before entering the Rift. There was a small flash, and the Rift started to ripple and shift. Admiral Anderson instantly knew something terrible was about to occur and grabbed the intercom, selecting an open frequency.

"This is Admiral Anderson. All ships are to move away from the Rift immediately. I repeat, move away from the Rift. It is showing signs of instability."

More flashes jumped back and forth through the Rift, and the command ship started to break up. Explosions and streaks of light bounced around the great hulk as it tore itself apart over a period of several minutes. The Rift remained but continued to emit unstable radiation as it shuddered and destroyed its prey like some carnivorous worm. Almost as quickly as it had arrived, the enemy ship was gone, leaving an unstable Rift in its wake.

The crew of the warship cheered at the sight of the enemy's destruction, but the Admiral, ever the worrier, thought of the reports he'd been seeing over the last hours. He looked to the XO of the ship.

"Get the order out to our forces in this sector. I want all bases, moons and landing sites to be reinforced and secured as a matter of urgency. It's time we took control of this place."

* * *

The last defenders of Hades waited as the sound of footsteps increased. The acoustics were surprisingly good there, and Teresa's mind wandered as she considered the many things that could be accomplished in this underground refuge, other than combat and death, of course. She looked to Spartan and the others, and her memory flashed back to the dozens of warzones they had fought on together. She and Spartan had encountered their first bloody battle on a captured Confederate moon base. It seemed fitting that they were now about to face a final confrontation on yet another. The difference of hundreds of light-years seemed insignificant next to the violence of their situation. The sound from the nearest opening became louder, and each of them carefully trained their weapons, waiting for the moment.

"Steady!" Spartan called out, though it wasn't needed.

His group were professional to the last. More noise and then several bursts of gunfire. The sounds became louder, and then came the lights at the entrance. They were close. Each of the bloodied fighters trained their weapons on the numerous breaches. Hunn was completely out of ammunition now, threw his carbine to the ground and pulled his razor sharp glaive from his back. Gun and the other Jötnar watched him and then did the same. Even Spartan dropped his weapon and picked up the blade he had only so recently borrowed.

"Here they come!" shouted Teresa, and before the rest even blinked, she'd cut down the first two to come through the gap.

Hunn burst out from cover and charged across the open space towards them. Spartan and the others watched in awe as he made the distance, even after being struck four times in his chest. He arrived just as the rest of the enemy force rushed out and disappeared into the middle.

"Now!" roared Gun, and with a great bellow, the small group charged across and jumped into the furious melee started by Hunn. Limbs and heads were hacked off with every slash of their weapons, while none but Hunn were forced to their knees by injuries. The armored butt of a rifle struck Spartan in the belly, and just as quickly, it seemed as though their desperate fight would be over. As he dropped to one knee, he noticed the T'Kari doing their best to emulate the Jötnar as they threw themselves at the last wave of enemy attackers moving from multiple access points.

Gun brought his glaive down with such force that it crushed the helmet of the soldier and cut down to the shoulder. The man dropped to his knees, lifeless before his head even touched the ground. Teresa sidestepped another and emptied the last of her ammunition into two soldiers before being stabbed in the leg. Spartan tried to reach her, but three more soldiers blocked his path. With a supreme effort, he pushed himself upright, but two figures passed by in front and leapt upon the soldiers. It was Ayndir and one of her warriors. They attacked with little skill or grace, just the ferocity of anger, and a vain attempt to emulate Spartan's team.

"Spartan, down!" shouted Khan as he limped about in the middle of the battle.

Spartan knew his friend well and didn't even hesitate at his cry. He dropped to the floor to witness the sight of the soldiers being cut apart by glaives. Even so, one of them managed to bring Khan down to one knee, yet he refused to go down. Another figure blocked his view, and Spartan immediately grabbed to pull them away from Khan.

This isn't the way it should end, thought Spartan, as a hand grabbed him and pulled him out of the way.

He looked up, ready to grab at his foe to find a Vanguard Marine, the Alliance's equivalent to the strength and power of a Jötnar. The marine smashed his fist into the nearest enemy and then stomped past to finish off the others. More Vanguards and conventional marines surged in behind him, and as quickly as it had started, the battle for Hades was over. Spartan tried to stand, but a familiar face appeared from the middle of the battle. It was a blood soaked marine in standard PDS body armor, but as he approached, the man deactivated the visor to show his face.

"General?" spluttered Spartan in surprise.

General Rivers smiled at him and reached down to help his friend to his feet. More and more marines continued to enter, and he was sure Colonel Daniels had moved off to assist in a short skirmish, but the General caught his attention. He called out over his external speakers.

"This is General Rivers, Alliance Marine Corps. This battle is over!"

There was a short pause as those still in the fight struggled to believe the words they'd just heard. Dozens of hands lifted to the air, waving their bloodied weapons. Even the T'Kari, who seemed totally alien to the concept, raised theirs and cheered in unison.

The newly arrived marines helped the wounded to their feet or moved them into a more comfortable position. Spartan, Teresa and Gun moved towards the General, and Khan pulled himself over to check the badly wounded Hunn.

"What about our people on the surface?" asked Teresa

as she approached Spartan and the General. The marine commander smiled at them, but her exertions were more pronounced than either of them had seen in previous battles. He took a deep breath before replying.

"They are all safe. We found just one enemy ship in low orbit during our approach. Not that it was much of a problem, it was trying to get away."

He leaned against one of the broken pillars and pulled off his thickly armored helmet.

"This was a pretty close run thing. It looks like Admiral Anderson and his friends turned up at just the right time. We've been hiding in the debris field for hours, waiting for a chance to come and help. Any vessels that were caught out on their own were destroyed in a matter of minutes."

"Anderson?" asked Spartan.

Ayndir and a small group of the other T'Kari approached as he continued his explanation.

"Yes, he brought in reinforcements and forced them to withdraw into the Rift. One ship, ANS Devastation, commanded by Commodore Lewis, managed to hold them back long enough for Anderson to mobilize a reserve."

He then nodded towards Ayndir.

"Our friends here fired something into the Rift as they tried to escape, and it collapsed, destroying their ship in the process. This battle is over, my friend," he said with genuine warmth.

Khan and the other wounded Jötnar staggered over to

Spartan, eager not to miss out on the end of the battle. Instead, they found themselves stood next to Ayndir and three of her people. Spartan beckoned towards them.

"This is Ayndir, of the T'Kari."

She bowed slightly in an overly flamboyant gesture and then spoke quietly.

"We thank you for your help, General. There are few of the T'Kari remaining here now. I have received word from our scout ships, and they confirm the distortion has been disrupted. It can no longer be used for travel. The Great Enemy cannot come back this way for some time. They will have to create a new tunnel from another system in the meantime."

General Rivers nodded.

"Excellent, how long will it last?"

Ayndir shrugged.

"Every distortion is different."

"I don't understand," said Spartan, "Why not stop their distortions and keep your worlds safe?"

Ayndir smiled at him.

"Using this weapon has told the Enemy we are still here. We, and the rebels, have been fighting them for centuries. They send agents to our systems and start civil wars. They rarely fight their own battles."

General Rivers spoke briefly to one of his marines and turned back to Ayndir.

"This has happened in our own system. We have just

come out of our own Civil War with the machines and their servants."

Ayndir looked surprised at this.

"Your people survived a war, one started by the enemy's agents?"

He nodded in reply.

"Yes, it was hard, but we fought them to their last world. We found a Rift, distortion as you call it, directly to this moon."

Ayndir waited for a few seconds.

"Then our people are brothers. We are linked by this distortion and by our experience with the Great Enemy." She then looked back at her own people.

"Each of these moons has a small colony of T'Kari, and we have a small number of remaining scout ships to patrol these planets. Our two peoples will be stronger together than apart. I have been authorized by our Council to offer our technology and support to your people, in exchange for your protection."

General Rivers looked at Gun, Teresa and Spartan before returning to Ayndir.

"You wish to live under the protection of our people? The Centauri Alliance?"

Ayndir looked back at the small number of surviving civilians and spoke quickly. A short discussion took place, and she looked back to the General and the Spartan.

"My people have seen your honor and your military

skills, especially those of Spartan and his giants. We have neither the strength nor violence of your people. We only survive because our last citizens have been in hiding. You have already seen our graves and the battlefield on the surface. They were once our great cities. The T'Kari were once a people of twenty billion. Now we are less than fifty thousand. If you will protect this system, then we will ally with your Alliance."

General Rivers looked at Gun and Spartan, both of them nodded slowly at the proposal. Gun lifted his arm.

"What about our people already here? My people have started building on the high-gravity world."

Ayndir smiled.

"We do not own these worlds. All are welcome to live here, in peace. Go back and tell your leaders that the Centauri and the T'Kari are friends."

Gun grabbed Khan and Hunn's arms and lifted them up high into the air. All three roared as loudly as they could manage, much to the dismay and annoyance of the General. He moved one step closer to Spartan, Teresa and Khan but was forced to shout over the noise of the Jötnar.

"Your sons, Wictred and Jack. I have news."

The group of three all shared the same look of weariness and concern, but of them all, Khan did his utmost to appear stoic.

"They escaped the destruction of one of our medical frigates and are being treated aboard ANS Beagle. They are both up for a commendation in the battle."

Teresa grabbed Spartan and pulled him close, even though the movement brought groans of pain from them both. She embraced him firmly and listened to the rest of the General's news.

"Those two did well, very well. Between them they destroyed an entire warship."

Ayndir heard his words and shook her head in amazement. The General then looked directly at Spartan.

"I think you might have competition in the destruction stakes, old friend!"

THE END